---- ★ ----

Within six seconds I was rethinking this whole stroll around the graveyard. To begin with, I didn't see a single grave worthy of a digital click from even a throwaway camera— unless I wanted promo for a bad slasher movie. This cemetery must have been intended for the dregs of society. Every headstone was chipped or cracked into pieces. Not even foot markers had remained intact through the centuries. Broken bottles decorated the headstones and vines strangled the larger pieces of stone, effectively blocking inscriptions and epitaphs from the few curious souls seeking a shred of history.

I slowly surveyed this small cemetery. And it hit me with such force I sank onto the nearest block of stone that seemed intact enough to hold my weight.

"Johnny."

"What?"

"Are you seeing what I'm seeing?"

He nodded. "These headstones don't look like they've been destroyed through the forces of time, nature and neglect."

"I agree. It's like they've been deliberately smashed."

---- ★ ----

Previously published Worldwide Mystery title by
FLO FITZPATRICK

SWEET DREAMS

ARIA IN ICE

Flo Fitzpatrick

W⬤RLDWIDE®

TORONTO • NEW YORK • LONDON
AMSTERDAM • PARIS • SYDNEY • HAMBURG
STOCKHOLM • ATHENS • TOKYO • MILAN
MADRID • WARSAW • BUDAPEST • AUCKLAND

Recycling programs
for this product may
not exist in your area.

ARIA IN ICE

A Worldwide Mystery/July 2013

First published by CreateSpace.

ISBN-13: 978-0-373-26857-3

Copyright © 2011 by Flo Fitzpatrick

Printed in U.S.A.

ONE

A DENIM-CLAD butt perched in the huge, ancient oak just underneath the north wing of the castle. Legs attached to that butt were busily engaged in grasping tree limbs in an attempt to remain balanced in the branches.

I strolled over to the bottom of the tree and stood in silence until an entire flesh and blood body appeared on the limb some ten feet above my head.

Then I called out, "Pruning time? Or am I interrupting a burglary in progress?"

The butt, and the body, landed with a less-than-gentle thud right at my feet.

I smiled serenely down at the wannabe burglar. "Oops. So sorry. Did I startle you?"

Red hair in bad need of a trim. Stupidly sexy Irish green eyes. Currently glaring into mine. I'd just witnessed what had to be a painful, but most entertaining, performance involving an ungraceful descent from a tree. Since that fall had ultimately landed the acrobat on his backside, laughter was my immediate, if admittedly juvenile, response.

After a good thirty seconds of silence and stares, he spoke. "Excuse me, but is there some reason your hair is partially green?"

My smile changed to a scowl. "Yes, damn it. There is. This past Christmas I ran out of decorations but wanted to get a huge jump on next year's festivities, so

I figured chestnut and green was the way to go. You know…that whole concept of roasting over open fires and fir trees. I'm convinced green streaks will be the style for holiday ornamentation the world over in a year or two, don't you?" I took a breath. "Is there some reason you're being rude? Aside from the fact that my appearance caused you to stop your nefarious deeds, and ultimately land on your behind?"

He jumped to his feet. "Rude? Rude? *Me* being rude? How about you? Sneaking around, scaring the crap out of a guy and causing a near-fatal accident. How's that for rude?"

I raised the pitch of my voice just a notch without changing volume. "I was *not* sneaking around. I have a perfect right to be here and I'd lay odds that you most definitely don't, because otherwise you wouldn't be the one climbing out of treetops. Not to mention that if a truly klutzy tumble from the bottom branch can be labeled a near-fatal accident, you've obviously led a sheltered—albeit crime-laden—life."

We continued glaring at each other. Finally he winked at me. "We seem to be at an impasse. Tell me, are you planning to use that phone you're clutching so tightly in those delicate hands and giving the Prague authorities a buzz? I'd appreciate a head start if I'm about to become a fugitive."

I unclenched my fingers from around the cell. I had no idea whether a call to 911 in Prague would fetch the cops, the animal catchers, or the *kolache* delivery guys.

And really, what could I say once I reached the local authorities? "Yo! How's it goin'? Uh, sorry to bother you, but Mr. Johnny Gerard, whom I haven't seen in three damn months because of his stupid soap opera filming way-the-hell-out-of-town, now seems to be engaged in a felony, and has fallen out of a tree at *Kastle Kouzlo Noc* just under the north tower where I swear I heard Mozart only moments ago except no one is around and I have this strange gift of second sight so I'm not really sure if what I heard was an auditory premonition or a ghostly serenade but I'm kind of spooked and no, I don't see anything like the Hapsburg crown jewels peeking out of his pockets, and I'm really sorry to call—but while I have you on the line could you just transfer me to *Kolaches-to-Go*? I want to place an order for two cream cheese and one apricot-filled."

Johnny whistled. Doubtless he'd followed that entire fictitious call by reading my mind. He's good at that. He ran his fingers through my bangs. "I apologize about the hair comment, Abby. Honest. I'm curious though. Last time I saw you, your lovely locks were one color. Was this a deliberate dye job? Going for a retro-punk garage band look?"

"Remember I told you about the *Starlight Express* debacle in that theatre in Kansas?"

"Oh yeah. I was very jealous. Always wanted to play the *Pumping Iron* Elvis part. Although you did make it sound like the production staff was less than stellar."

"You would have been wonderful. You always are. And believe me, they could have used your exceptional talents because less-than-stellar doesn't begin to cover the idiocy I endured. Intense and constant diva dramas. I'll reveal all some night when we're not otherwise occupied. Where was I?"

"Kansas."

I shuddered. "Yeah. Nice state. Stupid theatre. Anyway, what I didn't tell you was that fool director, Bryce, decided all of the dancing, roller-skating characters should have exotic hair colors to represent the different types of trains. He sent me off to a demonic hair-stylist who chose green. Excuse me while I gag. Why the idiot didn't just order wigs is beyond my comprehension."

"Okay. Demonic hair-stylist. We'll get back to that because what I really want to know, Ms. Fouchet—why are you here in Prague?"

"The other thing I didn't tell you since you were roving around the world *incommunicado*—and why the hell was *Endless Time* filming in Africa—and why doesn't Kenya seem to have cell coverage?"

"I have no idea. Wouldn't have mattered. Remember I hate all phones but especially any device that can reach out and touch me anywhere anytime. Africa. Simple. Can we say soap insanity? Somebody saw some PBS channel special on safaris and decided Gregory Noble and his merry band of murderous wives, mistresses, fellow cops and assorted hangers on—or hanger ons—whichever—should hunt down a neo-Communist spy while riding around in an open Jeep across lion country. I barely escaped being fed to a hippopotamus. And I'm truly sorry that they scrapped your part of Vanessa after Christmas. You were supposed to come with me and I was miserable without you. But, go on, Prague—why?"

"Okay. Three days into rehearsals, I took a major header roller skating off a ramp that wasn't supposed to have a bump in the middle. I broke that same ankle that got wrecked back when I first met you when we were doing *Superstar*, so I came back to Manhattan and managed to rest up for about three weeks, and saw no need to distress you since I couldn't reach you anyway. I'm glad I didn't die. You'd've missed the funeral."

"Prague?" he prompted.

"Ankle. So I'm enjoying lying on the couch in the apartment with Cherry and Guido, who are supposed to be getting married but that's another story, and we're watching all the soap operas Johnny Gerard is *not* starring in and I get this phone call from Shay, who's in Germany choreographing *The Merry Widow* for a light opera company. She ran into a friend of ours, Ms. Bambi Bohacek. Bambi is owner of *Headlights Productions*, which is an indie film company, and she was looking for a patsy to play location scout. *Voilà!* Enter Abby to roam the Czech Republic looking for a place for Bambi's Gothic movie musical that Shay is going to direct, which is why I'm at *Kouzlo Noc* since it looks perfect as a creepy castle. Anyway, I've been hacking away at it—my hair that is—not the scouting—which is why I have this lovely, long, shag cut with the mixture of my natural chestnut and garish green. Satisfied?"

Johnny howled, "Damn, darlin'. A simple 'dye job gone bad' would have sufficed." The twinkle in his eyes quickly morphed into a glint I recognized. "I've missed you."

"Me too." I sniffed and dabbed at my eyes.

He grabbed me and proceeded to curl that lovely, long shag cut with a classic Johnny Gerard kiss that landed us both under the tree Johnny had plopped out of. Damn nice kiss with extras. It almost made up for his absence the last three months. Stinking-sexy-soap-star-smart-ass.

We broke apart and stared at each other.

"So, now that my presence has been explained, what about yours? Whacha doin' at *Kouzlo Noc*?" I snickered, "Burglar."

"Let's just say I had a good reason for being in the north turret."

"Ha. Knew it. You were breaking in and you weren't quick enough to come up with a cover story. Is this research for some other crazy stunt for Gregory Noble, Supercop?"

He shuddered. "Gad. I hope not. Then again, I wouldn't mind *Endless Time* funding some filming in Prague."

"Stalling, Johnny, stalling."

"Fine. I'm restoring a mural for Veronika Duskova, who is one of the owners of *Kouzlo Noc*. It's in very bad condition and in no way ready to be seen so she and I are a bit touchy about it."

"In the north turret?"

Pause.

"Well, actually, I was muraling in a different area."

"Not the north turret."

"No."

Pause. "Wait. This is new. 'Muraling.' Um. Is that a word?"

"No. Neither is 'muraled' although I'm sure both will now become part of the Abby vocabulary. Anyway, I got into sketching ages ago during breaks on the soap. Restoration was a logical step up in my artistic repertoire."

"Oh-kay. Should I even ask how you met the Duskova family?"

"Guess."

I pondered the question for about twenty seconds. "Yolanda Barrett. Prolific head writer for *Endless Time*. Right?"

Johnny gave me a thumbs up. "You got it. I have yet to meet someone truly interesting whom Yolanda hasn't managed to make a friend sometime in her life. We did a little filming in Prague a few years ago and she got to chatting with Veronika Duskova at a grocery store or something ridiculously mundane. They kept in touch. Veronika asked her if she knew someone who'd restore a mural for cheap. Yolanda said Johnny Gerard will do it for free."

"That's nice of you."

"Well, Yolanda also had an agenda."

"Duh." I smirked. "Which was?"

"There's a circus training facility about twenty miles outside Prague."

I held up my hand. "Don't tell me. Yolanda wants Gregory Noble to develop skills in—what?"

"Everything. Elephant riding, ring-master, fortune-teller; you name it. I love circuses. Considered joining one back when I was about twelve." He smirked. "You won't believe this because I neglected to show my process with balance when I fell out of this tree, but I guess high-wire and trapeze are my favorites so far."

"Makes sense. Great skills for a wannabe catburglar."

"Now, now, Ms. Fouchet. I am an innocent man. Really." He paused, then stared into my eyes. "What's freaking you out about the north turret anyway?"

I hoisted my tote bag to a more comfortable position. "Let me ask you a question."

"Go ahead. You want a list of the other amazing talents that lie hidden behind my shining presence."

"Shining ego," I snorted. "Johnny, my dearest darling, it's common knowledge you're capable of leaping tall buildings and staring down rays of Kryptonite, but I'll just have to suppress my admiration and curiosity. Back to my question. Did you hear anyone playing a flute in the north turret before you made that incredibly bad descent down the tree? For that matter, since you have some musicianship skills, were you by any chance...uh...flauting?"

He snorted. "Flauting? I'm damn sure that's not a word. And I can assure you that I was not playing the flute. Mind you, I can. As well as various brass instruments and a fairly mean guitar on occasion. But you did not hear me. And I didn't see anyone else in the north wing playing the flute, the harp, the piano or harmonica. No one else was even in that turret."

"I was afraid you'd say that."

"Why?"

"Because I'm pretty positive I heard a flute. A very fine flute sounding out more than a few notes from the overture of *Magic Flute*. And if no one was playing, and no one was in the turret, then the only explanation is *Kouzlo Noc* has a musical ghost."

His eyes widened. "A flute-playing spook is haunting the castle?"

"Well, I'm not sure I'd put it in those terms. Common theories say ghosts do not appreciate being called spooks. Kind of like spies, I guess. It sounds rude to them. Where was I? Oh. Yes. *Kouzlo Noc* is haunted."

"And you've determined this—why? Because, to paraphrase Irving Berlin, you're 'hearing music and there's no one there?'"

"I thought it was 'hear singing'?"

"It is. I *said* I was paraphrasing. You weren't paying attention."

"I was."

"Were not."

"Was too."

"Were not...what were we talking about and are you going to refrain from singing the refrain? Or beginning the Beguine?"

I realized I was indeed singing a few measures of the song he was referring to. *You're Just in Love.* "Sorry."

"Are you telling me you heard music from a non-living presence?"

"Uh—sort of."

"Cripes. Care to explain?"

"Remember that little talent I was bequeathed from Granny Dumas?"

"The foreshadowing premonition second sight thingee?"

"Yep. Guess what? It's more than possible Granny bestowed upon me a little extra giftie that lies dormant until one is past legal age. Like—uh—hearing music from folks who aren't with us anymore."

"Oh crap. This could get dicey."

"And dodgey. Not to mention possibly dangerous." I paused. "This isn't actually the first time I've had an experience bonding with the deceased."

Johnny's eyebrow lifted. "Do tell. Unless you want to count that premonition about me that thankfully didn't come true?"

"No, no. that was a whompin' big vision. This is different. I'm talkin' 'bout spook—excuse me—*ghost* communing when I was six and attending a fine Irish wake for my great-grandfather who was half Irish and half French. Minette's side of the family, which of course is no surprise since the Dumas' have all the weird voodoo genes. Where was I? Oh yeah. People at the wake suddenly began asking why I was singing the Canticle harmony to *'Scarborough Faire.'* Not the ancient regular folk song, but the Simon and Garfunkle arrangement from the Sixties. The anti-war version with the really cool lyrics that send chills down one's spine even at a very young age. Anyway, I explained that Great-Grandpa had taken the melody and I was being polite by singing harmony. Gramps had perfect pitch as well. Even after he died."

"Why am I not surprised?" Johnny said.

"Because I had visions thirty years into the future talking to your father last July?"

"Which I still find fascinating. Of course, I find everything about my petite little Abby fascinating but your Dumas abilities are sort of reality sci-fi TV fascinating. Now we get to add—what? Harmonious trysts with spooks?"

I frowned at him. "Now, now. I won't let you play ghost hunter with me if you're going to have a bad attitude about this."

"I shall be totally supportive. Although, as to flute-playing ghosts, I hate to be Mr. Practical but I do have to point out other possibilities—at least as to the why or how of ghostly sounds wafting out from the north turret."

"Such as?"

"What about the clichéd but reasonable suggestion of that old standby—the hidden tape player? Cell phone, MP3 player boombox held to head by the creepy gardener who roams the castle?"

"Yeah, yeah. Logical. All great explanations and I promise I plan to explore them all if I get to rent *Kouzlo Noc* for Bambi's company and sneak around in turrets. But I'm telling you what I'd heard and the techno-quality of your suggestions don't quite fit the sound of live. Even by a dead flautist."

He smiled. "Nice phrasing. Okay, howsabout your imagination kicked over into Gothicland because it's romantic and you love romance?"

"Aw, come on. Yes, I have a marvelous imagination, but I also have a fairly decent grip on reality—" I batted my lashes "—unless I'm around Johnny Gerard, who tends to get me into surreal situations even when he's not playing Gregory Noble."

Johnny patted my green and chestnut hair as though I was a toddler, then casually leaned down and proceeded to plant upon my lips a kiss that curled my toes as well as my hair. Just as casually, he let go. "Darlin', I personally love the ghost theory better, too. Tell you the truth, I'm very curious as to any spectral wanderers wandering *Kouzlo Noc*. Care to take a stroll around the castle cemetery and see what pops up?"

I winced. "Not sure 'pops up' is exactly what I need to see happening in a graveyard but I do like the idea of exploring." I linked my arm through his. "Lead on, burglar boy."

TWO

WITHIN SIX SECONDS I was rethinking this whole stroll around the graveyard. To begin with, I didn't see a single grave worthy of a digital click from a throw-away camera—unless I wanted promo for a bad slasher movie. This cemetery must have been intended for the dregs of society. Every headstone was chipped or cracked into pieces. Not even foot markers had remained intact through the centuries. Broken bottles decorated the headstones and vines strangled the larger pieces of stone, effectively blocking inscriptions and epitaphs from the few curious souls seeking a shred of history.

Graveyards aren't normally party sites, but this untended, ignored plot of land was—to put it mildly—sad. Johnny pushed aside a particularly annoying vine and we both nearly fell over partially-intact headstones. Since the epitaphs were in Czech the words were somewhat unintelligible to me, but the carved numerals were easily deciphered. 1721-1764. 1725-1780. Odd. The graveyard was such a mess I would have expected to find that the dates were more in line with much earlier centuries, perhaps even from the medieval period. Johnny knelt down to inspect a marker, while I sidestepped the two headstones and walked a few steps further. More 18th Century dates. I wandered through this forgotten piece of history, pushing away the dead greenery and the piles of dirt that clung to the stones. Everything was Seventeen-such-and-such to Seventeen-so-and-so.

I slowly surveyed this small cemetery. And it hit me with such force I sank onto the nearest block of stone that seemed intact enough to hold my weight.

"Johnny."

"What?"

"Are you seeing what I'm seeing?"

He nodded. "These headstones don't look like they've been destroyed through the forces of time, nature and neglect."

"I agree. It's like they'd been deliberately smashed."

I walked on, surmising that this destruction didn't appear to have been caused by kids out for a sick vandal romp through a burial ground, but by a person or persons who had been hunting for something. The cracks and the crumbles had been forced in such a way as to allow the perpetrators to literally search inside the stones. That wasn't the worst of this scene. It was obvious, once I took the time to really look, that each plot had been dug up; that some of the wreckage now lying in a sorrowful and frozen chaotic tableau on the ground were the remains of coffins—with parts of the original inhabitants now outside those original resting places.

I felt chilled. There is something so unholy, so sick, so uselessly mean about a grave robber. If one has to steal from the dead, then plan a heist on a museum where the personalities have been long forgotten.

Prague in the spring, yet suddenly cold as ice. I wanted out of this place. Time to let Johnny Gerard go paint the mural or whatever he wanted to do with the rest of this day while I headed up to *Kastle Kouzlo Noc*, talked to the owners about renting this castle for Shay's movie—and got warm. I shivered, looked around for Johnny, who'd wandered off to investigate broken angels, then carefully shielded my face from an open grave about eight feet away from me. No one had bothered to toss the dirt back inside. I closed my eyes, took as much of a breath as I could stand in this desolate and decayed area, sat up straight, opened my eyes again, and prepared to leave.

I screamed. There was a wool-trousered butt sticking up from the grave.

A torso followed the distinctly male derrière, then a neck appeared, and finally, I was reassured to notice, a real human head. Alive. Jet-black hair, amazingly well-coiffed for someone hip deep in dirt, hit just above neck-line.

I yelled with as much fury as my fright would allow, "Dammit! You just scared the holy livin' heart out of me! Doesn't anyone around here ever make a normal entrance?"

The man straightened and whirled around with such force I expected him to fall back inside. Golden brown eyes, like a superior feline, stared at me. I stared back, prepared to play "blink first" for as long as it took. Enough time passed for me to see the straight nose, the Cupid-shaped lips and the lashes that were triple mine (even with Volumized-Billion-Dramatic-Double-Layered mascara). The lashes pissed me off so much I was able to stay silent until the grave-popper spoke first.

"I'm very sorry if I startled you, young lady. I was engrossed in what I was doing and didn't realize anyone was above the crypt." The man paused. "What do you mean—normal entrance?"

I started to explain, then gave up. "Never mind. It

was supposed to be a funny theatrical reference but if you're not an actor, it's probably not even remotely amusing. Forget I said anything."

Johnny suddenly appeared next to me. "You okay?"

"Sure. Just startled by Mister Whomever here literally popping up out of the ground." I glared at the man. "So. That's a crypt, right, not an undone grave?"

"Of course. What a strange question. Why do you ask that?"

"Well, sure. Silly me. The fact that there isn't a solid grave anywhere to be found was a just a tad suspicious. What had you so captivated you didn't hear either of us above ground? What were you doing?"

"Working."

Johnny looked at me. I looked back at him, then at the gorgeous man in the dirt.

I smiled. "That sounds—excuse the term—cryptic. What exactly were you working on? If you don't mind telling us."

He smiled. Instantly he looked ten years younger and far less threatening. Neither thought reassured me. "I'm a historian. And I am currently engaged in a research project for the residents of *Kouzlo Noc*."

This sounded nice except that I'd just noticed the man was holding a dagger. Looked antique. I could feel my teeth grinding out of sheer nervousness.

Johnny obviously felt the same. "Do you mind placing that knife on the ground or someplace where it's not in your hand? No offense."

He looked at the weapon as if he'd just noticed it was there. "Sorry. I use this to chip away at some of the centuries-old encrusted dirt obscuring names and dates."

He laid it on top of a headstone above ground.

I began to breathe again. "Thank you. So. I'm intrigued. What are we talking about here? Are you writing a book? Dissertation? Or perhaps taking a leisurely stroll down genealogy lane?"

Again, the quick smile flashed. "That's a very good summary."

"In other words, you're not going to tell me."

"I didn't say that."

I groaned. "Enough. I'm about to meet the owners of this castle and try to present a dignified—uh—presence but I'm standing in the middle of a major horror show, so I'm not up to games involving wresting info from an avowed academic."

Those cat's eyes stared at me again from the grave. Again, I broke first. "Do you have a name?"

He relaxed. "I do. Corbin Lerner. I teach at a small eastern University."

He didn't say east of what. Could be Prague, could be Eden, could be Des Moines.

"I do some sideline work for the Duskova sisters. Those castle owners you're about to meet."

"Oh. Well, thanks. That rather sums it up. Neatly and with total ambiguity."

He wasn't going to tell me why he was sneaking around the graveyard. That much was certain. I tried a different tack. "I'm Abby Fouchet. Currently acting as location scout for a movie company planning to rent the castle from the Duskovas. This is Johnny Gerard, who is also doing work for the Duskovas."

Johnny tensed. The Dumas second sight didn't kick in, but it didn't need to. I got it. He wanted our romantic relationship kept secret. I didn't skip a beat. "Restoring a mural, isn't that right, Mr. Gerard?"

Johnny nodded. "Precisely." He immediately added, "So, Mr. Lerner, as an historian, do you have any theories as to why this graveyard only contains the dearly departed from the Seventeen-Hundreds?"

Lerner's shoulders lifted until his neck nearly disappeared into his collar. "That is interesting, isn't it? Veronika Duskova told me that years ago the family decided that the original gravesite was too crowded. So starting in Seventeen Hundred, all the deceased were interned here."

Something didn't quite ring true here—like *where's the rest of the dearly—and much more recently—departed and is their site a bit nicer and more refined?*

Johnny didn't buy it either, but only asked, "Did you find what you were looking for in the crypt?"

"Sadly, no. There are some interesting artifacts there, but the information I sought was not available."

"Can you tell us what you were looking for? Or is that a deep, dark secret?" I asked.

He gazed a bit too intently up at a tree branch that had nothing whatsoever of interest to distract him. He didn't answer.

I was about to take another stab at sticking my nose in where he obviously didn't feel it belonged (I have no shame when it comes to being curious) when I felt a light touch on my right shoulder. Normally I wouldn't flinch. But I was in a cemetery with a man who was bent on being stubbornly and ridiculously quiet about an old crypt and my boyfriend who was mysteriously bent on keeping quiet about his girlfriend—me. I jumped, whirled and prepared to beat the living fool out of who or what was behind me.

A woman glared at me from across a headstone that must have been hideous long before it was smashed. Skeletal images, flames and lost faces peeked through what was left of marble and granite.

She was dressed in a solid black Victorian-style gown and sporting what my favorite contemporary dance teacher at University of Texas had called the *"Early-Modern-Dancer-I-Have-No-Humor-and-I'm-Constipated-to-Boot"* look. A look that comes with a hard knot at the back of the neck hair and honest-to-God knitting needles sticking out from that bun.

I smiled at the newcomer. She wasn't having any.

"Yoong ladee! No! No! Vy iss you in graveyard? You must leaf now! Go! Go!"

THREE

I WRENCHED MY gaze away from the pitiful headstones and the two men then meekly followed the Woman in Black out of the graveyard. Neither Johnny nor Mr. Lerner followed. The woman did not talk. I kept my own silence until we arrived at the giant doorway about half a mile from the cemetery gates.

"Please. Uh, could you wait just a second?"

She turned. "Yes?"

"I'm truly sorry I was wandering in the graveyard. I love history and I didn't realize at first this must have been a family cemetery or I never would have intruded. I was just so devastated to see the destruction there and—sad. Since Mr. Gerard was with me, and he said he knew you, I kind of assumed that would be okay. Please forgive me?"

A glimmer of softness passed over the grim face.

"Ach, I deed not realize Meester Gerard had accompanied you. I wass rude. But eet iss sad, no? Hass been in family for centuries but last two hundred years people come and they ruin. Pleeze, do not tell my sisters I haf been here today—yes? They get most upset when I visit this place. We pretend no meet?"

I nodded. "That's fine. And by the way, I truly believe desecrating graves is one of the sickest things imaginable. I hope this never happens again near this beautiful castle."

She nodded as well, then gestured to a doorway we'd reached by a route I'd never be able to remember. I refrained from stating, *"Cool. I'm entering Kastle Kouzlo Noc—a Gothic novel come to life in 21st Century Prague. Possibly—make that probably—is home to a flute-playing ghost. Shay Martin is gonna love it."* If I was dumb enough to voice that inner monologue, what little rapport we two had established would be as wrecked as the grave Corbin Lerner had been using for historical pursuits.

"Gothic novel come to life" truly *was* the best description for what I was about to enter. The first thing I saw were the three scowling, dragon-headed door-knockers. The creatures were positioned underneath a plaque clearly stating to visitors that this was an entrance to *Kastle Kouzlo Noc*. Why three of these guys were needed when one dragon would have been sufficient to scare the stuffings out of invited guests or trespassing interlopers was a mystery that could be scary to solve.

"What does it mean? In English?"

"*Kouzlo Noc* iss Magic Night." She actually smiled, before gracefully crossing in front of me to stand directly under the dragons.

I was right. Even in English, "Magic Night" sounded like the perfect castle in which to film Shay's Gothic musical movie. With any luck, the inside of the castle would have the same quality of menace indicated by the doorknockers. It had to. Shay had sounded more than a tad desperate when I'd spoken to her two hours earlier. "Abby? Please, please perform miracles for me, okay? It's vital I get a castle that's huge, spooky, and preferably situated close to a mountain. Got that? Vital. With a capital 'V'. But it better have ultra modern heating, beyond modern bathrooms, and really damn cheap rent. Call as soon as you find one, so I can take a breath again. I'll be doing this maid-of-honor thing for at least another week unless the sweet intended calls it off again—which, incidentally, she did yesterday—but that's for another day's gossip. Anyway, I've got my cell with me, although roaming charges are killing me, and let's face it, you're definitely roaming. Oh, hell. Hang on a sec." A pause, then, "Sorry, Fouchet. Gotta go. Kathy's mother is yelling something about togas fitting the groomsmen. I'm hoping I heard that wrong and she really said 'yoga' and keeping the groom 'fit.'" Another pause. "Damn. I wish these people would speak English."

"You're in Paris, Shay. Remember? French is the native tongue? The 'R' in *croissants* is a 'W'? Be careful to whom you say *'tu'* or you'll end up engaged—or in jail—and your own sweet intended Fuji will not be happy."

I could hear the grin on her face. "Got that right. I do kind of speak the language, but I swear everyone in this wedding so-called party rattles off their French faster than Kathy snagged this idiot Jean-Claude. They do it to annoy me. Along with sending me to fittings to encase my way-too-voluptuousness in orange. Orange! Who the hell wears orange in a wedding? I look like a fat demented neon pumpkin. Anyway, talk to you later."

"Shay! Wait. Don't you want a progress report on these castles? I'll talk fast and keep it short. Really. I've seen three that are possibles. The first one is on a hill that overlooks St. Vitus Cathedral. Gorgeous. Although keeping the tourists away while we film could get to be a problem. Then there's *Castle Sykoretvka*, which has twelve turrets but apparently only outdoor plumbing which I guess messes up your beyond modern bathroom thingee but it's also got this really neat…"

"Forget it. If you haven't immediately fallen in love with one and declared it perfect for our set, then I don't give a flying—uh, *croissant*. I trust you. Really, I do. And Bambi trusts me. But, keep me posted. It'll help stabilize what's left of my sanity for the next week or so. Oh, Abby? Go for eerie. Super shadowy. Tons of scary ambience. Lots of towers. And cheap. Very cheap."

I heard a final "Kathy, your mother's making me crazy! If this wedding doesn't happen tomorrow, I'm outta here and taking the Italian crème cake and the Belgian best man with me," then a click as the phone went dead.

The woman was seriously deranged. She was also my best friend, my sort of boss for this location gig, and a gifted, if occasionally manic, director/choreographer. Shay knew that Bambi Bohacek wanted a Gothic Castle. Therefore, Bambi—and Shay—would *get* a Gothic Castle. Although, with the specifics they'd given me, there was a good chance I'd have to spend the next week peering at and poking through every domicile built during 13th Century Prague or Moravia. I was a bit clueless as to exactly what Shay wanted in terms of "beyond modern heating and bathrooms," but I'd jump that hurdle when I found a castle that met all her other requirements. I was damn certain however, that "port-a-potty" would not be a good choice for Ms. Martin.

I'd already spent four days traipsing through the homes of former Czechoslovakian aristocrats deposed by former Soviet officials. They were now all eager for income. Income that could easily be forthcoming thanks to an independent film company looking to rent a nice abode. *Headlights Productions* was willing to pay a fair price for a castle in Prague where they could shoot this rock musical version of an old Gothic romance novel, complete with dancing girls, dancing boys, wild dogs, tame horses, and a boat chase ending under the Charles Bridge.

As I'd tried to tell Shay, three castles had been placed on what I was calling my "Possible maybe list." Obviously, Ms. Martin didn't want "maybe", "possible" or even "Purty damn close." She wanted perfect. Fine. I would damn well find perfect.

With some effort, I pulled my focus back to the woman standing beside me, whom I assumed was a Duskova sister—and the scary dragon doorknockers. Before I could lay a hand on one of the beasts, Ms. Duskova yanked on a cluster of wooden wind chimes that must serve as the anchor of a long tapestry bell-pull. Saying a silent "thank you" to loom-weavers everywhere, I was rewarded by hearing the sounds of two measures from Mozart's *Requiem*. The huge iron doors opened as the last chord died away.

Two women stood in the foyer just inside. They were identically dressed in that same "Early Modern Dancer" humorless black with the knitting needles "do" just like my companion, but unlike her, they were smiling. They also possessed the most gorgeous complexions I'd see outside of BoTox commercials. They beckoned for me to enter. The first Woman in Black glided serenely past me, then disappeared down a long hall while I was making a mental note to tell Shay this entire trio would be terrific as extras for the scene where the Count parades around in his mask at the ball.

The sisters pointed in unison at my head and began to giggle. The taller of the two nudged her shorter companion. I heard the word *nezraly*. They had to be discussing why my hair was mixed with green streaks. It wasn't something I cared to discuss in any language. I was embarrassed enough without trying to provide an explanation in Czech.

I forgot about my hair the instant I was ushered into a room that was one part museum, one part dungeon, and one part medieval ballroom. Huge round columns served as the primary support for the arched ceiling. Each monstrous pillar was decorated with the image of a dragon cozily attempting to chow down on a knight or two. There was no artwork on the walls. Not even a single mirror broke the stark, ink-black wallpaper.

My focus was drawn to the corner closest to the entranceway where a harpsichord, decorated with 15th Century style Flemish panels, proudly stood. Paperweight busts of Mozart, Beethoven, Haydn and someone who looked suspiciously like a young Eric Clapton, held down loose sheets of music.

I nodded to one of the ladies and gestured toward the instrument. Both women began chattering in Czech. I couldn't understand a word, but the gesture made by the shorter speaker obviously was an indication that I was welcome to provide some music for us all if I so desired. I didn't attempt to sit on the fragile stool. I wasn't sure it could hold the weight of a cat and though Johnny teases me for being "teensy" (five-two, a hundred and two pounds of solid muscle even after a gargantuan Tex-Mex dinner) that's still bigger than the majority of felines.

I pressed the keys for a C major chord then winced

in pain. The harpsichord hadn't been tuned in at least a century. I do have near-perfect pitch, but even someone with a poor musical ear would shudder at the discordant sound. I stepped away, hiding my glee. Shay would declare it "truly awesome." Garishly pitched notes from this sad, neglected piece of musical history would add the right touch for the scene where the sexy, but scarred Count Zilania falls in love with his beautiful ward, Honoria.

The ladies led me further into the ballroom. I stopped when I saw what lay half-hidden behind a beaded screen at the far end of the room. It appeared to be a black marble coffin. I turned to ask where this piece of furniture came from (if one could call a coffin furniture) but was interrupted by the entrance of my original companion.

She slowly made her way down the gigantic staircase, lifting her ankle-length gown just high enough so she wouldn't trip, then glided across the ballroom to greet me with a beatific smile and I quickly realized she was serious—our brief encounter in the graveyard had never happened. Quick improv into "never seen you before we were at the front door together" land.

Her eyes bored into mine. "You are girl promised from real estate agent?"

"Yes. I believe Mr. Zelenka called this morning? I'm Abby Fouchet. Currently acting as location scout for *Headlights Productions*. Um. Did Mr. Zelenka tell you we're looking to rent for about four months?"

She nodded. "He deed. We are most heppy to meet you. Oh, I am zo sorry. I haf not the introduction myself. I am Madam Veronika Duskova, owner of *Kouzlo Noc*. These are my sisters, who lif with me. Marta and Trina."

The ladies bowed. I bowed. I felt certain that the siblings, aside from Madam Veronika, only spoke Czech. Marta, Trina and Veronika. M. T. V. The final lyrics of the old Dire Straits tune, *Money for Nothing,* came rushing through my brain.

I pulled my focus back to Madam Duskova. "Very nice to meet you. All of you. You have a gorgeous home. I assume the castle has been in your family for years?"

Veronika nodded. "For plenty centuries. We haf live here through King Karel IV in 14th Century, und ze Hussites and Hapsburgs und Emperor Jozef through communists." She spat. "Pigs. Und now, wid new Czech Republic. Iss better. Zey do not understand yet aristocracy, but iss better than Soviet rule, no?"

The woman couldn't have been much over seventy but from the way she stated "we" I had the impression she and her two nodding sisters had resided in *Kouzlo Noc* during every one of those centuries. I shivered, hoping I wasn't about to have an out-of-body experience into the Seventeen-Hundreds. The last time that happened I experienced a little exchange of dialogue with Johnny's father, Kieran, thirty years into the future. I preferred to stay in my own time. Veronika saw that little body shake.

"Ah, I haf no manners. You come in and haf tea now. Iss chilly out, no? You Americans. Never do you dress warm enough here. I put fire on as well."

She gestured toward a walk-in fireplace big enough to roast a large-sized boar. Doubtless more than one pig had met his doom there courtesy of hungry Duskovas. Tongs with gargoyle heads rested alongside a poker at least six feet tall. The top of the poker featured the unfriendly visage of a dragon—first cousin to the doorknockers. I wondered how many murders had been committed using that dragon as weapon of choice. The shorter sister (Marta?) picked up the poker, presumably to sift through ashes before starting a nice fire. Veronika and Trina ushered me across the hall into a salon.

I released the breath I'd been holding since first seeing the poker in the hands of someone a foot shorter than the deadly instrument. The ladies led me to a sitting area complete with café table, dainty chairs, reading lamps, and a window seat offering comfort and doubtless a spectacular view of the countryside and river below.

I turned to Veronika. "Do you mind if I sit on the window seat? This view is truly breathtaking."

Marta appeared, without the poker, just in time to join her sisters in nodding. Veronika spoke for all. "Iss nice to see view. Hass been in family many year. Tapestry made by ancestor from Emperor Jozef. No one buried under seat for two centuries now. I get tea for you now."

FOUR

VERONIKA AND HER sisters exited the small space, leaving me gaping at the embroidered fabric that topped the window seat. The scene depicted was that of a sienna-colored horse bearing the image of a knight prepping to throw a silver lance at a group of beige and brown-clad peasants. The lance appeared bloodstained and the peasants were obviously scared witless.

I swallowed hard. I had no desire for the murdered spirit of some hapless enemy of the Duskova family to rise up from the window seat and plead for my intercession in his quest for justice and vengeance.

"Cream and sugar?"

I turned to watch the taller sister (Trina?) who was inching her way into the salon. The slow pace was doubtless due to the fact that she was struggling to carry a huge platter of pastries, cream and sugar pitchers, and dainty napkins stamped with the visage of dragons. Sis *Numero Dos,* Marta, was close behind her, bearing a tray with what had to be a teapot. Hard to tell. It was hidden by a "cozy" displaying an agitated black rooster crowing at his harem of six depressed chickens decked out in canary yellow bibs. Veronika allowed her sisters to play servant while she smiled and gestured toward a dainty chair on the far side of the café table. I smiled back.

"Thank you, ladies. Yes, cream and sugar would be

lovely. And, oh my! *Kolaches*. I love them. Especially the ricotta cheese and poppy seed."

Veronika's eyebrows shot into the top of her tightly bound hair. "You haf had *kolace?* You haf been in Prague how long?"

"Oh, it's not from being in Prague. I grew up in El Paso, Texas but had buddies from Austin to Dallas which meant stopovers in West—this little town that's primarily Czech. West is really the name of the town, not the geographic location. The owner of the film company, Bambi Bohacek, comes from West and she's always getting her mom to send kolaches as care packages to New York. There's a marvelous bakery not too far off the interstate that makes fresh kolaches daily and Mrs. Bohacek just goes in and buys them out. Yummy. I'm beyond addicted to these guys."

Veronika's eyes glazed a bit. "Ah."

Any conversation we'd've attempted came to a halt while we drank very strong tea from very delicate cups. Then the sisters watched, squealing with delight, as their crazy American guest devoured five of the kolaches. They did not partake. For those uninitiated as to the delights of Czech baked goods, kolaches are a sweet breakfast pastry. They can be filled with fruit, cheese, poppy seed, almond paste, or for a heartier meal, with sausage. I'll eat any of them with whatever stuffings are inside.

I finished with a particularly fat little treat made with apple filling, sat back, thanked God for great cooks, then politely dabbed at my mouth with the linen napkin. Madam Veronika Duskova knew a satisfied customer when she saw one.

It was time for negotiations to begin.

"So, Mees Fouchet…"

"Abby. Please call me Abby, Madam Duskova."

She nodded but did not return the favor of casual address. Madam D she was and Madam D she would remain—at least to her face.

"Ab-bee. How much iss film company weeling to pay for use of *Kouzlo Noc?*"

I named a price. It was a nice price. I'm a good performer, trying also to be a good location manager, but I'm a lousy bargainer. I knew Shay would adore this castle. The distance from Prague was right. The turrets and stairs and moat had a great fantasy look that was needed for outside shots. The ballroom was tailor-made for the inside musical numbers. The harpsichord alone would be worth renting the whole castle, even if a single note never sounded. The marble coffin was a bonus. In a word—perfect. I wasn't going to quibble over price. For all her "go with cheap, Abby, Bambi is so poor," grumblings, Shay was well aware that Ms. Bohacek had some very wealthy backers lined up for this project. *Headlights Productions* could afford to pay the Duskova family a tidy sum for the privilege of invading their castle for a few months.

But before I signed over any of the company's funds, part of my job was detailing precisely what we were buying.

"Ladies. *Kouzlo Noc* seems to be just what we're looking for, but I need to ask whether we'd be allowed access to any of the rooms upstairs. We don't want to toss anyone from a bedroom, but we very much could use several turrets, uh, towers. We also could use a small room for some of the more intimate moments in the movie. Not every scene will be a big song and dance number in the ballroom. And we'll also want some shots of the door areas with the dragons and everything. And probably the cemetery as well. I mean the newer one."

Veronika bit her lip, then turned and began a rapid-fire discussion in Czech with her sisters. I say "discussion" but it was really a monologue. Marta and Trina stayed silent. After much head shaking and nods and waving about of teacups (fortunately empty) all three ladies turned and stared at me. Trina and Marta picked up some embroidery work from bags nestled close to the window seat, then calmly began to sew. Veronika stood.

"Ve haf decided that you may use the south wing. There iss much rooms there along with stairs to turret. Good scene of outside too. Come. I show you."

I plopped my napkin and cup on the tray next to the rooster, then sped after her. I was nearly out the door when I stopped and turned. Trina was crooning into her embroidery. It sounded like Eric Clapton's *Layla*. She looked up at me and the sound stopped. She smiled. I blinked. And could have sworn she was singing this to me—and me only—as she was being carried out, God help me and her—in a black body bag.

Crap. A Dumas premonition vision zinging into my brain from wherever those damn visions come from. I quickly thrust that image from my mind. Veronika motioned for me to follow her up the huge staircase at the back of the ballroom. We took a left at the top of the stairs under a chandelier worthy of a set for any version of *Phantom of the Opera*. I got lost soon after we took a right, then another left before heading up the dizzying, narrow staircase that would have sent anyone with claustrophobic leanings to imagine the walls were closing in at a rapid pace.

We finally made it up the last flight and entered a landing, bookmarked at either end by solid doors standing at least eight feet tall. Veronika opened the door to our left with an oversized key from a metal key ring.

It was a simple guest room. A wedding-ringed patterned quilt, colored in soft shades of ivory and sage, lay on a bed that must be several centuries old. Head and footboards, stained in a light walnut, framed the box springs and mattress. A vanity, wardrobe, and small washboard, all in the same walnut color, were the only other furnishings in the room. It was immaculately kept, with a saccharine sweetness to it. It should work well for our heroine Honoria's bedroom when she arrives from London. Someplace more exciting and ominous would be needed for her seduction at the hands of Count Zilania.

I nodded at Veronika. "It's very pretty. So. What else is up here?"

Veronika marched across the landing to another room, without bothering to notice if I followed. There were no furnishings in the tiny space, not even a table or a chair. But this was a room with a view. I'd been enchanted with the scenery from the window seat downstairs, but it paled by comparison. An entire forest lay before me. Spires from the cathedrals in Prague off in the distance, jutting into the bluest sky I'd seen since the last time I was in Texas.

I didn't care if Shay used this room for Honoria, for Zilania, for one or more villains or the whole camera crew. I'd've paid any amount of money simply for the privilege to worship the countryside through this glass once a day for the next month. I leaned out the open window and breathed in the pure, crisp air. A chilly wind blew my hair back from my face so I retreated. Veronika started to shut the window but I stopped her. "Wait. Please. About an hour ago, I heard the most marvelous musician playing the flute. Sounded like it came from what I guess y'all refer to as the north wing? Who lives there?"

My question was greeted with silence and looks that chilled me more than the gust of wind had. "Dere iss no one. We are only people at *Kouzlo Noc*."

"But I'm sure I heard music."

"I do not hear anyting. Perhaps our gardener is playing, how you say, 'see dees.' He likes music from America. Must be that you hear, no? He iss here today."

I knew what I'd heard and it wasn't the family gardener strutting around listening to some rapper from the States with a CD player held on his shoulder while he planted and pruned in the lilacs (or whatever blooms bloomed at the castle.) The music hadn't come from below. It had come from a castle wing. It was very classical. It was also very Mozart. Wolfgang Amadeus. The one, the only. The tune had been an aria from *The Magic Flute*.

Johnny had denied being the musician. Veronika had denied any music being played except on a boombox. I knew better. A ghostly flautist was playing for my benefit.

Perfect. I'd stumbled into a Gothic tale while trying to rent a Gothic castle for a Gothic film based on a Gothic novel. The intrusion of Goth was making me dizzy. Doubtless, a headless flute player was being held in chains in one wing and no, that's not logical because how the hell can one play a flute without lips which would normally be attached to a head? A beautiful damsel in distress would be found in the tower of another wing, cranking out arias from Mozart's last comic opera while hoping a gallant prince would hear her songs and arrive with sword in hand to rescue her from her sad fate. During some dark and stormy night, the murdered peasants depicted on the bloodstained tapestry on the downstairs window seat would pop out and hunt down their oppressors. The dragon-headed doorknockers would take human form in the guise of a black-clad demon-possessed tortured hero. Finally, the Victorian governess trio of the sisters would burn the place down à la Jane Eyre's Mrs. Rochester.

Veronika stared at me as though I'd brought the madwoman's matches. I hoped I hadn't just opened my mouth and aired my fantasies to *Headlights Productions'* new landlady.

I smiled. "Well, at least your gardener shows good taste. Can't do much better than Mozart."

Not an ounce of color could be seen on the woman's face. She struggled to catch her breath. She gulped at the air around her. She arranged one of her hairpins trying to subdue a non-existent errant lock. Her hand went to her chest and for a moment I thought CPR was next on the day's agenda.

"Veronika? Beg pardon. Madam Duskova. Are you all right? Did I say something to upset you?"

"No. No. You say not'ing bad. I…I…perhaps am winded climbing so many stairs."

"I'm so sorry. Do you want to rest for a bit? I have no problem staying up here looking at this view for awhile."

"Iss okay." Her spine stiffened. "We set price, yes? With south wing, and west and east wing. No north wing. Iss no available. Cemetery included, but no north wing. Add thousand *koruna* to rent and we haf deal."

I tried frantically to remember the exchange rate for the Czech Republic with American dollars and decided this would not be the time to make a joke about *koruna* and Corona beer.

"We have a deal. Our director, Shay Martin, will be in next week, but I have her power of attorney to sign whatever contracts are needed."

"Good. We go downstairs, now, yes?"

It was a dismissal. I didn't care. In silence, I followed her to the landing, then down the stairway from hell, musing the whole time about why Veronika had gotten into such a tizzy over a harmless comment about Mozart. Unless she knew the flute-player was indeed not part of life's present tense.

Veronika literally marched me to the back door. We murmured a few pleasantries and determined how and when the contracts for renting the castle would be signed. Then I was outside staring at the dragonheads and the tapestry pull. I felt like the relative who's just been informed the family disowned her for burping during Thanksgiving dinner.

"Well, fine," I addressed one of the dragons. "Ms. Veronika Duskova is a strange bird, but I have achieved victory for *Headlights* and gotten Bambi and Shay their friggin' spooky castle. I shall see you and your fire-breathing brothers in a day or two with contracts in hand, but in the meantime I'm heading down to the Vitus Bar for a stiff drink—and I don't mean tea."

The closest dragon assumed an expression amazingly similar to the one I'd last seen on Veronika's face. I turned my back and gazed up at the north turret where I'd heard the haunting music. The north turret that Madam D had clearly stated was off limits to everyone. This time no denim-clad burglar could be seen. Johnny had just vanished without bothering to say good-bye.

Which was damn tacky of him. What was up? Did he plan to contact Yolanda, head writer for *Endless Time* and rent the castle for the daytime drama? Start a ghost story which would knock ratings off the charts? *Kouzlo Noc* was already about to be besieged by actors and a slightly obsessive compulsive director. Add a spooky legend and sell it to a crowd of theatrical types and you'd have a mad dash for sleepovers in the north wing.

I needed nicer jammies.

FIVE

"SMART-ASS, SECOND-STORIED wannabe, semantic-twisting, art-restoring, soap-starring sometime swain!"

The waiter looked startled. I shook my head.

"Not you. You're wonderful. You've let me camp here for an hour drinking boozy hot chocolate and eating kolaches and you will receive a marvelous tip. Sorry. I'm just ranting to myself."

The waiter smiled cheerfully at me, then set the Prague Castle–representative ceramic mug down in front of me, turning the handle exactly where I could grab with ease. Soft wisps of steam swirled around the fresh whipped cream floating atop the hot chocolate and Kahlua—my third cup in an hour. I inhaled the cinnamon and cocoa scent and blessed Shay for sending me to Prague even as I cursed Johnny Gerard.

My waiter nodded as he handed me a fresh linen napkin. It wouldn't surprise me to learn that furious drool had collected at the sides of my mouth. I'd start foaming soon. Johnny. Leaving me to fend for myself with Veronika Duskova after the meet in the graveyard. Sliding down trees on his way-too-sexy bottom. Being silent about us as "us" and whatever strange doin's were doin' at the castle. Going off for three stinking months instead of staying in Manhattan (albeit jobless since *Endless Time* might well have fired him) and marrying me.

Restoring a mural. Right. A mural that was *not* in

the north wing. A mural that wasn't "up to speed" according to Mr. Gerard so no one could see the ancient wreck until it was done.

I growled again, but was interrupted before any barking began.

"I beg your pardon. Aren't you Ms. Fouchet? The girl who's finding the castle for the movie?"

Two blue eyes were staring at me from under a delightfully curly and undeniably natural blonde head of hair. I hurriedly wiped off the rest of the foam around my mouth, then gazed into the lovely eyes of the man who called my name. He looked familiar. It hit me. I'd seen his picture recently. He was the lead actor Shay had hired; the man who'd be playing the role of the mysterious Count Zilania. I knew he was from Vienna, but couldn't remember his name.

He was beautiful. I was dumbstruck. I did manage to nod and gesture toward the empty chair across from me but had to swallow my bite of cheese kolache before I was able to speak. Aside from good manners, I had no desire to humiliate myself in front of the god from Austria by trying to talk with my mouth full. He politely did not start conversing until I finished. "I am sorry. I should not have interrupted you while you were eating."

I shook my hand. "Not a problem. I just wasn't expecting any of the cast to show up before Shay made the announcement as to exactly *where* to show up."

"Ms. Martin is fast. She told me she'd hung up the phone with you within minutes of then calling me. I was already in Prague at the hotel and she was excited that I could get a head start on exploring *Kastle Kouzlo Noc.*"

"Aha. I wondered. Did she call anyone else?"

"She said she was contacting Lily Lowe, the actress

playing the heroine. Apparently Lily is also in Prague, but she grew up here and she has family here still so Ms. Martin wanted to tell her to view the castle very soon."

I nodded. He smiled as he reached across the table to take my hand. Thankfully, it was clean of all remnants of goo, ricotta cheese, and whipped cream.

"I have bad manners." He inclined his head. "I am Franz Hart. Playing Count Zilania."

"I'm Abby Fouchet. Good to meet you."

We shook hands, then he leaned back in the chair and signaled the waiter to trot over for another order of hot chocolate and pastries. I couldn't eat another bite, but decided it would be rude to leave him. And to gaze with admiration at that face? Heck, that was worth staying at the table another hour or so. *To heck with you, disappearing, keeping-mum Johnny Gerard.*

He took a sip of cocoa, then asked, "How did you and Shay Martin get together for this film?"

"We're roommates. Met at a dance class in Manhattan several years ago. She needed a third for the apartment so I moved in. We have a very—interesting—third roommate named Cherry Ripe who was supposed to get married to Guido Marricino two months ago but postponed until the Marricino matriarch can make it to the wedding. She lives in Trequanda, which is some hill town in Tuscany. She doesn't get out much. The matriarch, that is. Cherry gets out a *lot*. Which could be another reason for the postponement since Guido gets a little anxious that his bride-to-be might still prefer the single life."

I was rambling. His eyes were slightly glazed, somewhat like Madam Veronika Duskova's had been back at *Kouzlo Noc.* But he smiled, then asked another question.

"Shay said you were from Texas? I was in Amarillo when I was shooting a musical movie two years ago."

"Musical? Really? Um—country music?"

Before Franz had a chance to respond, another voice chimed in over my head. "I personally love country music. Not as much as I love classic rock or classic classical, but hey—give me a steel guitar and a head full of big bleached blonde hair and I'm there."

I turned.

Johnny. Before I had a chance to react—either to the man or the comment, he'd grabbed a chair from an empty table nearby and plopped his denimed butt down.

"I'm Johnny Gerard. Ms. Fouchet and I met—earlier— at the castle."

That was true. Of course he'd left out that our first meeting had been in Manhattan not long after Shay and I had met and that apart from some angst and murder and jealousy over other women (I have trust issues) and solving crime, corruption and murder, then his contract with a soap opera sending him to foreign lands without me, we'd been together for the last two and a half years. I can keep a secret, although I'd've liked a good reason as to why I couldn't reveal that Johnny and I were a couple.

Johnny stared at Franz, obviously waiting for introductions. Neither male looked happy. I coughed, then did the politeness thing. "Joh…uh, Mr. Gerard, this is Franz Hart, who's playing the esteemed Count Zilania for the film. I did tell you we're doing a film right? Anyway, Franz, this is the not-so-esteemed Johnny Gerard, who obviously is a bit out-of-date in his country music assessment since bleached blondes went the way of the dial-phone quite a few years ago. Mr. Gerard is in Prague…um, why are you in Prague exactly? Something to do with *art?*"

Gerard casually leaned forward and used his finger to wipe a bit of whipped cream off my upper lip. I'd had no idea it was there. I turned redder than his hair. He settled back in his chair, turned and looked directly at Franz.

"I'm restoring a mural for the Duskovas. It was a mess to begin with."

An "Ah" was the only response from Franz.

There was silence from all points of the table. There was also hostility between the two men that appeared to have no source.

Franz quietly asked, "So you have an interest in *Kouzlo Noc,* Mr. Gerard?"

"Johnny. Please, make it Johnny."

Franz's mouth tightened ever so slightly. "Johnny. Yes? *Kouzlo Noc?*"

He smiled. "I have an interest in the arts, Mr. Hart." Silence again.

I slugged down the last of my cocoa and tried to fill the quiet with chatter. "Well, since you have an interest in the arts, you'll like this. The Slovak Opera company is performing *The Magic Flute* starting next week at the Estates Theatre. I, for one, can't wait to see it. Even in German the name is just thrilling. *Die Zauberflote.*"

Johnny raised one brow. "Flutes on the brain, Miss Fouchet?"

I echoed the tone he'd taken with Franz. "Abby. Please, make it Abby. And there's nothing on my brain—or conscience. I just happen to love that particular opera."

I nodded at Franz. "Uh, Franz? You a fan of Mozart?"

"Mozart? Of course. I am from Vienna, after all."

"Good point. Of course, that implies major Strauss waltzes above all else."

I smiled. Franz smiled. Johnny smiled. We were all so chummy here.

Franz asked, "Why the question?"

"Oh. Well, since *The Magic Flute* is playing at The Estates Theatre for the next few weeks, you'd probably want to see it in Prague. I do."

"But of course!" Franz exclaimed. "The Estates is a beautiful theatre. Built in 1783 in the NeoClassical style."

Johnny wasn't interested in talking architecture. Nope. He wanted to talk Wolfgang Amadeus Mozart, who, by a far too coincidental coincidence, had lived in the mid-18th century—the same time frame as the graves in the cemetery where Corbin Lerner had been exploring.

Johnny leaned back in his chair. "Funny you mentioned Mozart, Abby. I'm actually gathering information about the first production of *The Magic Flute* when it was performed in Prague in the Seventeen-Nineties. Trying to learn about the various instruments used in that performance."

There was no reason for Franz to stiffen, but he did. So slightly that I wasn't sure he'd even made a movement. I was lost. The two of them seemed to be playing a chess game and I wasn't even the referee.

This little café served sweet goodies, but also doubled as a bar. My waiter returned just when I was about to dive in and get nosy. I kept silent. Johnny ordered a bourbon and coke, and Franz went with white wine. I threw caution and calories to the wind and asked for my fourth Kahlua and chocolate, wishing the amount of Kahlua was more than just a taste. Then we all sat back in our chairs and played "avoid Mozart" for the next hour.

Johnny started with "Franz? You're playing the hero for this movie Abby's involved in?"

A nod.

"So, how'd you land the role?"

Franz relaxed. "I sent Miss Bohacek clips from the last two films I was in. Both leads. Both in German, but she saw in me the mysterious nobleman she wanted and sent her recommendation on to Miss Martin." He added, "I also sing and dance, which is good for this movie."

Johnny took a sip of his drink. Franz let him swallow before asking, "And what exactly do you do, Mr. Gerard?"

"In the off season, when you're not breaking into castle turrets." Oh lordy, had I said that out loud?

Apparently not. Neither man looked at me with any change of expression.

Gerard finished his entire drink, waved to the waiter for another, then smiled with absolute ease. "Many things. I'm an actor and singer." Understatement. Johnny had both a Daytime Drama Emmy and a Best Actor Tony under his belt. "I'm also a musician. I've done studio recordings; sometimes I play down in Soho with a group."

This was news. When had this started?

Franz and I spoke at once.

Him: "What instrument do you play?"

Me: "What's the name of the band?"

Johnny answered me first. "Band is called *Noble Posse*. We're very eclectic in our choice of music. Classic rock, early garage punk, big band, C & W." He shot me what I call his "Irish choirboy caught naked with two Irish milkmaids in the church vestry" look. "I use a different name though in the group. Gregory Noble."

Typical. Another plot twist for the cop who does everything. I wondered when Johnny had filmed these musical episodes for *Endless Time*. Before, during or after his African safari? Why hadn't I been invited to at least watch since my character of Vanessa had been cancelled?

I smiled, a bit grimly. "I like it. Sounds fun. I'm impressed."

"Thanks. And it is fun." He glanced at Franz. "I play guitar. Other stuff as well, but that's my primary instrument." He smiled. "So, Franz? Tell us about Vienna, would you? I've never been there, but heard it's gorgeous and the people are friendly—and the pastries? Wicked."

Franz complied with the request and began to regale Johnny and me with a guide through Olde Vienna, talking about the great sights such as the Spanish Riding School where the Lipizzaner horses are trained. I heard about St. Stephen's Cathedral and the Baroque Schonbruan, aka the Hapsburg dynasty palace. My attention was wandering after the list of orchestras in the city, but I perked up at the mention of the Giant Ferris Wheel, which was portrayed in the classic movie, *The Third Man*. And I began to drool when he described the dream dessert of carboholic freaks the world over—*Sachertorte,* named for the restaurant that originally served the dish.

Franz did not mention that Vienna had premiered *The Magic Flute*. He also did not mention that Vienna was the place where Mozart died; or whether that death had come by means of a cup of poison administered by rival composer Salieri, by simple ill health, or perhaps by someone with motive even nastier than jealousy.

When Franz finished his whirlwind tour through Vienna, we all simply sat in silence. Other than the Ferris wheel and the visions of torte running through my head, I had no idea what other bits of info Franz had given us. My mind was in the Czech Republic, not Austria.

Suddenly my mind was also at *Kouzlo Noc.* An "Abby-vision" was flashing before me. I could see the north turret of the castle—and I could see someone falling from it. It was a short vision but vivid. I shivered.

I needed to vanquish that image. Mentioning Mozart again was bound to stir things up a bit and center my focus outside of bodies tumbling from tall windows.

"So, Franz? What's your favorite part of *The Magic Flute?* Were you aware it was first performed in Vienna?" I turned to Johnny. "But of course, you, being the consummate musician, probably can sing the durn thing in German, too. And while I'm being nosy, Mr. Gerard, you said you were doing research on the opera's first Prague performance. Why not the original from Vienna? For that matter, why the research?"

Johnny's response was a crock as far as his real reasons for studying the Prague version. He avoided any mention of why he was researching the bloody thing to begin with. "Because the Prague production contained a few elements in the orchestra that were not heard in Vienna. Especially for the flautist. Don't you just love the flute?"

I was now sorry I'd mentioned the stinkin' thing and worried that Johnny would bring up my far-out theory about the ghost at *Kouzlo Noc* who could well be a flautist. I began to blather. "I love *The Magic Flute*. Of course, anyone who loves opera loves that one. I don't get all the symbolism, and I wish Wolfgang Amadeus had thrown in a few more arias and less recitative, but the Papageno/Papagena duet is way too much fun, and you can't do better than that aria by the Queen of the Night. So, aside from me, who's planning to see this current production by the Czech Company? I've heard that this version will have modern costuming and more of a present-day approach, whatever the heck that means."

Johnny folded the napkin he hadn't used, left it on the plate he hadn't used, then stood. "I have tickets for the gala opening Friday night. Care to join me, Ms. Fouchet?"

Franz also stood. "I plan to attend that myself. Perhaps I can escort Ms. Fouchet since we are staying at the hotel together."

He made it sound as though we were sharing a room and I had no desire to be labeled his sleep partner/lover when that label was absolutely false. Johnny wasn't normally the jealous type (unlike me) but he did have a fine Irish temper and I could easily visualize him picking up Franz then tossing him into the dessert tray. Of course, if Johnny would just own up to the girlfriend/boyfriend truth of our relationship then Franz wouldn't be so quick to make insinuating comments about his and my current residences.

I shoved my chair back and jumped to my feet. "Well, isn't that a kick, Franz. I had no idea we were both at that hotel. Guess Shay arranged it?" I smiled so my comment didn't sound harsh. "Tell you what, guys.

Why don't we all meet at the theatre Friday? I'm sure a few other cast members from the movie would like to join us. Shay said at least three of the leads, plus our composer for the movie, should be here by then. Are tickets hard to get?"

Johnny replied, "I bought two tickets for you and me less than an hour ago. Sorry, Mr. Hart, but you're on your own for yours. They should still have seats available for your other cast and staff." He glared at Franz, who appeared clueless as to how he'd wronged Johnny Gerard.

I quickly said, "Cool. Hey, look at the time! I've got stuff I need to do. Johnny, I guess I'll see you Friday? And Franz, we can meet tomorrow if you're coming out to get a look at the castle? I need to take some notes for Shay on what scenes should be shot where."

Franz brightened. "I very much will want to see the castle. So tomorrow perhaps you can guide me?"

"Sure. It would be my distinct pleasure."

Johnny bowed, then growled. "Ms. Fouchet? Friday—or sooner."

He turned and stalked off.

I reached under the table for my bag. Franz politely extended his hand. "May I carry that for you?

I smiled at him, but shook my head. "No, thanks. I'm wandering off to check out this old bookstore I saw in a guidebook. I love hunting through old stuff like maps and histories. And I'm hoping they'll have some other Gothic tales that were written in countries other than just America in the Sixties and Seventies. I'd love to be able to bug Shay with strange ideas." I paused. "Uh, I'm sorry that Johnny was a bit abrupt about tickets and stuff."

He eyed me with curiosity and some other emotion I couldn't define. "Just how long did you say you and Mr. Gerard have been friends?"

I did more spinning than an Olympic skater finishing a routine. "I ran into him a few hours ago at the *Kastle*. He was, uh, looking at some rare tree there."

He was looking at that tree up close and personal with his backside and that tree was about as rare as a pine in East Texas, but it was almost the truth. I added, "I gather he is doing some restorative artwork for the owners there."

Franz quietly stated, "He's quite the Renaissance man isn't he? I should study him for future use as a character."

I held off from stating, *"Honey, been done. Tune in tomorrow—or whenever Johnny Gerard is back in Manhattan filming—and watch the quintessential Mister Do-It-All, Gregory Noble, outwit villains while surviving jumping out of planes with slashed parachutes then skiing down the Alps promptly upon landing."*

"Well, Ms. Fouchet. Oops, sorry. Abby. I'm going to attempt to purchase tickets for the opera. I shall see you tomorrow?"

I nodded. "Sure. I'll give the Duskovas a call and give them a heads up that our leading man would like a preview of the set—or at least what will be the set."

"Thank you. And thanks for mentioning the opera will be performing here. It will be fun to see."

He turned and left the café. I wasn't sure "fun" was a word I'd've chosen for this upcoming night at the opera. If the tension became any more palpable between Franz and Johnny, Friday evening promised to be as much fun as climbing into the bloodied, tapestried, coffin optimistically called a window seat at the Duskova sisters' castle.

SIX

I'D LIED TO Franz about my reasons for digging through old books. I could care less about Gothic novels from any other period or country. Shay would do what she wanted to do with the movie without extra research on my part. *Kouzlo Noc* and Mozart were the topics inflaming my curiosity. Madam Duskova and Franz had acted wacky whenever the composer was mentioned and while I hadn't had the chance to toss in Amadeus' name to the cryptic crypt explorer, Corbin Lerner, doubtless he'd've done the turn-pale-and-blanch bit just like Veronika and Franz. On the other hand, Mr. Gerard's freckled complexion hadn't changed a whit during Mozart discussions. He was too busy tossing grenades into the air and watching how and where everyone— everyone being Franz—ducked. I was determined to do a bit of semi-academic exploration about *Kouzlo Noc* and its possible connection to Wolfgang Amadeus Mozart's last opera. Something was way weird.

Especially when it came to music. There's nothing wrong with my ears. I have a tendency to lose earrings on a regular basis, but the audio portion of my eardrum works just fine. I knew damn well I'd heard someone playing a tune from *The Magic Flute*. Madam D had nearly jumped out of the turret when I brought up Mozart. An historian was exploring a graveyard that coincidentally happened to contain markers from

the same era as the composer's life. My conclusion—
unless there was a musical ghost living at the castle
(okay, technically, not "living" there) someone was trying to create that illusion. I wanted the skinny on who,
when, why and how.

A tiny store declaring itself to be *Jozef's Knihu* (Joe's
Books) had been listed in my guidebook as a great place
to find out-of-print novels, antique maps, and, most important to my quest, biographies of old Czech aristocrats. Good possibility for tomes concerning cultural
activities in Prague through the last four centuries. An
added bonus was Jozef's location: three blocks away
from the café where I'd been scarfing down a load of
pastries while exchanging barbs with two testy males
for the last hour.

For no good reason I took a few furtive glances
around me before stepping foot inside *Jozef's Knihu*. No
wannabe burglars. No beautiful gods from Austria. No
humorless historians. No landladies in black. I ducked
inside before any of the aforementioned folks jumped
out from behind statues in the street. A grandfather
clock nestled between two enormous shelves of books
chimed the hour. Four p.m. I had no plans for the evening. Johnny hadn't bothered to even ask if I was free
to meet him. I shoved that thought away. I would wade
in and prowl until I was tossed out whenever closing
time hit—which, in the Czech Republic, would doubtless be after midnight.

It became quickly apparent that my biggest problem in locating the books I needed was that all the
shelves had Czech titles announcing subject matter. I
plopped onto a footstool in front of Shelf One, pulled out
my handy *Louie's Lingo* and prepared to fight through

names and nouns until I found the words for biography and culture. I got stalled on the "Eating Out" section for a moment, entranced with some of the exotic-sounding dishes that could be found at funky little restaurants all over Prague. Barely half an hour from Abby's last snackfest and food was overtaking my thought processes. I needed to start dancing again soon or I'd outweigh the armored knights guarding the ballroom of *Kouzlo Noc*.

"Excuse me? Miss? Do you need help?"

I looked up. A gentleman who appeared to be in his seventies loomed over me, smiling, leaning on a cane that reminded me of the one my grandfather had stored in the closet back home. Major crow's feet crinkled his eyes. He had white hair and a luxurious white beard. His expression was kind and the English impeccable. He looked like what God would look like if the Deity owned a bookstore.

I nodded. "Thank you. Yes. I do need help. Can you read Czech? Oh heck. Dumb question. Sorry."

His smile grew broader. "I am Czech. I read and speak and write Czech. I also read and speak English, French, German and Italian. What are you searching for, young lady?"

I squirmed just a bit. "Um. Well, I'm looking for oh, uh, old Gothic romances from the Nineteen Sixties or Seventies?" I explained about *Headlights Productions* doing a film.

The man stayed silent. I knew guilt was stamped all over my face. "And, also…this is a bit strange, but I'm trying to find any books about *Kastle Kouzlo Noc* and the Duskova family. *Headlights* just rented the castle."

He shot me an odd glance, pointed to one of the

stacks in the back of the shop, then lightly took my hand in his. I was afraid without his grip on the cane he'd topple over, taking the clock and a few shelves with him, but his stance stayed firm.

"There is one volume on *Kastle Kouzlo Noc*. But, tell me—why are you this interested? Are you an historian or genealogist as well as a movie person?"

What hesitation I had lasted only a second. One trusts God when God asks a question. One does not lie to God.

"Honestly? There's something odd at *Kouzlo Noc*. For one thing, people get loony when I mention Mozart. They hush up or they sidestep the issue or they just out-and-out lie. And I discovered an 18th Century graveyard near the castle that's been ripped to shreds, which was disgusting, sad—and odd. Talk of genealogy just doesn't sound right to me. Consequently, I have this feeling that all is not kosher at the castle. So to speak."

His smile now lit up the dim bookstore. "In that case, I shall save you some time and effort and tell you the legend of Mozart and *Kouzlo Noc*."

"Really? That would be marvelous," I told him. "Especially since I'm not sure what I'm hunting for."

He motioned for me to sit back down on my footstool then pulled a high-backed chair away from the wall. He settled himself there, gently laid the cane next to the chair and took a breath. Obviously this man was a storyteller. I only hoped he would tell a tale that could explain why everyone got snarky when flute-players, Mozart, and *Kouzlo Noc* were mentioned in the same sentence.

"First, young lady, are you aware that Mozart's *Die Zauberflote* was given its Prague premiere in 1792?

Almost a year to the day that the original opera was performed in Vienna."

"I wasn't sure of the dates, sir, but I did know the first performances were in Vienna, not Prague, even though Mozart was in Prague only months before. Is that right?"

He nodded as vigorously as he could, his white hair bobbing enthusiastically after my response. "Very good. Yes, Mozart was in Prague composing an opera in honor of the coronation of King Leopold II. He did not want to do this, you understand, but he was in need of money and he was already in ill health. Perhaps he knew his death was not far off. He was very depressed at this time. His soul was so low, in such a despair that he'd even written a family member telling them that *'everything is cold—cold as ice. Everything seems empty.'* It breaks my heart to this day. Such a fine young man. I believe this is why *The Magic Flute* became, in truth, such a hopeful opera—to overcome his own misery."

He nearly had me in tears myself over this poignant quote from the young, brilliant composer but he continued, "It hurts me deep in my heart that Mozart was never able to see *Die Zauberflote* performed in Prague at the beautiful Estates Theatre."

"Oh my gosh! That's where I'll be seeing it."

"Yes? Ah, that is good. You will get more of a flavor of what I am to tell you, although most music lovers believe National Theatre is better equipped for large operas nowadays than is the old Estates."

"I'm sorry. I interrupted you," I said. "Please, go on."

"You did not interrupt in a bad way; you shared your happiness and I'm very pleased. It is quite nice to hear that excitement in your voice when you talk of going to the opera. Sadly, I have heard that most Americans your age are more interested in hippy-hoppy video music than the lovely classics."

We were straying from his story, but since God looked disappointed over my generation's bad taste, I felt compelled to reveal that my Dad and uncle are both very musical and I was raised hearing Haydn and Bach issuing forth from the radio in Dad's office while Appalachian Mountain tunes were the order of the day when Uncle Don taught them to his bluegrass band. And lastly, my cousin David (Don's son) blasting away on his trumpet for his mariachi band.

"Bluegrass?" God beamed at me. "I am a big fan of bluegrass myself. Although, I am not familiar with 'mariachi.' I will have to purchase a CD or two and listen."

"I'll get David to send you a few. He's got all the really good ones."

We smiled at each other in perfect understanding. Then, without skipping a beat, or a thought, he continued, "When it was announced in Prague that *The Magic Flute* would be performed here, the city went wild. Citizens of Prague had always adored Mozart and mourned his death with much intensity. The singers for the opera had already been chosen. Many of the musicians had been picked as well. But this is where the story really begins."

I held my breath waiting for what had to be a sad, spooky tale.

His voice was melodic and I was entranced. "During the end of the 18th Century there lived a wonderful flautist, a man named Ignatz Jezek. He grew up in Prague, learning music from the finest teachers. He was a gifted musician on many levels, but with a flute to his lips, he was a genius, someone who could play music that truly lifted the soul of man.

"Ignatz was more than an exceptional flute player. He was a craftsman. He had been in Vienna when *The Magic Flute* premiered. He even spent a day visiting with Mozart. The two had become quite good friends when Ignatz met the composer the previous months when Mozart had been in Prague working on the coronation piece for Leopold II. Ignatz wanted to be part of the opera's history when *Die Zauberflote* came to Prague and he wanted to give a gift to Mozart that no one else could give. So, he handcrafted a special flute, one he intended to present to his friend when he next came to the city."

I bit my lip. "But Mozart never returned."

"No, he did not. Mozart passed away only months after *Die Zauberflote* was performed in Vienna."

"So what happened to Ignatz Jezek and his flute?"

An expression of sheer joy made the man's face look like that of a teenager. "Ignatz learned that *The Magic Flute* would be in Prague in May 1792. So he brought with him the flute he had made and offered it to the company to use as they wished. I have heard that the manager was thrilled and touched by this gesture—this gift of love. But he told Mr. Jezek that the flute would be put to better use if the flautist himself played it as part of the orchestra. He hired him at that very moment."

This was a very romantic tale but I started wondering where the Duskovas fit in, and why Ignatz Jezek was haunting the place. I said as much to the gentleman, without mentioning Ignatz's presence at the castle piping tunes since I didn't want God labeling me a lunatic.

He smiled at me and my impatience. "This is where

the real story, the legend, if you will, enters the picture. For, you see, even in 1792, the rumors had begun that Ignatz somehow had created a truly enchanted flute. An instrument with mystical powers. A magical flute for Wolfgang Amadeus Mozart."

I sat up. "Wow. I had a feeling this was going to lead to mystery and magic. This is marvelous. So, what's the rumor about the magic? What are the powers?"

"I myself do not know. I do not believe anyone knows for certain. At the time Ignatz made the flute there was much interest in alchemy in this part of Europe and to many, alchemy meant turning objects into gold. I am certain there is more to the magic than monetary treasure, but perhaps that is because a man such as Ignatz would not have been tempted to infuse music, especially a gift to his dear friend and mentor, Mozart, with the evils of greed. But then, Ignatz and Mozart were both freemasons and alchemy was an interest of many of the masons of the time so perhaps this is the correct theory after all. Whatever the power is, magic of some sort resides in the flute. This I do believe."

"What happened to Mr. Jezek? And the flute?"

He looked as stricken as though what he was about to tell me had happened the day before instead of over two centuries ago. "Both Ignatz Jezek and the flute disappeared late in 1793. No trace of either was ever found. His children mourned for him for many, many years."

His sadness hit me now as well. "How awful."

"Indeed." He paused. "Ignatz was living with his sister and brother-in-law at the time."

"Wait. Let me guess—these in-laws didn't happen to have the last name of Duskova, did they?"

"You're very quick. They did. And since 1793, there

has been speculation that Ignatz knew he was going to die and that he hid the flute somewhere in *Kouzlo Noc*."

I paused, then asked, "So, the pursuit of wealth and treasure often being the nature of the human beast, I gather that this magic flute has been the dream of fortune hunters and plunderers throughout the years?"

"Indeed, yes, young lady. Family members of the Duskovas. Visitors to the castle. Anyone who had even an inkling of the story. Of course, through over two centuries of living, most people forgot. If anyone even remembered Ignatz Jezek, they'd sigh, *'Ah, a tragedy, this brilliant musician gone missing forever, but it happened years ago. On to the next tale.'* As for the flute? Since it disappeared so completely, there began to be much speculation as to whether it had even existed in the first place. People do not believe in magic that much anymore, so the treasure-seekers gradually did not come to *Kouzlo Noc*."

The words came involuntarily. "Until now."

We looked at each other for a very long moment.

Jozef softly coaxed, "Please. Did something happen to you this morning? You saw—what?"

I couldn't deny it. Not to my new friend the kindly Deity. "Not saw. Heard. Someone playing or playing a recording of a flautist trilling the opening of *Magic Flute*. Somewhere in the north wing of *Kastle Kouzlo Noc*." I looked deep into the bookseller's gentle grey eyes. "No wonder Veronika was so freaked when I mentioned Mozart and music in the same breath with the north wing. Being a Duskova, related to the man even remotely, she must have lived with that legend her whole life and understands that now Jezek's flute would be worth quite a bit, whether or not she believes it will do tricks and turn the castle into gold. This explains why that ghastly cemetery looks as though it had been ransacked more than once in the last two centuries. I met an historian searching in a crypt, scraping dirt off of names with a dagger, and I'll bet you anything he believes that flute is there. Perhaps along with the body of its maker." I shivered.

"What about you, miss? What do you believe?"

I closed my eyes for a second as I remembered that moment when I first heard the music. "I listened to the man. Well, that is, I heard someone play and whoever he was, he's still the consummate musician. I don't care about whatever power the flute possesses, intriguing as it is. I'd lay odds though that Ignatz Jezek was murdered and he haunts that castle. Perhaps he wants justice. Or he just wants the chance to play his flute? Whatever his reasons, it appears he never left *Kastle Kouzlo Noc*. And for centuries he's been fending off greedy seekers of treasure because I'd wager that even if no magic is inside that flute, it's worth a potful of money. And a new crop of interested parties appear to now be on the scene."

I didn't add that not only was this century's treasure hunt already in progress, but that I was about to be thrust into the thick of it. Franz and Johnny had circled each other like dogs near a nest of squirrels. Johnny was buddies with Veronika Duskova. He was also no slouch in the nosy department. Probably was helping the Duskovas search for the flute, though why he couldn't just tell the truth about it pissed me off. Corbin Lerner had been, to use a bad pun, silent as the grave, when questioned as to why he wanted to explore the 18th Century cemetery. The Duskovas were just too adamant about not showing me the north wing. Maybe they figured if Ignatz did his trilling there, the flute must be hidden close by, since the graveyard hadn't yielded any bodies or musical instruments.

I felt ill. I suddenly knew that *Kouzlo Noc* hadn't seen the last violent death. I needed air and a walk back to the hotel to let the story seep into my brain.

The old man hugged me and I thanked him for telling me about Ignatz, then started to leave. Something stopped me. I turned. "I'm sorry. My manners are better than this. I'm Abby Fouchet. I forgot to ask your name."

He pushed himself up with the aid of the cane, then stood—his back straightening with pride. "I am Jozef. I am the owner of the bookstore." His flashing white teeth and twinkling eyes turned his old features into those of a man in his twenties. "And my last name is Jezek."

SEVEN

THE DRAGON-HEADED DOORKNOCKER glared at me with a truly sinister eye this morning. Perhaps my perceptions were colored with the new information I'd received yesterday afternoon about the mysteries within *Kouzlo Noc*—or perhaps the durn monster knew that my reasons for coming back to the castle so soon weren't quite as innocent as I'd made them out to be when I called Veronika an hour ago to ask if I could drop in to "make notes" for the film. At the time I'd thought Franz would be with me for his promised tour of the castle, but he'd left a message with the front desk clerk at my hotel telling me he had errands to run and would try to meet up later.

Relief. I didn't want to have company if I got my nerve up enough to sneak away from the Duskova sisters and take a peek into the north wing of *Kouzlo Noc*. Especially if I happened to bump into a ghost warming up his flute for a morning performance.

Shay hadn't called me back since yesterday afternoon when I'd phoned Kathy's home in Paris to give her all the info about renting the castle. Now, standing under the watchful eye of the dragons, I figured I'd give my buddy another try before I tugged on the Mozart bell-pull and got ushered into the castle to be swallowed up by spirit-searching pursuits. Shay is usually very good about returning calls, so I was a bit worried.

I didn't need any extra angst before starting my flute hunting for the morning. I hasten to add I wasn't interested in finding a treasure trove, although that would be a perk for the Duskovas, who plainly could use one; I just wanted to find out what happened to Ignatz Jezek.

I dialed Shay's cell, but again, only got her voice mail. *"This is Shay Martin. Spill it."*

I yelled into the phone, "Shay! It's getting better and better. Not only is this place spooky, huge, scary, gorgeous, and cheap—it's haunted. I met a very aesthetic, attractive historian—who's a possible graverobber. And Franz, your Count Hoo-haw whatever. Who is some serious eye candy, albeit jumpy when the name of Mozart is mentioned. And guess who's playing Gregory Noble detective? Yep. I'm not supposed to be seen as his engaged woman, which pisses me off, but at least he's here and not tango-dancing with some African princess in Kenya so I'm a happy little locator. Although I'm wondering if Franz and Corbin are skunks going after treasure and this whole exercise will end violently. I've already had two strange visions, neither of which left me with nice feelings. Hanging up now. I'm about to tackle the dragons in the den and, if I'm lucky, have a nice duet with a ghost."

The arrival of anyone responding to my tug on the bell-pull was taking forever and I was getting nervous. Had I upset Veronika too much yesterday by snooping in the graveyard? Or mentioning the music I'd heard?

After an eternity of playing "blink first" with a non-blinking dragon, the door opened. But this was different from yesterday's scenario. Veronika was the one who opened the door and Veronika was edgy and tense and tearful. Her eyes were red and her voice cracked when she asked if I'd like refreshments, but I forestalled her attempts to add to my waistline. "Is it all right if I just wander today with my notebook? I need to jot down what rooms would work best for each scene. I don't want to disturb you and I don't want you to vary whatever your routine is."

It wasn't a total lie. I did plan to make a note or two about the rooms on my way to look for Ignatz Jezek and his flute. Hopefully, she'd taken the hint that this was to be a solo tour by Abby Fouchet, location scout.

Wasn't happenin'. Veronika literally began to sob.

"Madam? What's wrong? Have I done something to offend you?" I gushed out, genuinely worried that I'd screwed up. Perhaps the walk in the cemetery yesterday had been too big an intrusion on the Duskova's privacy? Or even asking to wander wasn't a great suggestion?

Veronika clutched my hand. "No, no! Iss not you. Ach, I am so sorry. We haf much tragedy this morning."

"What's the matter?"

"He. We. Oh, dear God, iss so sad. He iss dead!"

Genuine worry raced into genuine alarm. Corbin? The non-existent CD playing gardener? Or—my heart took a nose dive. I barely kept from screaming. Johnny?

"Veronika. Please! Tell me. Who is dead?"

"We haf hire piano tuner from Austria you understand, to fix piano because it iss very bad to hear."

I nodded. If the piano was anything like the harpsichord, "bad to hear" was an understatement.

"Iss today. Only just before you come, we find Gustav—that iss name—on the grounds. He was lying dead. A dreadful accident."

I hadn't noticed any ambulances when I drove up to the castle in my rental car but they could easily have taken another road. Perhaps since this poor man was already dead, there'd been no need for sirens. I said as much to Veronika.

"Oh. We did not haf police or doctors. Mr. Lerner and Mr. Hart—you haf met him, yes? They took Gustav in our car to village below."

This did not sound right. "Um, Madam Duskova, how did Gustav die?"

"Perhaps his heart give out?"

I envisioned a Jozef look-a-like, grabbing his chest and gasping out a last breath on the grounds of *Kouzlo Noc*. Truly said. I'm a cry-at-commercials type girl so I instantly began blinking back a few tears.

Veronika saw my sympathetic reaction and instantly turned into mother of the year. She patted my hand and began to rapidly console me. "You must not worry, Abb-ee. You not meet this man and though you haf kind heart, please do not be concerning yourself. Do not be distress."

I had no idea how to handle this. A man I'd never met who had been at the Duskovas for what? A few hours before he died? How much mourning was proper? Would it be rude if I kept to my original plan to tour? Did I need to sit with Veronika and Marta and Trina? Did I need to help with funeral arrangements? Or contacting family? Prepare music for a wake?

I kept silent for a few moments. Finally I said, "Well, is it all right if I still roam over the castle a bit? I'm sure there are arrangements to make with this man's family and I can stay out of your way. Or I could help with those arrangements if you need me to?" Not the brightest response but I truly felt at a loss concerning manners in this situation.

She didn't appear shocked over any lack of funeral etiquette on my part. She simply nodded, said, "Please. Roam as you need," then sat down on the ghastly window seat, pulled a piece of fabric out of a bag I hadn't noticed before, and began embroidering. Marta and Trina also produced bags and embroidery implements. The trio barely noticed my exit into the hall or which direction I took once I'd waved thanks and good-bye.

I can state without blushing that I headed right for the north wing. I admit it. I confess. *Mea culpa, mea culpa.* I wanted to find the room that seemed like a good choice for Ignatz Jezek to use as a music studio.

The north wing was much like the south wing, except that the stairs were rotting and the hallways were even narrower. No wonder Johnny had used a tree for his exit. It was safer than trying to avoid the cracked wood and gaping holes. A trip that should have taken five minutes stretched into twelve. I already had one bum foot. A second injury received in questionable circumstances—*But really, Mr. Claims Person—I was on the job! I happened to be hunting for a ghost flautist who hangs out in this really spooky Czech castle. Uh, thought he could join the film orchestra on his days off. Heck, he has a magic flute—isn't that worth more shattered bones?*—would not look good on my insurance records.

I reached the top of the rickety stairway. Five doors; all closed. The hallway was silent in a way that suggested no living person had filled the space with sound in two centuries. I shrugged away the chill attacking between my shoulder blades, marched to Door Number One and flung it open.

Empty. No furniture. No murals, no window seats. If

my Ignatz hung out here, he'd be bored in ten seconds. I turned around to face Door Number Two right across the hall. I peeked inside and was instantly disappointed. I could see furniture but the assortment was definitely 21st Century. No self-respecting spook would take up residence in this space. I headed down the hall toward Door Number Three.

I stopped. Music. Definitely. And not just any music—the instrument I heard was a flute. I closed my eyes and listened until I could make out the melody. Mozart. *The Magic Flute.* The Papageno/Papagena duet, which is the frothiest, lightest piece in the opera. My head bobbed to the tune as I quietly opened Door Number Three.

"Oh yeah." Any ghost would be proud to call this home. It wasn't luxuriant; it was the comfortable residence of a gifted musician.

Two identical floral damask-covered divans faced one another from the east and west sides of the room. A large instrument that looked like a cross between a harpsichord and a glockenspiel sat smack in the center. Diagonally across from the instrument was a music stand looming above a heavy, dark, carved wooden chair. A leather-bound book lay on the seat as though the reader had just plopped it down to take a quick break for a look-see outside. A window seat with a tapestry far less violent than the scene from the Duskova parlor took up at least eight feet under three side-by-side windows. The shape of the moon had been etched into each piece of glass. The walls were decorated with two huge gilt-edged mirrors and several pieces of artwork bearing the name Boucher. I'm no art historian, but even *I* recognized Boucher. This was not a poster print, but an original work. Or a forgery, but a damn good one. Johnny doing more than murals?

The music that had drawn me to Door Number Three had faded to an almost imperceptible level while I'd been taking my survey of the furnishings, but I could still make out the melody. What the heck. I opened my mouth and sang about four bars. The acoustics in this place made the Metropolitan Opera House in New York sound like a garage. I began hunting for any tape players, pods, or CDs run by remotes that might explain where the music was coming from, although I was convinced I was correct in my first hypothesis—Ignatz Jezek was haunting the place and giving concerts to ghost listeners with second sight.

A different piece of music began to play. I strained but the song stayed tantalizingly out of reach. Not classical, that was for sure. It sounded like a show tune. I closed my eyes and let the sound drift over me—and it clicked. *"Night and Day."* Cole Porter. Written in the Nineteen-Thirties. Interesting. Could ghosts play tunes that hadn't even been composed until the ghost had been dead two hundred years or so?

Sheet music had been left on the music stand. I leaned down to check any fun titles and instead found a flute rested calmly in the crevice of the stand. I nearly screamed, *"Magic flute! I've found it!"* On closer inspection, it was clear this wasn't the Jezek flute. If the metal material hadn't convinced me, then the date of 1981 and the inscription *"Michna's Music Shoppe"* sealed the non-magical and clearly modern nature of the instrument.

I turned my attention to the leather-bound book I'd seen resting in a chair. I was in the process of lifting it so I could at least check out the title when voices sounded from the hall. I'm not normally into klepto-mania but I decided to make an exception, just in case whatever had been left here was important. I quickly opened my bag then placed the manuscript inside.

Marching through the front door were three men I'd not expected to see together—at least not now and not here. Johnny Gerard, Franz Hart and Corbin Lerner.

"My, my. Larry, Curly and Moe?"

Johnny snickered. Franz looked confused. Corbin bit back a smile. Well, hot damn. The man had a glimmer of humor somewhere inside that handsome exterior.

I stared at each one in succession, finally asking, "So, guys. Is everything okay? I heard you were help-ing out with this poor man—uh—Mr.—uh—Gustav?"

Franz spoke first. "We took his body down to a lit-tle village not far from here. There will be a memorial Mass there tomorrow, we were told."

"Yeah, that's what I heard. I mean—about the vil-lage. So, what are you doing here in the north wing? Hunting for me? And why aren't you running errands, Franz? Thought that was on your agenda today?"

Franz stiffened. "I decided to come early and alone to get a feeling for the castle and when I got to the door, Madam Duskova was rather hysterical over finding this man on the grounds. Someone suggested coming to the north wing, which could be of interest to the movie."

I nodded toward Johnny, then Corbin. "And Curly and Moe? Popping in on the way to murals and mau-soleums?"

Johnny calmly headed to the window. "I was taking a nice tour around the castle. Three hours of carefully painting a mural to appear centuries old can become tedious. Saw ol' Fritz here with Madam D and decided to join them to see if I could help with Gustav's body."

Franz glared at Johnny. "Franz."

"What?"

"Franz. Not Fritz. That would be a nickname of a Frederick."

Johnny. "Yes, I suppose it would."

I pointed at Corbin. "What about you? Did you just follow the crowd? Was there ever a leader?"

Corbin shrugged. "I saw someone in the window and was worried that a burglar was sneaking into the north wing so I wanted to warn Veronika since no one is supposed to be here."

I opened my eyes wide. "Really? I thought no one *lived* here. Is there a ban on touring? Or is that just the graveyard?"

Franz frowned. "We are not allowed in the grave-yard?"

"Well, I'm not sure there's an actual edict stating that. I just had the feeling the Duskovas would prefer we avoid it." I paused. "Perhaps for safety reasons."

Franz nodded, as though this actually made sense. "Ah, of course." He then motioned toward Corbin, bury-ing the topic of the very recent death at *Kouzlo Noc.* "Pardon me, but I never asked what you are doing for the Duskovas at the castle."

Corbin quietly stated, "I am a historian."

Silence. More silence. Everyone looked at me. I felt like I'd become the hostess for this party and was ex-pected to draw out the shyer guests to reveal the inti-macies of their lives and work.

No way. I smiled and said, "Shouldn't that be 'an' his-torian'? Doesn't the 'h' count as a vowel in that word?"

Corbin did not answer. Franz looked at me as though I'd lost my mind. Johnny, bless his heart, joined right in. "I believe either usage is proper. The 'a' or the 'an.' I taught English part time at a private junior high school when I was at Columbia and I seem to recall that was one of those innocuous little pieces of grammar that drives people crazy but has no set answer."

"You taught grammar?"

"No. I taught English literature but grammar occasionally raised its annoying head."

"Aside from inanimate substances having heads, isn't grammar plural? So wouldn't it be 'their' annoying heads?"

"Grammar is of one. So it stays singular."

We could have danced around this pole another thirty minutes. Johnny and I were having a great time. I'd almost forgotten why I was in the north wing and the fact that some poor piano tuner had died and had been discovered below only a few hours earlier. Franz was not having a great time. He was on a mission to discover Corbin's and Johnny's real interest in *Kouzlo Noc*. I gathered that silence had been the order of the day during that very odd trip to deliver the corpse of one piano tuner with a bad heart.

Corbin didn't look pleased. He stopped our banter with a single statement. "Miss Fouchet. Veronika tells me you're interested in the history of the castle. Correct?"

"When did she say that?"

"After you and Mr. Gerard left the graveyard yesterday."

Franz coughed. "Graveyard? You met Abby in a graveyard?"

"Yes. She was…what was the explanation, Miss Fouchet?"

I casually leaned against the windowpane. "Hey, I was being a good little location scout. Looking for exotic shots. Then again—that particular graveyard? I was nosy. Simple." I squared my shoulders and prepared to drop a bomb. "And of course, I was interested in discovering who'd been playing the flute earlier somewhere near the north tower. Though I thought I saw a gardening troll with a trowel, who was then lost in the cemetery."

Franz and Corbin both whipped their heads around to me. Franz spoke first while Corbin merely raised an eyebrow. "You heard a flute?" That was quickly echoed by Corbin, "A flute? Where?"

I didn't have a chance to answer, which was just as well since I had no desire to tell either Franz or Corbin that I'd heard music with no one actually holding it in hand—or at mouth—and that I wished I'd never mentioned that instrument in mixed company. Dumb move by Fouchet.

Fortunately, I was too busy thanking all the deities for the interruption created by the entrance of the tall newcomer, who came striding toward me with a grin of pure, delicious evil. Shay Martin. Choreographer, director and instigator of trouble whenever possible.

EIGHT

As I'd informed Franz yesterday, Shay and I really did meet in dance class before she'd persuaded me to join her at the residence on Seventy-Ninth and Amsterdam along with our other roommate, Cherry Ripe, a former topless dancer at a Manhattan club on Eighth Avenue. Shay and I had become friends in class, then bonded into true sisterhood through various emotional, physical and vocational traumas suffered in and around Seven-D. Which Shay joked was her bra size. She *is* a big girl for a dancer, which is one reason she turned to choreography and direction. The other is that she's damn talented at both and sure as heck making more money than we lowly players.

She crossed the room in three graceful strides and enveloped me in an excruciatingly tight bear hug. "Little Abby! What a damn weird and wonderful room. Does anyone live here other than dead people?"

I hugged her back and ignored her statement and question. "Sass-shay! Not that I'm not thrilled to see your smiling face in Prague, but exactly why are you in Prague? I mean, now, not in a week, like after the wedding?"

We drew apart. She growled, "Because that idiot Kathy and her even more idiotic fiancé, Jean-Claude Lafitte the Nineteenth or whatever, had another huge fight and called off the wedding for the sixth time in five days. I said, *'Nuts to this. I'm not waiting around playing peacemaker until the two of them decide either to elope or just shoot each other.'* I'm tellin' ya, it'll take a Nobel Prize winning mediator to solve the war between them!"

She suddenly realized we were not the only two folks in the room. "Who the hell are the hunks? *Chee— wow—wah!* Oh wait. Franz! You sexy man, you look even better than you did at the screen test."

I squinched my face with a *"Damn, Shay, just be rude and embarrass the guys, why doncha?"* expression.

She shrugged. "What? If these guys don't get that they're foxier than critters at a Virginia hunt, they're either blind or too arrogant to own up to it." She winked at Franz and asked, *"Vas is los?"* I gathered that was Shay's German translation for "What's up, dude?"

She turned to Corbin and scrutinized him intently. "The historian. Gotta be. No one can get away with the dashing professor look except for a dashing professor."

I groaned.

She winked at me, then shook Corbin's hand. The man simply looked stunned.

Shay then held her hand out to Johnny. He took it and immediately pressed her palm to his chest. I coughed. Shay caught it and remembered in time none of us were supposed to be friends or lovers of Johnny in a previous life for whatever bizarre reasons he had yet to reveal.

"Hmm. You must be the burglar. You're way too sexy to be Abby's ghost."

Terrific. She'd just released the "G" word. As an Abby possessive.

I suddenly realized that Franz and Corbin hadn't

even registered Shay's comment. They were too busy staring at the girl who'd followed Shay into the room. I hadn't seen her since I'd been lifted off the floor by my buddy who had effectively hid the newcomer now posing prettily by the door.

I started to cross to her to say "Hi," then stopped dead. I turned back to Shay and whispered, "Is this Lily Lowe? Um. She bears a rather startling resemblance to someone from the ice cream commercial you choreographed and I supposedly starred in."

Shay was trying, unsuccessfully, to look innocent. "She does?"

I narrowed my eyes. "Yes, Shay. She does. Remember Hannah Hammerstein? Of course you do."

Shay shrugged. "Well, now that you mention it, Lily does have a trait or two of Hannah's."

Understatement. Lily was a walking clone of Hannah. Hannah the blonde-haired, blue-eyed dimwit with the turned-up nose, the perfect red lips, the legs to the neck of her five-foot-seven-inch frame, and the disposition of Rasputin on PCP, meth and acid. Hannah had been the bane of my existence from the day she hijacked the role of a popsicle (not for her dancing, which was lousy, but those stinkin' legs made up for it and the director of the commercial was beyond hetero-male) then tried to steal Johnny away from me the first time he arrived at the warehouse shoot to take me to dinner.

I took a breath and prepared to be pleasant to Lily Lowe. It wasn't her fault she was Hannah Hammerstein's doppelganger. And since Lily did look the part of "Honoria" for the film, I had to acknowledge that Shay had done a nice job of casting.

"Hi, Lily. I'm Abby Fou…."

"Yes. You're the…scout." Her tone was sheer boredom, spiced with a smidgeon of derision.

"Well, that's one duty. Did Shay tell you I'm helping with the choreography for two dance sequences since she's pretty tied down with directing?"

Lily waved a graceful hand in the air, dismissing me. "Yes." She marched on dainty feet over to Franz and placed that tiny hand on his arm.

"I can't wait to dance with you, Franz. I can tell you're marvelous just by taking one glance. The perfect Count Zilania. Kissing will be lovely."

Whoa. Lily wasted no time. Hannah Hammerstein all over again. I waited to see what form her feminine wiles would take as she oozed toward Corbin. Franz remained speechless.

Lily smiled up at Corbin, who loomed with great panache over her. He leaned down and kissed her hand. Smooth.

Lily giggled. "Oh my. And who are you, charming man? Are you playing the villain," she glanced over her shoulder at Shay, "what's the villain's name, Shay?"

"Harold."

Lily shuddered. "What a dreadful name for such a handsome man."

Corbin shook his head. "And not mine, Miss…Lily. I'm only a humble professor, here to do a bit of work for the Duskova family."

"Oh." The tone change was barely perceptible, but I caught it. I couldn't tell if Corbin had or not. Apparently he had, because he bowed to the actress and added, "Just as well. If I had to perform opposite you on screen I'd be so consumed by your presence that I doubt I'd be able to remember a single line."

Smooth. With just a hint of sarcasm creeping in.

Sarcasm which sailed right over Ms. Lowe's yellow hair. She was about to turn her simpering wiles on Johnny but I tossed in a question to grab her interest for at least a second or two and keep me from maiming the leading lady within four minutes of meeting her.

I turned to Shay. "Got our new movie title yet?"

She fluttered her lashes. "Quite possibly."

Something exceedingly trashy was coming up.

Have I mentioned that during breaks at Seven-D, when we weren't engaged in watching *Endless Time,* rehearsing for shows, eating ridiculously calorie-laden meals or discussing our love lives, we'd rediscovered the enthralling world of the Gothic romances? I'd learned that both of us had fallen for the Gothics when we were eleven. Shay in Wisconsin; me in Texas, but the same passion for cheap thrills and dumb heroines. We'd inhaled Gothics primarily written in the Nineteen-Sixties and Seventies, the quintessential era for dark heroes and sweet heroines who found lasting love after initially fearing, distrusting and almost killing one another— accidentally of course. Our favorite—and coincidentally a favorite of Bambi Bohacek—was a two-hundred page drama simply called *"Honoria."* It was the reason we were now in the Czech Republic making this film. The plot was not unique: sweet and lovely heroine, orphaned after her professor father's death (mother died when heroine was toddler) is sent to the scary home of one of her father's ex-students, the even scarier, psychologically and physically scarred, semi-alcoholic, but brilliant, lord of the manor. What the plot lacked in originality it more than made up for with character and word skills. The writing was great, the heroine damn spunky for a Gothic female, the hero sexy, dark and—heroic, and the Bavarian setting was—cool.

Shay had been given free rein by Bambi to name the movie. We'd been debating titles over the phone for weeks now. The top contenders were *"Turret of Dream Shadows"*, *"Damsel in Darkness"*, and *"Nightmares of Count Zilania."* Shay refused to go with the simplicity of *"Honoria"*. It wasn't cheesy enough.

I shuddered, wondering which of these would be flashed across a large screen in about thirteen months.

Shay winked at me. "Don't look so concerned. I came up with a wonderful name. Even you will agree it passes the cheese test."

I wasn't sure if that were a good or bad thing.

She paused for dramatic effect. *"The Naked Mistress of Dark Silhouette Tower."*

Franz, Corbin, Lily and I all just stared at her for a moment. Johnny didn't stare. He was carefully clutching his sides and biting his lips. Shay was right. Brie, cheddar, or Swiss—the cheese smelled strong, but the title grabbed one nonetheless. It also scared me more than Count Zilania after a night imbibing whiskey.

I chortled, "Wait! Wait! That sounds like a porn movie. Since when is Honoria naked? And is Honoria still Honoria or did she get a name change?"

Shay fluttered her lashes, then sneered. "Be serious, Abby. Naked sells. Porn, romance, internet. You name it. If it has no clothes, it's a winner. Although, we're keeping this PG-rated. Lily will stay in her stays. As for Honoria? Are you nuts? Of course I'm changing the name. Honoria sounds like a Victorian venereal disease. Our mistress of the towers is now Kelsey."

"Say what?" I exclaimed. "As in 'Grammar'—as in *Frasier* reruns?"

Instead of responding, Shay flashed every tooth she owned in a smile directed at Johnny. "So, Mr. Gerard? What do *you* do? For a living. That is," her volume lowered, "when you're not casing castles or being a supercop."

I waited for the "art mural for the Duskovas" response. It never came. Instead, Johnny stated, "Well, in about a month I'll be designing the set for *The Magic Flute* for the South Sarasota Retirees Light Opera Company."

I coughed. "You have got to be kidding."

He winked at me. "I am absolutely serious. It's a great gig. Fantastic pay."

"I'm not talking about the pay or the gig. I'm just reeling from the idea of an opera company composed of the geriatric denizens residing in the swamps of Florida."

"Sarasota does not have swamps. And you'd be amazed at the vocal talent of some of the elder performers."

I closed my eyes. "The mind staggers. Actually, I'm sure there are some incredible voices. I just can't quite visualize the Queen of the Night as a ninety-plus great-granny belting out those F's at the end of the aria where the wicked Queen tries to get Kathyina to kill Sarastro."

Johnny chuckled. "Well, a few of the tougher arias have been transposed down to ease the chords of the aging divas. But they're still damn good."

"I believe you. Hey, keep me in the loop if they decide to do a nice musical comedy and need a short dancing alto. After a few months being chilled in Prague, I'll be ready for some nice hundred-degree temps. Even if it's a job wrestling alligators with any seniors who are doubtless smuggling Viagra in gator bellies."

"When the hell did seniors in Sarasota suddenly start messing with alligators and smuggling?" Shay asked.

I grinned. "They didn't. I just wanted to change the topic before my brain turned completely to oatmeal contemplating naked mistresses in turrets and short, elderly character actors warbling the Papageno duet."

Perhaps it was time to shepherd the flock of actors, directors, and historians downstairs to the parlor in search of kolaches and tea laced with anything 80 proof or above. Preferably before our collective presence was noted by the M.T.V. siblings who were already nervous about visitors in the castle. Understandably so.

Too late.

"Vat iss all dees people doing here?"

We turned to face the door. Marta, Trina and Veronika had managed to stand toe-to-toe in the admittedly wide space. All three ladies were glaring. For some reason, the glare was directed at me.

NINE

My FIRST INCLINATION was to lie. Something on the order of "I got lost." A simple lie. A glaringly, patently false lie—but simple. Then I glanced around the room. Every face bore an expression of guilt identical to a group of five-year-olds caught naked, with crimson-colored finger-paints, in a white room with a copy of *Grey's Anatomy* open in the literally red hands of the smallest child.

I couldn't lie. The next face that flashed before me was that of Sister Martha Mary Margaret from fourth grade. The one whose eyes always asked, "You want extra cheese with that Whopper?" The one with the ruler. *Digressing here, but why hasn't a killer nun ever been plopped into a game of Clue? "I win! I win! The answer is Sister Mary Mendacity—in the classroom—with the nail-spiked ruler."*

I opened my mouth to state the obvious. *Kouzlo Noc* had been invaded by treasure-hunters, curious theatrical types and the new leasees who put the "nose" in "nosy".

It was simple. It was direct. It was even true. Up to a point. Before I could utter a word, Johnny neatly stated, "Abby got lost. We all came to find her."

There were holes in those two sentences bigger than the New Jersey Turnpike after five years of blizzards but Veronika glided right past them.

"That iss all right then. But everyone now leave this room. This iss not part of film and bad thing hass happened here today. Death iss not good. We should be mourning Gustav."

Six sinners meekly followed Madam Duskova and her siblings into the hall and out of the north wing. I tried bringing up the rear on the off chance that I could sneak away for one extra peek, but Veronika kept in step beside me as though she could see inside my evil mind that intense impulse to check out the space I knew damn well had once belonged to Ignatz Jezek. The fact that countless other flute-seekers for two hundred years had doubtless trooped through this room looking for the "magic flute" didn't deter me. None of them had had the ability (I assumed) to hear Mr. Jezek play. Not to mention I was pure of heart and therefore could not fail in this quest to find the flute and bring Jezek's alleged killer to justice. After a couple hundred years. And since I'd just stolen a manuscript I hoped belonged to Ignatz Jezek I was certain I'd've solved all the mysteries by this evening at the latest.

I didn't get all A's back in college in "Scenery Chewing" (aka Acting 101) for nothing. I can pretend innocence with the best of them. I smiled at my fellow trespassers as we wound through the gothic architecture of *Kouzlo Noc* and never once let on that anything odd was emanating from the north wing. I refrained from singing the song only I was able to hear (still Cole Porter) when we entered the sitting room in the main of the castle. I even managed to compose myself enough to start introductions once the matter of tea and goodies had been neatly disposed of and Marta and Trina headed for the kitchen to whip up a gentle but more solid repast.

"Veronika? Have you met Franz and Lily? They're playing Count Zilania and uh, Honoria, or Kelsey, or whatever the heck the heroine will be named. And have you met Shay Martin, who's directing the movie?"

Eight people looked at me with sheer astonishment. Oops. My polite introductions were redundant. Franz had been here long enough to help with Gustav's body. And, unless Lily and Shay had entered with my ghost— unseen of course, Veronika and her sisters had met them the instant they bonded with the dragons at the back doors.

I smiled. "Never mind." I reached for a kolache. Mozart's *"Kyrie Eleison"* from his *Requiem* sounded from the front door bell-pull. Trina carefully placed her tray (kolaches plus scones) on an overly-laden table then headed out. Ten seconds later she was back and she wasn't alone.

A beautiful young man followed her into the sitting room. A room that was getting very crowded with primarily gorgeous persons. Corbin looked a bit tense, but courteously offered the embroidered chair he'd been sitting on to the newcomer. Franz appeared to be sizing up the competition. Johnny merely took another bite of his lemon scone. Shay waved. Lily literally fluttered her lashes and straightened her shoulders so her silicone-filled centerfold chest would garner even more attention.

This latest testosterone king looked to be in his early thirties. Blonde, with green-gray eyes. The hair was styled in what I'd call "early surfer" and he had the lean build of just such an athlete. Must be Mitchell Herbert. Composer for Naked Honoria or Whatever.

Introductions were made all around. Mitchell seemed taken aback upon meeting Johnny and Corbin, since neither of the latter gentlemen had been expected to be part of the film crew for Naked Honoria or Whatever. His manner was a mass of nerves. He dispensed with any niceties and dove into business, turning to me with, "When do you need the first piece of music? I finished composing the number for Honoria's first gala event at the castle. Oh damn. I just remembered. I don't have a tape ready yet, so I guess it won't do much good, though, will it?"

"Did you write it out?"

"Of course."

"Cool. If you've got the sheet music and it's legible, I can get started with that. The tape is better since I don't have to be charging back and forth reading and I'll need that for rehearsals unless you care to accompany, but the music will be fine for starters."

"You're telling me you can read music? Really?"

"Yes. Problem?"

"Um. I'm just not acquainted with many dancers who read music."

My hackles rose. "Well. I do. Read music, that is. But I'm exceptional—for a dancer. Sing. Act. Dance. Scout locations. Makes me a quadruple threat. And while a tape definitely will be better when I'm choreographing, I have no problem reading the music and hearing it in my head as I'm arranging steps. Although I would like to get together and discuss nuances."

Shay bit her lip. "Watch out for Abby, Mitch. Her temper matches her red cowboy boots and she gets irritated when her abilities are questioned. Didn't I mention that she sight-reads music like a Met mezzo?"

Mitchell nodded. "Sorry. Making assumptions. Probably not a good practice."

I kindly stated, "That's okay. I'm glad I'll be able to get started right away. This will really help Shay out."

Every ear in the room had been listening to the exchange but now that it appeared fisticuffs were not in order, chatter broke out between small groups of twos and threes. Lily and Franz got cozy. Shay, Corbin and Johnny entertained the Duskovas with American gossip.

Mitchell stayed beside me and dropped his volume for me only to hear. "I am sorry, Abby. For the last month I've been dealing with a group of supposedly classically trained singers who don't seem to understand the difference between Keys of 'C' and 'D' and the Florida Keys. Guess that translated to jumping to bad conclusions. Also, I'm not a good traveler. Today has generally been crappy."

"Really. It's okay. You didn't say anything that terrible and I can be a total snob when it comes to my prowess at sight-reading." I smiled.

"Can I make up my *faux pas* to you by buying you dinner at some elegant restaurant this evening?"

Oh yeah. Surfer boy at a nice restaurant. Could I make Johnny jealous enough to where he'd quit being secretive and take his rightful spot as Abby's loving fiancé?

I answered, "Well, not this evening—although that sounds nice. I'm going to the opera tonight."

"Oh? To see?"

"The Magic Flute."

"Any tickets left?"

That was abrupt.

"Ask Franz. He checked that out yesterday."

Before Mitchell could ask me the who, what, and wheres of the production, Shay grabbed him and began discussing a few of her ideas for Count Zilania's songs. Everyone else was still engaged in what appeared to be stimulating conversation.

I was ignored. Which is probably not a good enough excuse for starting to sing the last measures of the *Queen of the Night* aria from *The Magic Flute* to myself. The last measures are pretty much a technique exercise, popping up and down the scale singing *"Ah-ah-ah"* in very crisp staccato time.

Conversation stopped. The sisters looked distressed. Mitchell looked puzzled. Lily, Franz and Corbin looked surprised. Shay and Johnny just looked amused.

"Uh oh. My bad. So sorry. Didn't mean to interrupt all the intellectual discussions around here. But that tune has been in my head since yesterday," I said, as I fluttered my eyelashes in an appearance of sheer innocence.

Shay chortled. "Not bad. Of course I have no ear so what the hell am I doing with the compliments?"

I bowed and ignored her. "It's a lovely little aria. Sounds rather like a flute near the end?"

Silence. The Duskovas, Franz, Corbin, Mitchell and Lily all continued to stare at me. Shay snorted. Johnny went a few steps further. He began to sing the Papageno part of the duet of the same name from the same opera. He knew I couldn't resist. I immediately chimed in as Papagena, the mate of the bird catcher.

The stares could have continued for hours (certainly Johnny and I were not ready to stop warbling) but our impromptu concert was interrupted by Mozart again. The *Requiem* notes from the doorbell sounded and effectively ended the duet. Veronika took off like a runner stealing home base. All the others began talking again.

I heard a lot of discussion about the weather and best places to eat in Prague. Nothing about music. Nothing about flutes.

Within thirty seconds, Veronika was back with another visitor to *Kouzlo Noc*. My friendly bookstore owner, Jozef Jezek, was led into the parlor by a beaming Madam D. He was carrying about six books, wrapped in a rope that swung from his right hand. I hesitated before greeting him. Did everyone know his relationship to the flute-player? Did everyone know the story? Did he want anyone to know that *I* knew the story? I was giving myself a headache with all the questions and secrecy.

He took care of that. "Miss Fouchet. Good to see you again. I have found only one Gothic romance novel from Germany. But it was indeed written in the Nineteen-Seventies. I have not read this, so I do not know if it will help you for your movie, but I have brought it—along with the texts Veronika had requested the last time she graced my shop. They are on Medieval Architecture."

Smooth. If I hadn't already been blessed with a terrific father, I'd've bargained for adoption on the spot.

He handed me a hard cover book complete with a dust jacket. Even at first glance I could tell it was in German. But no one knew I couldn't read that particular language so my excuse for getting chummy with Jozef Jezek and his bookstore would remain confidential. Except for Shay and Johnny, of course.

Conversation began again. The groups shifted. Lily decided to charm her hostesses and began a lively discussion with the Duskovas about the film industry in the Czech Republic. Franz was eating the last scone. Shay was flirting with Corbin. Mitchell and Johnny were admiring the tapestries. Jozef drew me aside and quietly tapped the book with his index finger. "This particular novel should prove to be of interest."

"The Seduction of Countess Marissa?" I lifted my brows.

Jozef dropped his volume. "It's a very pretty dust jacket, no? But it doesn't really belong to the book."

I glanced around the room. No one was paying attention. I quietly slipped the dust jacket front piece away from the book. The title revealed was a textbook. *Freemasonry and Mozart—A Duet for the Centuries.*

"Thank you," I whispered. "I'll give this a read as soon as I get more than fifteen minutes of free time."

Jozef smiled. "If you find it boring, you can always read about Countess Marissa being seduced—in between studying the symbolism of *The Magic Flute*. The dust jacket gives an entire synopsis of the novel." He glanced around the room. "I only wish I could decipher some of the meanings of the symbols of freemasonry enough to perhaps explain the truth behind Ignatz and his flute."

I asked, "Why don't you ask the Duskovas?"

He shook his head. "Veronika and I have discussed Ignatz many times in the last ten years. She discovered my bookstore back then, and we learned about our mutual ancestor and we both have become anxious to find out the truth." He paused. "Before someone with sinister motivation finds it."

I hugged him. "I feel the same. I just didn't realize that you and Veronika were friends. I had no idea until you walked into the parlor only minutes ago that you had any kind of relationship with the Duskovas—in this century that is. Not to be nosy, but I must express some surprise that you and the Duskovas are on good terms considering the family history."

He winked. "The official feud ended sometime in the late 1800s and since neither the ladies nor I were around then we thought it best to ignore any unpleasantness that happened in the centuries preceding that time."

"Including the possible murder of Ignatz Jezek?"

"Ah. Well. It is certain that none of the Duskovas currently residing in *Kouzlo Noc* had anything to do with my ancestor's demise so a bit of forgiveness is in order."

"Got it. So, what symbols should I look for in this book?"

Before Jozef had a chance to begin a lecture, we were joined by Shay. Ms. Martin, naturally, jumped in with both of her size eleven feet. I was only thankful the rest of the crowd was busy elsewhere.

"Mr. Jezek? You're the great-great-great—well a bunch of greats—grandchild of the ghost? Right?"

I groaned. "Dammit Shay, do I have to start adding duct tape to my bag to slap on you when you can't keep your mouth closed for two seconds?"

Shay waved me away. "You're such a wimp. Let's get real. We're in a spooky castle. You've got spooky genes. Put those together and that means there's got to be a ghost. Where there's a ghost there's a treasure, at least in this case. So, what's the loot and who does it belong to?"

I gazed up toward the heavens, but got no help from the Almighty. The earthly deity, Jozef, was unsuccessfully trying to stifle his obvious amusement.

I glared at my best friend. "I have no idea what the treasure really is, but if there is one I'd imagine it belongs to Mr. Jezek here—being the great-great-great heir."

Shay snarled, "Knew that. I'm just nosy and in the mood for a good treasure hunt since I missed out on a good wedding because of that idiot Kathy and her moronic mother and the groom with the sex appeal of a dead goat."

"Ah. Well. I'm glad that's settled."

"Lily and company alert. Headed this way with a parade of males," I muttered. "Cool the ghost tales."

"Hey, I can be subtle." Shay lowered her voice— slightly—for one last question that, fortunately, only Jozef and I could hear. "Not to start things up, but while we're into honesty, isn't there something else involving the flute here? I mean, it's a particularly valuable flute, right? Not in monetary terms, but in—well— some terms. Could be gold. Could be the power of— oh—love through the ages."

Shay being subtle. Not.

Jozef responded, "As Abby and I were saying, the only thing we are sure of is we must find the flute before persons who have souls of evil discover either the whereabouts and the magic and mystery it holds within."

TEN

I OOZED TOWARD the door to begin a graceful exit from *Kouzlo Noc* before Shay could start shouting, "Ghost hunt!" to the castle-dwellers and cast and hangers-on. I had no idea if anyone could have heard Jozef outside of Shay and me but I was nervous that one of those present would decide to step up some greed-filled treasure-seeking before we good guys could succeed in our quest.

Shay set a time for cast and crew to meet back at the castle in the morning for a production meeting. Business was finished for the day. I hadn't found my flute player and wasn't likely to get another chance until *Headlights Productions* was firmly entrenched within castle walls and I could snoop during dance breaks.

Now I had to stop obsessing over Ignatz for many "becauses." Because for at least one night, this night, I wasn't going to worry about keeping ears open for the sound of spectral fluting. Because tonight was the opera. Because Johnny had tickets. Because I was thrilled to see an opera in The Estates Theatre and anxious to discover if any clues to Ignatz Jezek's missing flute (and body) were hinted at in any of the scenes of *The Magic Flute*. And because I was damn glad I had a chance to dress up and change my location-scout attire of jeans and T-shirt for a few hours to date-attire in a real dress.

My schedule for the last few days had been to tramp around Prague and little villages nearby checking out spooky castles for Shay, so I hadn't been able to even dream about donning fancy clothes and high heels. But blessedly, my invisible fashion fairy-godmother had seen fit back in New York to make me pack a little number that should keep Mr. Gerard's mind off of murals, flutes and treasure. The salesgirl at the funky boutique in Manhattan had called the color champagne, and proclaimed it perfect for a chestnut-brunette (even one with steaks of green.) The material was a combination of lace and stretchy rayon, the skirt was handkerchief hemmed and the neckline was "sweetheart taking the plunge." I'd thrown in the pair of ecru lace granny boots I'd planned to wear to the wedding Shay was supposedly attending before she'd begged, pleaded and thrown herself on my mercy to go castle hunting instead. A 1950s vintage black velvet coat was warm enough for the short walk to the theatre.

I even had a cute little black lace beret that covered most of the green in my hair. Eye shadow, a ton of mascara, and a tinge of blush and lipstick—I was set. Bring 'em on.

"On" was definitely the operative word. As I entered the lobby of the hotel, I was dazzled by the sight of Johnny in a black tux. He looked—well—damn good.

I headed directly to him, curtseyed and fluttered my lashes. "My, my, Mr. Gerard, but you do clean up well. I'm impressed."

He bowed in turn. "Let me return the compliment." He stared at me. "Dang, Abby, let me go one further and tell you that you're a knock-out. Saint Agnes would be proud."

He dropped a light kiss on my cheek, then extended his arm, crooked at the elbow, to me. I placed my own hand over his elbow with as much grace as heroine Honoria would have managed in the late 19th Century. This was no night for rampant feminism. It was a night at the opera.

Which quickly turned into a farce closer to the Marx Brothers movie with that same title. As soon as Johnny and I left the hotel we were joined by none other than Franz Hart also decked out in splendor in a black tuxedo nearly identical to my stylish escort.

Franz yelled loud enough to engage all of Prague. "Abby! I got tickets. I thought I'd join you both and we can all go together, yes?"

The Estates Theatre, in the section of Prague called Old Town, was walking distance from the hotel. So our little trio walked. We tried strolling arm-in-arm, but the sidewalk wasn't big enough, so first Johnny took my arm and we left Franz to walk behind, then Franz cut in and a scowling Mr. Gerard was forced away. I waited for Johnny to stake his valid claim to Ms. Fouchet and watch Franz back off, but Mr. Gerard stayed silent on the subject.

Finally I pulled away from both. "Okay, guys. Enough. Tell you what? I'll drop back and you can just march to the theatre together. You're nearly the same height and your tuxes are matching black. You'll look like you're part of a gay dance team."

I love a sense of humor in anyone. And bless them, both Johnny and Franz took me at my word. They linked arms and sauntered down the street with matching strides and total nonchalance. I expected a tango at any moment.

We finally reached the theatre. Johnny's two tickets were next to each other. Somehow, Franz had managed to find a seat right there with us. I took the middle, glanced at my watch and breathed in my surroundings. The Estates Theatre. The very history of the place was overwhelming. *The Magic Flute* was not the first of Mozart's operas to be performed here. Wolfgang A. personally conducted the premier of *Don Giovanni* and Mozart's other operas, such as *Cosi Fan Tutte* and *Marriage of Figaro* were regular staples.

The Estate Theatre was indeed, as Franz originally told us, built in the Neoclassical style; lines with straight-backed chairs (no lounging in rockers like in today's sixteen-screen movie theatres) and box seats in tiers that surged up into infinity. We sat directly under an enormous chandelier that gave me the sensation of being bathed in one huge light bulb surrounded by a ceiling painting with colors in gold and red and cream. I sighed with pure pleasure over the entire décor.

I normally don't watch this opera contemplating who represents what, and whether or not a certain three chords in the overture represent three knocks in Freemason ideology. I wait for the Queen of the Night to sing her marvelous aria. It was written as a comic opera but it's one of the most stirring Mozart wrote for a soprano.

This night, squinched between Johnny and Franz, both of whom appeared so absorbed in the opera that they must be taking notes in their heads, I tried to concentrate on Mozart's intent. Find those symbols and solve a puzzle.

With great effort I watched and listened for every nuance related to Ignatz's magic with his flute. Did the symbols used, the morals presented, have a durn thing to do with flautist Ignatz Jezek haunting *Kastle Kouzlo Noc?* I paid close attention to any scene involving the magic flute; said to bring wild beasts under a spell rendering them tame. Also there was a lyric that caught my ear about night and day. Night and day. Same tune I'd heard earlier up at *Kouzlo Noc.* Was Ignatz trying to give me a clue about magic? Could his flute soothe savage animals? Could it change light to dark? Rust to gold? And had human savage beasts, in the guise of family or friend or colleague, taken an opportunity to destroy the young Prague musician/artisan then steal the flute and its magic for themselves?

I found no answers. My only insight was that any insight into the mystery would be solved at *Kouzlo Noc.*

The plot of *The Magic Flute* was originally based on a fairy-tale. A prince sets out on a mission to rescue a princess from her father, Sarastro, a man he believes to be evil. The belief stems from the words of the princess's mother, Queen of the Night. But the prince soon discovers that the man is a good man; almost a godlike character. When prince and princess meet, it's immediate love. Actually, before they meet it's love. They see one another's portraits and it's boom—Romance City. Sort of early online dating. But before they can live happily ever after, they have to undergo various trials to prove themselves worthy to rule over the kingdom the wise Sarastro relinquishes to his daughter and son-in-law. Comic relief is provided by the bird catcher named Papageno, who is searching for a "Papagena" so they can produce little papagenos. Yeah, the names get a bit confusing, especially during the Papageno/Papagena duet, but it's still hilarious to watch and see. It's one of those duets that sticks with the listener long after the opera has ended. Insidious. Fun—but insidious.

Masonic symbolism hits the audience at every turn, with numbers of three being very prominent; with light and day and black and white representing good and evil. I didn't understand half of it, but I did know that Freemasons of Mozart's time period went through various "trials" to prove they were worthy of joining the brotherhood. Entire books have been written explaining just what Mozart and his friend, the librettist and producer, Schikaneder, were getting at. I couldn't wait to read the book Jozef had slipped me that afternoon. The elderly bookseller himself had pored through it searching for clues to the magic his ancestor had crafted, but obviously he was interested in letting fresh eyes take a peek.

After about thirty minutes of angst over what meant what, I said, "Screw it" and spent the next two hours not worrying a damn about symbolism as I let myself be swept away with the marvelous singing and the production as a whole. I did tuck back in my brain for later perusal the intensity of this production's use of light and dark. And I also decided that return engagements to view *The Magic Flute* were in order in case the opera had something to do with Ignatz Jezek and the flute he'd hidden at *Kouzlo Noc.*

After the last standing ovation died down, the three of us headed back to the café where I'd enjoyed kolaches and cocoa earlier in the afternoon. Yes, the three of us. Franz apparently had decided he was the focal point of this little ménage and showed no inclination to leave me alone with Johnny Gerard.

Didn't matter anyway. When we got to the café, we

were greeted by no less than three familiar faces. Shay, Lily, and Mitchell were seated at a round table by a back window. Hand waves all around and Franz, Johnny and I made our way through the crowded restaurant to join them. Three empty seats awaited us. Very "Freemasonic."

"So, how was Amadeus?" asked Shay.

"He was marvelous. At least, his work was. As for Wolfgang himself? Well—he did not make an appearance—at least none that I was aware of, and let's face it, if he had, now that I'm hearing ghosts all over Prague, I'm sure I'd've been the first to catch any impromptu jam sessions," was my whispered and overly-long answer.

A waiter clad in an even more elegant tux than either Johnny or Franz was sporting arrived to take our order. I needed something stronger than cocoa and Kahlua so I ordered a gin and tonic. A double. I deserved it after what had been a durn stressful day.

"What about any surprise spectral guests in the orchestra?" Shay hissed while my two escorts for the evening were giving their orders.

"Shut it," I growled. "No. All present and accounted for. And alive. Will you quit with the ghosts?"

"For now, but you've got to fill me in on all juicy details of your talk with Jozef and your brilliant insights into *The Magic Flute*. Midnight. Tonight. Your room."

"Why my room?"

"Because I checked in without an advance reservation and my crappy room doesn't have a mini-bar. It barely has sheets on the bed and running water in the bathroom. I want comfort and booze when I hear ghost tales."

I nodded. "Midnight."

Seven pairs of eyes stared at us. Lily spoke first, mouth set in an oh-so-pretty pout. "What is so interesting that the two of you must be rude and exclude us?"

Shay smiled. "Just making snide remarks about people. So we thought we'd keep the noise level down."

There was no good response to that. Shay added, "Speaking of possibly snide comments, any takers on assessing our lovely hostesses at the castle? The sisters Duskova?"

Lily stared with a touch of acid in her tone, "They are perfect for the movie since they're already in costume. Hasn't anyone told them it's the Twenty-First Century?"

Johnny looked directly at Lily. "They're more than aware of that. But those 'costumes' are about the only clothes left after a half-century of Soviet rule where our aristocratic ladies weren't allowed to zip off to high-end boutiques in Paris for mini-skirts and black leather boots."

Lily turned as white as her flowered name. "I was very lucky to not be in Prague during much of the Soviet domination of my country. I was too young. But it did not occur to me that the Duskovas must have had a bad time for many years."

He smiled. "I'm sure it didn't. That's why I told you. The Duskovas are good people. Veronika can be a bit…"

"Testy?" I interjected. "Gruff? Frightening?"

"Serious. I was going to say 'serious.' But she has good reasons. She's held that family together through sheer hell. And managed to maintain a solid grip on the ancestral home, which is pretty amazing."

He had everyone's solid attention. Especially mine.

"So, Johnny, how *did* she hold on? Sheer luck? So

many other castles were razed during World War Two or abandoned during Soviet occupation."

"She's a smart woman. Her grandfather was a practical man and Veronika took after him. When the Russians descended on Czechoslovakia after the Germans finally gave it up, Mr. Duskova offered the use of the castle as a headquarters and home for various high-ranking Soviet officials. He was fortunate that these particular gentlemen were more interested in comfort than destruction. *Kouzlo Noc* was not burned. *Kouzlo Noc* was not vandalized. *Kouzlo Noc* was a nice haven from Prague with nice members of the Duskova family to act as servants for the Communists who invaded their country. Marta, Trina and Veronika grew up in the house of their ancestors in the role of underaged maids. Pleasant, huh?"

Mitchell nodded at him. "I had a chat with Veronika this afternoon when she was explaining the history of that marvelous harpsichord." He turned to Shay, "Off topic, but can we get that repaired and tuned? It really would put the polish on the scene in the ballroom where Zilania and Honoria are singing the love duet while his stepmother and Harold are sword-fighting outside."

"Sure. Abby already gave me the scoop on the harpsichord and I've budgeted all repairs in." She shook her head, "Of course, we have to find a tuner—I can't believe the one Veronika hired died on his first day out there. Sad and creepy."

Silence all around. For no reason I suddenly felt sick to my stomach. Out of focus. I closed my eyes as the vision of a man falling from the north tower at *Kouzlo Noc* pushed into my mind. I shivered, then tried to pull my focus back to Shay, who was addressing Mitchell. "So, back to topic, what all did the lovely Madam D have to say during your get-to-know-one-another chat?"

"She told me about all the Duskovas who'd gone before. Quite a bunch. Knights in shining armor. Members of court for kings. Members of another kind of court with various barristers and judges. Musicians."

I sat up and forced my vision away. "Really? Musicians? What did she say about that branch of the Duskova tree?"

I must have sounded too eager. All eyes were now focused on me. "What?" I growled. "I'm just curious since we're doing a musical there. That's all."

I'm not a great liar. And it wasn't a great lie. It was really pretty stinkin' bad. Fortunately, my old friends and new acquaintances were more interested in Mitchell's remarks on the subject than my obvious desire to delve into the mysterious pasts of Duskova musicians.

Mitchell was answering. "She didn't get terribly specific. She did say that a couple of family members had played with some of the best orchestras across the country—and in Austria as well."

"Did she mention… Ow!" I howled when my leg was kicked under the table. The kick had to have been aimed by Johnny who was sitting opposite me. It confirmed what I already knew. He knew about Ignatz Jezek. But since he'd been needling Franz about Mozart I found it somewhat unnecessary to kick me to keep me from talking about Ignatz. I was sure everyone knew anyway.

I smiled at the startled faces. "Sorry. Cramp in my foot. Sitting too long at the opera. You were saying, Mitchell?"

"I wasn't saying. You were asking."

"Oh. Yeah, I guess I was. I just wondered if she mentioned who, er, uh, played the, er, uh, harpsichord and when it arrived at the castle?"

Mitchell shook his head. "No. She didn't. But she did say that a cousin or in-law or something of the family from the late Seventeen Hundreds knew—was even friends with—Wolfgang Amadeus Mozart. How's that for a name dropper?"

ELEVEN

"GIRL TALK!"

I groaned. Midnight, and true to her word (Shay is always punctual) my best friend stood at the door of my hotel room laden with two boxes of pastries and three bags of potato chips.

Against all wisdom, better judgment, and several years of history with the woman, I let her in. "My God, Shay. You're holding at least sixty thousand calories in one hand there. Didn't we just part company less than an hour ago at the café after swigging down a few stiff drinks and inhaling three portions of dumplings and potato pancakes?"

"Oh, shove it. We've had an hour to let everything settle and I can't abide girl talk without munchies. Besides, *you* got to work off those dumplings and potato pancakes with your little walk home with Johnny."

I paused in the act of opening the mini-bar to bring out non-alcoholic sodas. "Are we 'drink' drinking—or since we're playing tourist tomorrow, which actually happens to be today since the hour of midnight is upon us, would we prefer to see Prague without a hangover? And just what do you mean, I 'got to work them off?' We didn't go jogging through Old Town or skateboard through Letna Park, Miss Smart-Ass."

Shay snickered. "Alcohol. Preferably bourbon. The potato chips will soak up all the lethal effects. And as to my comment, you did indeed walk back to the hotel with the divine Mr. Gerard, correct?"

"Yes, I did. But since the hotel was a total of twelve blocks from the café and I was in four-inch-tall granny boots I had no business being in with an ankle still healing, I wouldn't say that qualifies for high-impact aerobics."

Shay chortled, "Ooh, little girl—with Johnny Gerard I would expect *any* activity to be high-impact aerobics. And you looked like you were more than willing to partake of some sort of activity that involved heavy breathing."

She had that right. I hadn't completely lied, though. The stroll to the hotel had been exactly that—a stroll. After I'd eaten a third helping of potato pancakes, Johnny and I had taken leave of our tablemates. Just in time to greet Corbin Lerner entering the restaurant. We'd smiled, pointed him toward what was now the movie cast table, then departed.

Johnny hadn't wasted any time in upping the conversation ante once we were alone. "Interesting that Madam D told Mitchell about the musician who knew Mozart, isn't it?"

"Is it? Mitchell didn't say 'flautist.' Shoot. This 'buddy of Amadeus' could have played slide trombone in a marching band."

He chuckled. "Could be. Perhaps for Coronation Balls for big name Emperors?"

"Yeah. Exactly."

"Then again, she could have been talking about your favorite ghost."

I glared at him. "Out with it, Johnny. Has Veronika confided in you?"

"About? Subjects such as your own cryptic statements about hearing music coming from the north wing? Flute music?"

"That's answering a question with a question."

"It is, isn't it?"

"Are we going to do this routine again? Just tell me if she's said anything else. I mean, you've been muraling at the castle, right, for a couple of weeks?"

"There's that word again. Muraling."

I shrugged as we passed what I'd just noticed was *Jozef's Bookstore.* "I'm sure it's a good word. If it's not in the dictionary, it damn well should be. Don't avoid the question. What has Veronika told you?"

"Nothing."

"Oh yeah, like I believe that."

He smiled. "Veronika has not given up the ghost, so to speak. However you did not ask what I picked up independent of the divine Ms. D. There are other sources of information on the subject close at hand."

My ears perked up. "Yes?"

"I believe you're acquainted with one of them. We just passed his shop and you turned a lovely shade of red which clashed rather badly with your green streaks."

"Jozef did hit the castle with gifts this afternoon."

"Now who's fencing?"

I assumed a look of innocence. He didn't buy it. I sighed. "Fine. Yes. I spent a lovely hour or so with Mr. Jezek in his shop—a very nice shop by the way—clean, well-stacked—where was I? Oh, his shop. Jozef regaled me with a few very entertaining tales about a certain musical ancestor of his—one Ignatz Jezek, contemporary of Wolfgang Amadeus Mozart."

"And Mr. Jezek told you about the magical flute."

"Yes. Although he was very honest about being stumped as to just what that magical flute did. The magic of it, so to speak."

Johnny nodded. "So we have a mystery to solve."

"Several. Was Ignatz murdered? Is the flute really magical? If so, what exactly are those powers? And the biggie—where is the flute hidden?"

"You left out where is Ignatz's body hidden." He paused, then plunged on with a surprising statement. "Or the rather sickening question as to whether Gustav's very recent death has anything to do with this latest quest or even who all knows about the legend and who out of the *Kouzlo Noc* crowd is about to jump into the hunt."

My eyes had opened on the first part of his statement. "Wait. Gustav's death? I thought the old man had a heart attack? What are you talking about?"

"Old man? Who told you Gustav was an old man?"

"Oh hell. Now that you ask—no one. I kind of assumed it when Veronika said he'd had a heart attack. I pictured this sweet, elderly piano tuner keeling over as he left the castle."

Johnny winced. "Ah, Jeez. I wish that were the case. Unfortunately, there are several wrong assumptions."

"Like?"

"Like Gustav was probably in his early thirties. Not generally the age for heart problems. Not only that, but did Veronika happen to mention where on the grounds he was found?"

"No."

"Try just under the window of that infamous north wing tower."

I nearly sank to the ground. "Oh my God. That's

what I saw. I mean who I saw. Gustav. I had a vision of someone falling from the north turret window. I didn't get the connection because I really thought Gustav was an old man who'd died of natural causes. Johnny, do you think he was pushed?"

He quietly stated, "I don't know. I didn't see his body. Veronika, Corbin and Franz were the first on the scene. I'm going by what Veronika told me, which was that he was—and I'm paraphrasing—'awfully banged-up, like every bone had been smashed.' Not the norm for a heart attack victim."

I stared at him. "So you're theorizing Gustav did not simply fall. I mean, I didn't see the beginning of this event, just the middle. Thankfully, not the end when he was on the ground. You believe he had help doing a Louganis out that window?"

"Bingo." He spoke quietly. "Why do you think I haven't let on that you and I are more than 'met one afternoon by the cemetery' friends? I truly think evil is surrounding that castle and since folks know I've been hanging out there for more than a day, I can see it headed my way, so I'd prefer it didn't touch you. Honestly? I wish you guys would fly back to the States tomorrow—much as I'd miss you—before anything else happens. I realize you've got a job to do here so I'm not going to be a noodge—yet. Especially since I have no proof of anything concerning the death of Gustav the piano tuner. But, you do have a talent for getting into trouble with villainous types so I'd feel better if you were safely ensconced in Seven-D whipping up brownies with Cherry and Guido."

He held my hand and swung it in his like we were first graders wandering through a carnival. We continued to walk. "So, lovely Abby, give me the scoop on you hearing ghosts. This just sort of sprang up?"

"It's the Dumas genes. I can't help it if there are latent little gifties no one talks about. Mind you, I haven't had any ghostly encounters other than the one with Great-Grandpa I told you about the other day. But I have to confess there are some durn strange folks on the Dumas side of the family. My cousin Julien, for example, who became enthralled with the idea that the Fouchet children were one-quarter Indian as well as a quarter Irish and half French, and now goes on spirit quests twice a year with his shaman guide. A shaman guide Julien claims died back in the earliest days of the American acquisition of the West. Julien calls him Bubba for no good reason I can see. The guide isn't even remotely from the South or Texas. He died somewhere in California."

Johnny howled. "Bubba? Well, he sounds friendly."

I chuckled. "Oh he is. A cozy ghost guide. I have to admit that Cousin Julien is pushing the 'give me a break b.s. meter' with that one. Let's see. Then I have another cousin, Remy, who's sort of a savant. He does mathematical equations faster than a computer. And now he's practicing trying to move stuff with his mind. Kinesis."

"Kinetic movement?" Johnny repeated.

"Yeah. Tossing items around a room. Sort of like a benign, wimpy poltergeist. I told him four Thanksgivings ago it'd be really cool if he could actually succeed and then do something useful like set the dining table for the mass of Dumas and Fouchets arriving."

"How big are the movable objects he plans to toss? Is this dangerous? Can I borrow him for painting a wall?"

"So far no huge objects. And remember, he hasn't

actually managed this one yet so no Sci-Fi reality shows are asking for his services yet. Paints? Sounds easier than a lamp—but sadly, Remy has no aesthetic taste so you wouldn't want his help with muraling—ooh, there's that word again—although give him a year or so to start decorating apartments needing renovations."

"I'll keep him in my mind for my next move. Which—if all goes well—will be with you."

We grinned at each other. "From your lips, Gerard. Anyway, we must top the list with Mother Minette and her sneaky ability to call me when I'm in the middle of something either romantic or sinister, although that seems to have lessened since I took over the business of premonitions in the family. She's into other occult interests."

"Oh crap."

"Oh yeah." I took a deep breath. "She's getting up close and personal with the departed. Swears she has whole conversations with them. Helps the troubled pass to the next realm. Father Gonalez, our parish priest, says he's not sure whether she should be up for sainthood— or burned at the stake."

Johnny stared at me. "Interesting. But she does seem several steps further down the line than you do."

"Good point. But, I swear, if we can't figure out where Ignatz Jezek hid that flute using the little clues I believe he's dropping for my benefit, I'm calling Minette and asking her to zip over for a séance."

He kept his voice and expression deadpan. "There's always our old buddy, Jane Doe *aka* Madam Euphoria. Unless she's too busy driving her brother's cab to help."

"I miss her. She and I were getting together at least once a month in Manhattan in that great soul food place she introduced us to. We'd discuss life, death, channeling spirits and where to find the best clothing and cosmetic bargains around. The wench moved to New Orleans two months ago. Said the vibes for contacting the departed are much better there."

I repeated much of the conversation I'd had with Johnny to Shay as we devoured some sort of gooey, cream-laden pastry and spicy potato chips, but did not tell her how the evening ended. That once we reached the hotel Johnny had discovered what can best be termed a secluded corner of the lobby behind an atrociously large ficus tree, had calmly, firmly and most definitely planted several high-impact aerobic kisses on my lips, then sauntered back outside with not a single backward glance.

I didn't need to tell Shay. The sneak had been watching our arrival from a barstool diagonally placed across from the atrocious tree. She'd seen it all—including moonstruck Abby swaying in her shoes and staring off at the departing gorgeousness of Mr. Gerard for at least two minutes. Even if she hadn't, she'd witnessed plenty of those activities back in Apt. Seven-D when she'd burst in on us without bothering to knock first.

Shay waved a chip at me. Onion dip flew across my shoulder. "Yo! Miss Abby. How was the perfect kiss? Perfect? After three months of *no* Johnny smooching?"

"I *knew* you saw us."

"Well, duh. Mind you, I was not trying to spy. I merely wanted one last brandy before heading upstairs to unpack and prepare for girl talk. Not my fault Johnny chose that portion of the room to lay one on you."

"How far didja have to lean for a good view?"

"Far enough to need a masseuse for my entire torso

for the next month. But it was worth it. Enough aerobics in that kiss to qualify for ESPN any night of the week."

I sighed. "Gerard is a man of many, many talents. Kissing is one of his best. I just wish he'd quit pretending around the film cast that we're pretty much strangers. He's gone all 'Gregory Noble' on me in some sort of dumb macho 'keep the little woman safe' bit."

She nodded, opened up the last bag of chips, then held it out to me.

Two bites in, I stopped. "Know what just hit me?"

"A flying crispy potato?" was the chewy response.

I ignored her. "We know that Johnny knows about the flautist. Veronika knows and she knows that I know. Oh lordy, did I just say that? I wonder if she knows that Johnny knows? Anyway, she knew when she was so wonky about my snooping in the north wing and hearing music that did not come from any 'see-dee'. I'm sure her sisters know. I'd imagine this is a tale told to the Duskova family since Ignatz Jezek first went missing. With me?"

"I don't *know*," she snickered.

"Stop that! Okay. Franz's eyebrows twitch when Mozart is mentioned. Not a normal reaction. Corbin Lerner is helping Veronika dig up graves in the cemetery that holds the dear-departed from the Seventeen-Hundreds, so I'll betcha he's in for treasure and he's been damn silent about anything to do with his—doins'. I can't tell about Lily or Mitch though both seem a bit jumpy— could just be their normal personalities. But at this point we have a majority of treasure seekers at *Kouzlo Noc*. And a real live ghost!" I sobered immediately. "Plus a possible murderer as well."

Shay managed to swallow her last overly large mouthful without choking. "Murderer?"

"Oh yeah. Did I mention that Johnny said that Gustav the piano tuner, who was not the elderly gent I thought he was, was very banged up when discovered on the grounds near the north—let me repeat—*north*—tower?"

"And Johnny Gerard claims he was pitched?"

"Yep. I think he's right. Assuming he's the man in my vision, which seems like a yes. Dang, Shay. *Headlights* has just become involved in a race to uncover a few truths, possibly a body or two, and one of the world's greatest finds. Folks have been killed in the last two hundred years over this flute. And very likely in the last couple of days. It's possible that half the cast is in danger and the other half are dangerous and we have no idea who the bad guys are."

Shay cackled in sheer delight. "This is why I love being on location."

TWELVE

SHAY AND I made it out of the hotel for our day of touristy activities by ten the next morning. Whether it was the excitement of seeing the sights of Prague that had banished the dregs of alcohol from our heads or we'd eaten so many chips and pastries that the bourbon hadn't had a chance to soak through, the reason didn't matter. We were hale, hearty and ready to dive into historic buildings and "ooh" and "ahh" over statues erected by Emperors from centuries ago, then stop now and again to partake in more gastronomical delights.

First up on the agenda was the area closest to our hotel. Our hotel was smack in the middle of part of Prague called Old Town, with its attractions of Gothic cellars, a Gothic chapel and my favorite—the Astronomical Clock. I love clocks. I have a cheap cuckoo clock from a tiny store in Munich. I have a replica of Big Ben I found in a museum shop in London. An embarrassing armadillo clock from Juarez. But this was a timepiece to end all time. There are really two clocks, one on top of the other. A statue of Death pops out on the hour and pulls a cord that starts bells ringing and cocks crowing and little statues dancing all over the place. Even Jesus and his apostles make an appearance.

I immediately decided I had to find the nearest tourist-gouging souvenir stand and buy a miniature for my collection. Shay is used to this particular obsession

of mine so she patiently followed me to three different
stores before I found the right clock and only made one
snide comment to the harried shopkeeper who pulled
out five different examples before I was satisfied. "My
friend was scarred by a metronome at an early age. You
have to excuse her."

The clerk didn't care. He made a good profit from
Ms. Fouchet, who chose the most expensive of the
clocks he displayed for her perusal.

I was happy. Shay was happy I was happy. And we'd
managed not only to see the Astronomical Clock but to
buy its tiny facsimile all in the space of twenty minutes.

Which left us plenty of time to wander through cathedrals before lunch. Well, one cathedral. St. Vitus
Cathedral, to be exact. St. Vitus is one of those places
you can roam through for days and still only get a taste.
Just the statues of saints outside are enough for a *Gilli-
gan's Island* "three-hour tour." A bronze door depicting
scenes from the castle's history is almost the first thing
one sees when entering from the doorway that gazes
upon the Second and Third Courtyards of Prague Castle. The choir loft, with a big mama pipe organ, looks
down on—what else—a royal crypt. But the *"Oh, Mil-
dred! If you go to Prague you must see"* attraction is the
stain glass Rose Window in what is considered the Neo-
Gothic area of the cathedral that boasts smaller chapels.

That was where Shay got what I call her "Contestant" expression. Generally, when this look crosses her
face, a light shines in her eyes and she straightens her
shoulders, puffs out her expansive chest, then makes an
announcement rather on the order of a beauty contestant answering that all important "What do you wish
for?" question. Only with Shay the answer is never

"Peace on earth." Ever since she started directing films last year, her answers run closer to, "Let's stick that actor in a burning building for the next scene. Stunt men? What stunt men? We can't afford stunt men. John Smith, the actor I hired at a reduced rate from Bayonne, New Jersey, can handle it. Yo! Abby? Do we own a fire extinguisher?"

Under the Rose Window, I watched, with no small amount of trepidation, as Shay's expression skipped the preliminaries and round two, jumping directly to Final Contestant mode.

"What now?" I asked.

"I'm ruminating on my own genius. This would be a marvelous place for Kelsey to hide from Harold. Our very evil villain, who hasn't been hired yet, by the way. So—picture this. She could sneak into the choir loft for a few hours but then get so drawn to the Rose Window that she kind of forgets she's on the run from Harold the Horrific. But she'll hear someone playing the pipe organ and then she can swing out using a rope, crash through the window, and of course, Harold will find her and there'll be a massive fight."

"Under the Rose Window, a damn old masterpiece Shay Martin's leading lady has just shattered."

"Sure."

"Well, I'll bring you dumplings in your jail cell after the Czech government slaps you in irons for even suggesting such an affront on the Cathedral."

"Oh. Well, I guess there are certain considerations to…"

"Consider?"

She ignored me.

After three hours of the obligatory "oohing" and

"ahhing" over oodles of patron saints staring down at us while we stared up and admired more centuries-old stain glass windows, my stomach was growling and I needed sustenance.

The timepiece chimed in with a tiny birdie that popped out, cuckooed to announce it was two in the afternoon and definitely time for lunch. We obeyed the summons. We pulled out our handy guidebook and chose a *kavarny* that promised homemade *gulas* and pastries more disgusting than anything served by the Duskovas on their best cooking day.

"This is nice, Shay. Sitting. Eating. Not running around worrying about castles and ghosts and story-lines and killers and creepy graveyards. That ceme-tery, by the way, is a place which makes 'dismal' look like a party."

"That whole castle is kind of gruesome, Abby. Even if you hadn't heard your ghost fluting or tooting or whatever the heck he was doing in the north wing, I'd've assumed the place was haunted on nothing more than the general eeriness of ambience. It's so creepily per-fect. The very fact that more than one Duskova has ei-ther dispatched an enemy from those towers or been tossed himself screams *'Ghosts Live Here—Get Your Tickets Now!'*"

We both fell silent remembering the probable new-est member of unearthly spirits, the unknown (to us) musician, Gustav, who'd met his Maker only days ago.

I was about to start a discussion about murders most foul, when I was distracted by a small tourist bus in front of the café. Passengers were popping out one after the other and the outfits were, typically, a plethora of bad taste. I sat up straight.

"Oh. My. Sweet. Sainted. Granny."

"What?"

"Johnny Gerard, in the flesh. At the bus."

She squinted, since the sun was partially obscuring the bus and the man. "Ah. Yes. It is indeed the dashing soap-star muralist."

"Is that anywhere in Websters?"

"Muralist? Of course. Hey, we've all been using it. Although Daddy would not approve."

Shay's father is Chair of the English Department at a large university in Wisconsin. Both Shay and I take great delight in creating words to make Daddy Martin shudder even though I'm rather fond of the man.

Johnny had spotted Shay's waving arm and was making his way through the crowds lined up for a table until he could lean on ours. He grabbed Shay's palm and kissed it, then calmly used those lips to directly kiss mine. Lips—not palm.

"Well, golly gee! A real kiss from Gerard in public! Are we out of the closet now?"

"Only in front of Japanese tourists. So, how y'all doin' today?"

"We're good," Shay responded. "Wandering through Old Town seeing historical sights and planning to do the lunch and dinner excursion of Prague that we're making up as we go along, and I'm watching Abby spend too much money on clocks and we're trying to decide if we want to hit a museum or the Jewish cemetery or see the ghost of the Mad Barber who haunts Karlova Street. How 'bout you? You look like you were shepherding a flock of tourists over there by the bus."

"I sort of got caught in their group instead of the one I was supposed to be in this morning. And, naturally, they all watch *Endless Time* and are thrilled that Gregory Noble has joined the tour. They elected me to be guide."

"Guide as in *'This is the cathedral where Saint Agnes dyed her hair red and don't get lost and meet me at the bus at two o'clock?'*"

"That about covers it. I look upon this as research for the next four hundred nutty occupations Yolanda sticks Super Detective Noble into before next year's ratings."

"Which reminds me," I interrupted. "What wacky device did Yolanda use to get you off the show for the time you're in Prague, then traipsing down to Florida to design for the seniors? Please tell me not another coma?"

Johnny began to whistle. "Nope. No more comas. For at least a year."

"Go on."

"I've disappeared."

"Disappeared? As in Gregory Noble got eaten by a large lion while on safari and we're waiting for the cowardly beast to cough him up whole in a few months?"

Johnny loved it. "I wish. Nah, this is almost realism. During the last safari episode, Greg Noble takes off after the Communist spy—Cade Kern—remember him, Abby? He played Letitia's brother last year?"

I nodded. "So Letitia's brother is now an agent for the former KGB?"

"Oh yeah. Except Cade is doing the National Tour of *Wicked,* so he needed a way out of the show."

"With you."

"Precisely. When last seen, Gregory Noble is chasing the man he's learned is 'Vladimir Borodin—agent' into the jungle. Of course, I'll come out unscathed and heroic in a couple of months once my gig with the Sarasota bunch is over. Cade will be in 'Oz' singing his little heart out. His body will not be found in case the producers decide to bring him back after his tour is done."

I couldn't help lift my eyes to the heavens. Pointless to comment since I was secretly still pissed—and jealous the soap had dumped my part a couple of months before Johnny headed off to Africa.

Shay teased him with, "So, Noble, where else should we expect to see you during your stay in Prague? Will you be presiding at the courthouse later today? Preaching at Mass this Sunday at the Church of Our Lady Victorious? Uh…?"

I joined in, "Waiting on tables at Pravda? Cooking the goulash and potato pancakes at the Café Kafka? Driving a riverboat up the Vltava? Wrangling the miniature *przewalski? 'Working at the car wash, yeah'?"*

"Don't knock the ability to multi-task, ladies. I have incredible life experiences stored within under this charming exterior. Feel free to partake at any time." He winked at me. "And, you'll be thrilled to hear that as Gregory Noble I spent two weeks at the Prague Zoo caring for the *przewalski* before arresting their trainer for diamond smuggling. Just wish *Endless Time* had taken longer for those episodes. I really enjoyed that gig."

Shay screamed. Softly. "Stop it you two! What the heck is a pretezalitskytitsky? Pretzels with special sauce?"

Johnny was finishing a swig of coffee, so I answered. "Miniature horsies. Remember? I told you about them when we were doing the guide book thing this morning at breakfast?"

"Well, yeah, you told me about teensy horsey-doos

but you didn't start blathering in Czech. Most annoying." She hopped to her feet. "I'm dying to see them. Sometime after lunch?"

"We'll see the horses, Shay. I have to admit the admittedly awesome culture of this day is beginning to wear. Nice, cute, cuddly little animals sound like a welcome relief."

Johnny glanced at his watch. "Oh nuts. Sorry, ladies. Have to haul it even though I'd love to stay and eat strudel and drink coffee and personally escort you to the zoo but I'm subbing at the *National Marionette Theatre* in an hour. They normally don't perform weekdays, but this is a special event. If you're up for just a bit more culture, drop on by. We'll be performing the Verdi version of *Macbeth*. With really eerie and scary witches. You'll love it."

THIRTEEN

THE INVITATION HAD been too good to refuse. Johnny Gerard at the puppet show. He hadn't said whether he was subbing for the ticket-taker, the popcorn-seller, or the guy who dangles strings for dancing puppets on high. Either way this took precedence over tiny horses, no matter how cute they were.

I didn't see him when Shay and I took our seats, but I quickly heard him. The man was bloody well singing. And singing bloody well—Johnny's an amazing baritone. He was dangling a puppet and singing the role of Macduff, who is really the hero in the play and the opera.

I nudged Shay. "Thank God it's Verdi and they're singing Italian. I love Mozart but if I'd had to hear *Die Zauberflote* or even *Cosi Fan Tutte* in German or something today, I'd've gone and jumped back into the Vltava River to catch the next boat."

"Ssshh. You'll get us thrown out. Especially if you say anything derogatory about Wolfgang."

I whispered, "Never. I just *said* I adore the man. But everyone needs a rest from symbolism and magic now and again. I'll bet Mozart would've watched bad Slasher flicks if he'd had a DVD player. So, a nice murdering, flat-out greedy Scottish king is quite refreshing."

We stayed silent after that, enjoying the music and the really intricate movement of the puppets. The artistry of all the performances erased thoughts of the Austrian composer. In fact, the name of Mozart didn't even float across my mind until long after Birnam Wood had come to Dunsinane and Macbeth had met his well-deserved fate.

The witches were marvelous. I wished Minette had been there since she's also now big into Wiccan magic (which she smoothly juggles with Catholic theology without incurring the wrath of the priests in Texas. A minor feat of magic in itself.) These "Wyrd" sisters reminded me of my initial introduction to the Duskovas, which isn't the nicest thing to say, but in my defense, it was the costuming that made the comparison so sharp. This version of *Macbeth* was set in the Victorian era, so the black-garbed-governess-with-buns-for-hairdos-look had been chosen for the three puppets singing about toils and troubles.

The curtain call was for puppets only. No humans allowed. The wooden actors danced back onstage and bowed and curtseyed to an enthusiastic crowd. Johnny's face wasn't seen, but his hands still worked Macduff. He got a standing ovation from the crowd. No great surprise.

We waited for him outside on a bench where we could watch the citizens of Prague along with the tourists buying sausages and potato pancakes. The performance had been scaled down to last only about ninety minutes, so it was just now five in the afternoon and the sun was still shining. Shay and I soaked up the warmth and talked about the various performers we'd just heard, especially the witches and how good they'd been.

Johnny found us at the bench not more than ten minutes after he'd finished the show.

"Well?"

"Loved it," I told him. "I've never really thought about puppetry before—especially with opera, but this was fantastic. Some of the puppets were more real than some singers I've heard at the Met. And all the voices were really, really good. Even that chap who played Macduff. I'm impressed."

Johnny blushed. "Thanks, hon." Then he chuckled. "Did you like the witches? Did they remind you of anyone?"

I chortled. "Ha! I was just telling Shay that our hostesses, or landladies or whatever from *Kouzlo Noc* probably loaned the theatre their entire wardrobe for this. And didn't that one witch with the raspy voice look just like Veronika when she's pissed?"

Shay cackled. Johnny smiled, then looked somber. "What's sad is those 'outfits' the Duskovas have are pretty much it for them."

"Yeah, I do remember you mentioning to Lily Lowe that the Duskovas didn't exactly have a chic wardrobe left after Soviet rule. Nor the money to go out on a shopping spree, I'd wager."

"They're one step above abject poverty. I'm doing the mural for free and Corbin Lerner has a grant for his research so the Duskovas aren't paying him. If you guys hadn't found the castle and rented it, they were looking at being forced to sell and find some tiny flat in the city. That wardrobe is probably left over from the days when they worked for those few members of the Communist Party who used the Duskova castle as a nice hotel."

"That stinks. Really. Veronika is spooky but it could be she's just been through so much she's not sure how

to play gracious lady of the manor anymore, so she's
got the Victorian governess routine down to an art."

Johnny agreed. "She does, doesn't she?" He turned
to Shay. "If there's any way you can get the sibling trio
into your movie and pay them, as well as paying rent,
it would be a godsend to them. I gather *Headlights* has
some major backing for this flick?"

She waved her hand dismissively. "Of course. I already have it planned to perfection. Our girls will be in
every crowd scene and I'll just use Marta as the maid
who waits on the heroine when she comes from London. Lays out the clothes, the warming pan, all that
good stuff."

"I'm not sure Marta speaks English, Shay," I interjected.

"Pish-tosh. Not a problem. A few 'miladys' will suf-
fice. It's the look I want and Marta's got it."

"Damn straight." I nodded. "Say, I forgot to ask you
earlier, but do you think Bambi would have any problems using the Duskovas as our food service, too? I
mean, they whip up some mean goodies and it would
probably be cheaper than hiring some caterer to come
tromping all the way out to the castle every day with
a big van to feed the ravenous actors. I already mentioned this to Veronika and she seemed to like the idea."

Johnny brightened. "That would really help them.
And they can cook more than just kolaches, strudel and
scones. Wait 'til you taste Trina's special cheese dump-
lings. I'm trying to convince them to open up *Kouzlo
Noc* as a bed and breakfast once the movie is done. But
I love the idea of using them as extras and as chefs."

Shay held up her hand. "I'll ask Bambi as soon as I
track her down. I think she's still in Mumbai. I expect

she'll tell me to employ the lovely ladies every which way I can. And costume them as well. Satisfied?"

Johnny held out his hand to Shay. She took it, with some suspicion. He turned her wrist so her palm faced down, then leaned over and kissed her hand. It had the desired effect. She giggled. I groaned. Johnny the charmer.

"What?"

"Can't you just shake on the deal like a normal person?" I asked.

Shay growled at me while simpering at Johnny. "Hush, Abby. I love this hand-kissing routine. So European. So romantic. So..."

"Words fail her," I said sarcastically. "Well, if you two are through with wheeling, dealing and smooching palms, can we go find some dinner somewhere? I'm starving."

Shay, never one to pass up the opportunity for eating, jumped up from the bench. "Great idea. I'm all for romantic gestures, but they pale in comparison to the thought of a nice bowl of *gulas* and a plate of those little slices of ham with the horseradish smeared all over them."

Better and better.

I rose. Johnny rose. "There's a great place that's not in any of the guide books not far from here. Trust me?"

Johnny Gerard—actor, muralist, Japanese tour guide, zookeeper (well, miniature-horse keeper), marrionetteist-singer supreme and gourmet extraordinaire.

Trust him? *"Lay on, Macduff.'"*

FOURTEEN

As ADVERTISED, DINNER was wonderful. Not only did this café, hidden in a back street that looked exactly like the alley for some of the scenes set in the film *Amadeus,* serve incredibly delicious food, but they boasted music as well.

Not opera. Klezmer. For those who've never heard this style of music before, I shall attempt to clarify.

Klezmer was originally Hebrew liturgical music played by roving minstrels throughout Eastern Europe, but evolved to include gigs at wedding ceremonies and then jazz clubs and there are now bands, even in the U.S., that tour like rock groups. The instrumentation is generally made up of violins, cymbals, clarinet, trombone and accordion and when words are sung, they're sung in Yiddish. Think "bar scene in *Fiddler on the Roof* with the bottle dance" then jazz it up some. That said, there are many different styles and sounds; just like American "C & W" can claim Hank Williams Jr., Dolly Parton, Garth Brooks, Tim McGraw and Carrie Underwood. Eclectic but huddling under and sharing that umbrella called "country."

At this café (named something so Czech with so many consonants I hadn't the slightest clue how to pronounce it) the Klezmer musicians were casually dressed in black turtlenecks and slacks and yarmulkes, which gave them the appearance of a Jewish Bohemian beatnik band circa 1950s. They were called *Klezmer Volny Rabin* and they were incredible.

I knew "rabin" meant "rabbi" but the adjective defeated me. "What's *Volny* mean?" I asked Johnny. I figured he'd learned some Czech for the soap episodes filmed in Prague. At any rate he had to have a heckuva lot better grasp of the language than I did.

He did. "Means 'free.'"

"Ah. Very post Communism political of them, huh?"

"Possibly." He chortled. "Then again, it could just mean that Martin, the owner of this fine establishment, doesn't pay."

Shay tapped his arm. "Do you suppose they're really rabbis?"

"Well, I can't speak for all of them, but the accordion player, Jacob, can be found teaching at the temple school most days. And Joshua, the clarinet player, is a cantor. Come to the Synagogue next Saturday and you can hear some fine singing."

I knew a crafty look had just surfaced across my face. Shay glared at me.

"No."

"What? No?"

"No."

"Shoot, Shay, don't tell me no. You don't mean it."

"I do. No."

Johnny put his hand between our faces. "Would you like to let me in on this little tiff since I have no idea what Shay is saying 'no' to since as far as I can tell, no topic has been introduced that would cause that word?"

I narrowed my eyes. "Shay is being stubborn."

She stuck her tongue out at me. "Am not. You're being nutty."

"Children! Children. Stop. Give me a break here. What are you going on about?" Johnny nearly shouted.

Shay shifted her glare to him. "Abigail wants to add the singing Rabbis to the film."

Johnny's expression became one of fascination. "Where did that come from? I didn't hear her say anything even close?" He stared at Shay. "Do you suddenly have the Fouchet gift for extra sensory perception? Can you now read minds?"

I snorted. "Try rooming with someone you're also in class with twenty-four-seven. Identical twins don't have the communication Shay and I have." I added with a sneer, "Not that it helps when one of the duo is digging her heels in and not agreeing to what could be a defining moment in the movie."

"Defining moment?" she yelled. "You want a bunch of bearded guys with beanies to parachute in à la Gregory Noble or have 'em pop out from behind that marble coffin and start jamming to the tune of *Sunrise, Sunset* while all around them counts and countesses and maids and butlers dance a *hora?*" She brightened. "Wait. When the whole vision comes clear, it's not that bad an idea. In fact, I'm getting to like it. It's inspired! I'm so glad I thought of it. Let's ask these guys if they could use a few extra bucks and get their names splashed onscreen."

I shot Johnny an "I told you so" look, then contentedly settled back in my chair to sip coffee and enjoy the music, which was quite a bit livelier and had more jazz influence than *Sunrise, Sunset*.

I didn't stay content for long. The Rabbis were taking a break and the violin player was approaching our table. Johnny motioned for him to sit. The musician, who

didn't seem to be a day over sixteen, introduced himself as Benjamin, the "real" rabbi's younger brother, and
gratefully accepted the coffee Johnny had just ordered.

"You play beautifully," I told him. "This is going to
become a fixed hangout for us while we're in Prague."

"You are here to visit for how long?"

Shay jumped in and explained about the movie, finishing by asking him to ask his fellow Klezmerites—
which probably isn't a word Shay's dad would buy
either, but I liked it—if they'd be interested in performing a number for the film.

Benjamin's eyes shone. "I would love to do that. I
would bet the rest of the band would be interested as
well. We are all great film enthusiasts and the chance
to actually be in one is not something to pass up."

That was settled. So we discussed various films
that had been shot in and around Prague, mostly the
American action films that made such great use of
the Charles Bridge in between blowing up historic-
looking buildings.

"No CIA explosive devices or spies in this one," Shay
told him. "No, wait, that's not quite true. In the novel
we're adapting, Count Zilania has actually worked as
a spy for the British government. I don't recall the author ever really explaining why though, so this could
be nothing more than glossing over that particular piece
of back story."

Benjamin smiled. "I do not care whether a troupe of
secret agents appear, I am just thrilled to be asked to
play." He tapped Johnny's shoulder. "Which brings me
to why I came to sit with you—other than simply to say
hello and meet these beautiful ladies."

Shay and I preened. He was a kid, but one preens when one is called beautiful by a male of any age.

Benjamin continued, "I need to get home and finish work for a test in my Biology class tomorrow. Would you mind sitting in for the rest of the evening?"

Johnny enthusiastically agreed, asked us if we could handle being on our own and getting back to the hotel without incident, then, after we assured him that we were not that helpless, he followed Benjamin back to the small platform that served as a stage. He rosined up a bow and began to play the next set.

I groaned.

"What? You're looking morose. Problems?"

"There are times when I see my wedding to Johnny Gerard getting as lost in time as Ignatz's flute."

"Why?"

"Because he gets everything right. I mean, he's done everything and is way too well-rounded to be human. Look at today."

"What? He guides Japanese tourists and still leads us to a Klezmer band who will play their wonderful tunes soon in our movie to the delight of millions the world over. Not to mention he's cute as a bug, talented, has steady income, is smart and makes you laugh. Y'all are getting married as soon as he's not flying around film-ing *Endless Time* for two seconds. What's the problem?"

"I feel like a dweeb next to him."

"Ah, come on. Yes, the man has more than his share of talents, but you're not exactly a one-gifted woman yourself."

"Oh? Really? Aside from breaking feet while roller-skating in bad productions of *Starlight Express,* what the hell else can I do?"

She shoved a bourbon and coke at me. (We'd switched from coffee after the food had arrived.) "You want the breakdown? The sizeable schemer? The entire enchilada?"

"If it will prevent you from using alliterative metaphors, yes, fine. How in hell can I keep up with The Gerard and his coat of many colorful careers—most of which are related to his beyond-normal soap character?"

Shay took a sip of her own drink, then toasted me. "I like that. Nice. Coat of colorful careers. Well, let me get to your jacket, buddy mine."

"Before you and I both end up in the Retirement Home for old dancers?" I countered.

"You're the one stalling. I'm ready to list your accomplishments any time you can keep your mouth quiet for longer than twenty seconds. I shouldn't do this. This is what your damn idiot agent Angela, who is also my idiot agent, should be doing. But be quiet and I'll buck up your ego."

"Okay."

"Really?"

"I said 'okay.' Now who's stalling?" I downed my drink. "I don't have other accomplishments, right? That's why you don't want to list them. It won't even take a twentieth of a second, much less twenty."

"Stop!"

"Okay." I closed my mouth, then immediately opened it again. "I'm morose."

"You're whacked. Be quiet or I'll disown you. Shoot, Abby, you're smart. You memorize songs and lines faster than composers and playwrights get them on paper. You can dance, you can sing, you can act. You *can* choreograph although I'm much better. Uh. You find locations. Well, you found one and you will doubtless find more in future times since you are somewhat accident prone and you do break your feet at least once a year, usually because some idiot director makes you do something idiotic. Where was I? Oh. You can walk into a bare house and decorate it in your mind within minutes of entering. You make the meanest batch of brownies on the planet as well as chili that can peel paint. You love animals and thanks to those episodes on *Endless Time* playing Vanessa Manilow, Olympic equestrian coming out of a coma, you can even ride a horse without getting thrown, bitten, falling off or making a total fool of yourself. Of course you turn into a blathering, blithering idiot around roaches and you have a tendency to be a wimp most of the time, then lose your temper and spout dumb epithets at people, but other than that—how'm I doing?"

I shrugged. "Johnny Gerard can paint murals. He sings, he plays violin and guitar and doubtless every instrument in a marching band. He can swing on a trapeze with ease. He's taught English. He can speak languages and is energetic and personable enough to help guide tours in a country not even his. Every damn female in every damn country in the world is hot for him. What am I missing so far?"

"Nobel-prize winner?"

I groaned. "Wouldn't doubt it. Hell, Shay, I quit. What's going to happen when we do get married? How soon will he get bored with me, the bone-breaking underachiever of the millennium?"

"Shit, Abby, you're such a dweeb. You're a nice person. And you're funny. And you listen and you don't judge people unless they happen to be leading ladies who resemble bitchy dancers you've known. You make all kinds of people adore you. And you're loyal. And in today's world, I wouldn't trade you as my friend for all the gold in Arabia. Or wherever gold comes from. And if Johnny is half as smart as we both agree he is, then he won't trade you either."

She added, "Not even for a dozen Hannah Hammersteins."

FIFTEEN

WE LISTENED TO Johnny jam with the rabbis for the next forty-five minutes or so, then decided to head back to the hotel and rest. We'd eaten too much, possibly drunk too much and we intended to get some work done tomorrow out at *Kouzlo Noc*. The idea was to wander, notebook in hand, from room to room, deciding what furniture needed to be brought in, what room worked for what scene—all real work needed for making the movie look as authentic as a Gothic novel turned musical flick with Klezmer musicians and rock singers could be.

It took us an hour to get back to the hotel. Of course, the café where we'd been bobbing heads to Klezmer music was actually less than a fifteen minute walk from our hotel, but we hadn't grasped that fact before we left the place (after trying to pay the check and being waved off by a smiling Martin, owner of the joint, who explained in halting English that the bill was already paid. By Mr. Gerard. Naturally.) We'd lied to Johnny when he'd asked us if we knew where the hotel was and if we'd have any problems finding our way there. We hadn't a clue. And we even knew it was a lie when we boldly assured him that we were independent, tough navigators who had the location of every café and hotel in Prague memorized down to the last square foot. Which sounded much better than admitting we were both so directionally-challenged we could get lost in an elevator in the Empire State Building. Johnny, of course, knew that but was tactful enough not to point out our deficiencies in front of the Klezmer band.

Once Shay and I reached the right hotel (with the aid of two guide books and four very kind Prague natives who spoke excellent English) we'd parted at the door of my room, agreeing to meet the next morning around eight to rent a car and head back up to *Kouzlo Noc*. I'd slipped the card key into the lock, taken two steps into the room and promptly collapsed on the bed for a well-deserved sleep.

That lasted about thirty minutes. I woke up and felt recharged. I checked the clock by the bed—and my new souvenir Astronomical clock as well—both proclaimed the time to be ten-thirty. A great hour for the nightlife in Prague to start revving into high gear.

I got up, took a shower, washed my face and re-applied make-up, then found a nice little basic black dress with a swirly hem and threw it on. Only then did I head to the phone and call Shay's room. I knew one of two things would happen. Either she would be in a deep sleep and I'd hear obscenities she'd learned from choreographing a Way-the-Hell Off Broadway semi-pornographic musical five years ago and be told to go away until tomorrow. Or—and this quickly became the case—she'd say, "Meet you in the lobby in five. Whacha wearin'?"

We were out the door in six minutes. We had no idea where we were headed but the guidebook we'd been treated to courtesy of our hotel's "social director" listed at least four great night clubs within close walking distance. We picked a name at random, *Club Krev,* and took off.

Club Krev was big and noisy and the décor just a bit bizarre. Apparently the owner had decided to cash in on the wave of vampire movies and books and cults that have been springing up in the last few years all over the world. *Club Krev* sported fake mirrors on the walls that did not reflect. Cloves of (thankfully) fake garlic hung down en masse from the high ceilings.

Coffins had been set up in front of the bandstand where a band was belting out tunes at high volume. The female singer was decked out in a black leather and lace corset and black lace thigh-high boots. The male members of the group were in Lord Byron–style white poet shirts tucked into tight black leather breeches tucked into tight black leather riding boots. Little replicas of bats swung from side to side over each table. And silver bow and arrow sets were tacked onto every inch of the wall that didn't have a mirror.

It appeared that every table was already taken, so we prepared to just stand by the bar and inhale the atmosphere. But when we heard a shout, "Shay! Abby!" we figured someone we actually knew was nearby and wanted to see us.

We were right. Lily Lowe and Franz Hart shoved their way through the mob of the dancing undead.

"Come join us. We have a table in the back. It's not as noisy there and we can hear one another if we want to talk."

Getting back was harder than it looked. Dancers were swirling not only on the floor reserved for the activity but in and out of spaces between tables. How the waiters were able to juggle drinks without incurring major injury to themselves or the glasses on their trays was a mystery. They were amazing. I hoped they'd be getting great tips.

The table was by the exit door, which reassured me immediately, since, while I like night clubs and dancing and partying, I get a bit paranoid about getting stuck in one of those places if, God forbid, a fire should break out. Franz noticed my perusal of the door.

"It's unlocked. From both sides. We checked."

I glanced at him. "You share my worries?"

Franz's face grew somber. "I survived a night club fire in Hamburg only three years ago. It was truly a miracle that no one was killed or injured, but it was the most terrifying experience I've ever been through and I don't wish to repeat it."

"Gotcha. I'm with you. Open door policy all the way."

Franz and Lily stole two chairs from an empty table nearby.

"The couple who originally staked this table haven't quit dancing or going outside to kiss for the hour we've been here. When they haven't been kissing in here on the dance floor. They do not even realize this table is where they first ordered drinks from," said Lily.

"Good. I don't want irate customers coming back and tossing Shay and me out on our respective butts. By the way, for you native Czech speakers, what does *Krev* mean?"

Lily smiled. "Blood."

"Oh, yuck," Shay wrinkled her nose.

"Well, it's a vampire theme club, so that was a good choice, really."

"All true, but still—oh yuck."

"Come on, Shay, ambience and all that. This place would be awesome for the film."

"Hmm. Let me ruminate on this idea for a moment." She closed her eyes for approximately three seconds, before opening them and delightfully declaring, "I could sneak in a vampire scene—not in the club here, but in *Kouzlo Noc*. Vampires are still good box office. I can just see the T-shirts for the movie. I could make Count Zilania a vampire? No, that's too cheesy even for me. But perhaps there's a way to hint that vampires have been stalking the heroine on her journey to London?"

Shay was off and running. There was no good point in responding to her flights of film fancy, so I didn't bother to say anything.

Franz had barely settled in the chair he'd swiped from the other table, before popping up again and extending his hand to me. "Want to dance?"

"Only for a bit. My foot isn't quite up to a lot of hopping around in heels. But yeah, thanks."

We found a spot that allowed two people to move arms and wiggle bottoms and not much else, and gyrated to the heavy metal rock sounds from the band. This was great. I needed this. I'd had too much culture and too much musical history crammed into my brain the last couple of days. I needed a break to go wild and listen to music that had no social significance and would never survive two-hundred-fifty years. Or even two years. The band was awful. I loved it.

Franz took turns dancing with me, Shay and Lily. I let the other two take extra innings since I really didn't need the stress on my feet and I was having fun watching. About the fourth time Franz danced with Lily, leaving Shay and me to sing with the band since they'd started playing top American hits, we were joined by two men—Corbin Lerner and Mitchell Herbert.

"Looking for us?" asked Shay.

"Yep. This if the fifth club we've hit tonight trying to hunt you down," was the response from Mitchell.

"Reason?"

"Boredom. Not knowing anyone in the city and wanting to be part of a group."

Corbin smiled at me. "I have been in Prague for three weeks now but I've mainly been up at the castle working in that awful graveyard. This is a good break for me."

"If you don't mind a nosy question, what exactly are you doing for the Duskovas? Other than jumping out of crypts at unsuspecting location scouts? I mean, don't they know their history by now?" I queried.

"I've heard this," said Mitchell. "Shay? Wanna dance?"

She was up and running before the "c" in dance sounded.

I prodded Corbin. "So? Your work?"

"Well, you saw how destroyed that cemetery was."

"That's an understatement. It looked like a third world country after a third world war."

"Nice way of putting it. Veronika told me the grave-yard has been vandalized for years and years, long before she and her sisters were even born. And when the Communists were using *Kouzlo Noc* as their headquarters, they cleaned up the original cemetery, but didn't bother with that one. Veronika said that it was originally built because the other cemetery got too crowded, but she was embarrassed to tell you the truth."

"Which is?"

"The graveyard, Saint John of Nepomuk Cemetery, was named in honor of the saint tossed off the Charles Bridge by Wenceslas the Fourth sometime in the Four-

teenth Century—not the Christmas 'good king Wenceslas' who had an earlier reign—became the cast-off
burial ground for the Duskova clan. Cast-off as in, um,
servants or various other working people who'd died
and hadn't enough money for a decent burial at another site. Or less-than-desirable folks who'd gotten
into trouble somehow near *Kouzlo Noc.* Duskova family
members who'd brought disgrace to the name through
various means. The usual stories of the maids who'd
been taken advantage of by barons and sons of barons
and died in childbirth."

I shook my head. "I knew that place felt sadder than
a normal cemetery. Unwanted. And the vandalism just
made it so much worse. So your job now is—what?"

"Discovering who was buried when and where and
in what plot their remains should have been kept. Plus
learning as much about the history of who, what, where
and when to document for the Duskovas. It's not literally genealogical research but that's what I'm calling it."

I paused. "Found anything really interesting?"

He paused. "Such as?"

"Oh, let me run with this. Um. Buried gold coins
underneath a skeleton with a pirate hat and a cutlass
and a big sign that reads, *'Treasure from the Spanish
Armada—Dive in, dude!'* Something of that nature."

I don't know if he bought that particular idea but he
did chuckle before stating, "No. The closest thing of
value are the jewels I discovered in a rotted velvet bag."

"Jewels?" I perked up.

"I use the term very loosely. Upon appraisal by a
local jeweler in Prague it was determined that the loot
is worth about a hundred dollars tops. Diamonds, but
very poorly cut and hardly worth anything at all."

"Ah well. I'm sure you'll stumble onto a cache of emeralds and sapphires around the neck of some serving wench dressed in the garb of a highwayman."

His laughter sailed across the table. "I can see why you and Miss Martin are making a movie. You obviously have a taste for romantic fiction."

"We do. After all, what's life without a touch of improbable romance?"

Shay, Franz, Mitchell and Lily all returned in time to hear my last remark.

Mitchell queried, "What are you guys yakking about?"

Corbin answered, "Abby is giving me a glimpse into the workings of a show business mind filled with glamour, mystery and fantasy. It's very interesting."

Lily spoke up. "Speaking of mystery, I have a piece of a puzzle that needs answering. Well, perhaps it could be said to be more along the line of gossip that furthers a mystery."

Shay brightened. "Gossip? Is this some lovely obscure bit of info about a rock star involved in seducing some other rock star?"

Lily almost sneered. "No, no. This is about someone we know."

We waited.

"It's about Johnny Gerard."

I sat up straight and took a sip of my drink (vampire teeth used in place of umbrellas in red liquid) and tried to ignore the pounding of my heart that was sounding louder than the bass of the band onstage. Shay shot me a quick warning look, then said, "Is this fun gossip—or something best left unshared?"

"Well, I wouldn't say it was fun, but it's important."
She looked at me.

We waited again. The woman had dramatic pauses
down to an infinitely fine art. Finally she spoke. "Johnny
Gerard has a prison record. He's an ex-convict."

Before my mind could register what that meant,
Franz added, "He's also here in the club. Well, actually he just climbed onstage. It looks like he's going to
be the guest DJ while the band takes a break."

SIXTEEN

THE REST OF the night at *Club Krev* hadn't been much fun for me. I danced with all the guys and I drank some new drink called Teeth of the Vampire that was good enough to rate a space in my memory for future reference. I chatted with Shay, Lily, Franz, Mitchell and Corbin about the movie and what the plans were for *Headlights Productions'* next few projects. I didn't care. I kept alternating between *avoiding* staring at Johnny Gerard who, naturally, was making a huge hit with the crowd as the guest DJ and *deliberately* staring at Mr. Gerard. I also wavered between wanting him to come over to our table and praying that he wouldn't see us this far in the back.

The latter turned out to be the prayer answered but I wasn't happy about it. Shay and I stayed at the club for about two hours after Johnny had done his forty-minute DJ stint and we hadn't seen him once he'd left the stage. Presumably, he'd just done the job and gone home.

Our own crowd left together about one-thirty in the morning and walked back to our respective hotels. Well, Shay and I, Franz and Mitchell were at hotels. Lily took a cab to the house of some relatives of hers and Corbin got into an old Jeep and took off for *Kouzlo Noc* where I gathered he had been given room and board for the duration of his work in the old cemetery.

Shay and I were silent as we trudged up the stairs

to my room. We both sank onto my bed as soon as we were inside the room.

"Damn. Damn. Damn."

"Oh Abby, don't start that again."

"Well? Prison record? I thought he and I had no secrets from each other. When the hell was he in prison? And why the hell didn't he tell me? Man! This little jaunt to Prague is getting weirder and weirder when it comes to the man I'm marrying—whenever."

She frowned. "Not buying it and you aren't either. You just want something to obsess about. So, damn well ask him tomorrow if it's A—true, and B—if so, what was he convicted of? Remember all the b.s. you thought about Johnny and Tracy when y'all were first dating? You put yourself through hell and all for nothing. Yes, you have some trust issues—which, playing shrink, I personally think were pushed into your tiny brain by your dear mother right after birth but that's beside the point. What *is* the point—for once can't you push aside and hear the man out? Be a good little American and not presume guilt?"

"Yeah, right. Great sentiments."

"Ah shit!" she exclaimed. "How many of those Teeth of Vampire drinks did you have? Lord Above and the good Sisters of St. Agnes, help us. Johnny Gerard is a pussycat and you're so nuts about him it's sickening to be around. So just go to sleep and I'll see you in the A.M. when you're sober and not letting your imagination takeover what's left of your zapped brain cells."

Good advice and I knew it, but it still took me another hour before I was finally able to get the words "prison record" out of my head enough to sleep.

They came back in my head when the hotel called me

at seven to tell me I had a visitor in the lobby. Johnny Gerard wanted to take me to breakfast.

I got ready in fourteen minutes. My hair was still slightly wet from the shower and my outfit, black jeans and a black turtleneck (I looked like one of the *Klezmer Volny Rabin*) wasn't the fanciest thing in my suitcase, but my make-up was on and I was as prepared as I could get for a nice morning repast with an Irish-eyed, well-rounded felon.

Johnny greeted me in the lobby with a red rose. Only Mr. Gerard could do that at seven-fifteen in the morning and still look smooth. He gave me the rose, then crooked his elbow so I could link my arm through. We exited the lobby without exchanging a single word.

The silence remained until we found a café three blocks away that had an empty table and wasn't filled with business people jabbing fingers at pocketsize computers and organizers.

Johnny poured coffee into my waiting cup, then sailed right in. "So Lily decided to make the shocking pronouncement that I have been in prison."

My eyes opened. I was wide-awake before I'd even tasted my coffee. "Hold up there, pardner. Were you skulking near our table last night and overheard? Been in communication with cousin Julien's shaman guide Bubba?"

"Nothing so crude. Nope. Shay called me at three in the morning to tell me what the sweetly vicious Miss Lowe had said."

"Ah."

He plopped a huge dab of whipped cream in my coffee and sprinkled cinnamon on top. Which is exactly what I'd done with my cocoa and Kahlua at the café the afternoon we'd run into each other under the tree at *Kouzlo Noc*. One of many reasons I adore him. He remembers little things like that.

He continued, "Shay did not ask for the story behind my incarceration. She said she'd let me give you the details and she trusted that I hadn't done anything 'really rude' like hijacking planes and dumping small children out over the Atlantic while I smoked Cuban cigars and had wild sex with a dozen kidnapped Rumanian prostitutes—or mowing down little old ladies crossing Trafalgar Square in London and stealing all their worldly possessions. Something to that effect. I told her to keep all those in mind for story lines on the soap so Greg Noble can catch the creeps that really do that stuff."

I hid my amusement and looked straight into those hypnotic green eyes of his. "And so…what *is* the true story behind your felonious past?"

He shook his head. "Two-fold. Revolving around circuses. I got into some trouble when I was eleven down in Houston. I was hanging out at some circus musing over a career as the Elephant Man and I ended up being friends with Serpent Boy, who was about my age. One afternoon we decided to take a joy ride in a customer's classic Corvette convertible while the customer was watching the antics of fifteen clowns in a Volkswagen towed by a sleepy elephant who had nothing to do with Elephant Man."

I snorted. "You desperado, you."

"Hey! We brought it back. Absolutely intact. Better even. We'd taken it to a car wash and got the thing cleaned for him since we hated seeing dust on a vehicle that fine. The customer was very understanding, especially since he'd been dumb enough to leave the top down and the keys in the ignition. Serpent Boy and I got the whipping of our young lives from his parents and my mom grounded me for a year, so that ended my days of benign carjacking."

"And the second half of that fold?" I asked.

"I was in Montana doing summer stock when I was still in college and I—well—I stole two lions from a different circus touring the Western states in the U.S. Those poor beasts were being abused beyond belief. So I snuck in and got them out with the help of a group who ran a rescue habitat for animals. We got caught. The owner of the circus rather gleefully pressed charges even though it was obvious the cops were in sympathy with all the rescuers. I refused to give up the whereabouts of Fred and Ginger, the lions, so I was indicted with a felony charge since the animals were considered worth in excess of $50,000. Two other actors from the company and I spent seven nights in the clink in Butte, where we learned of things best left forgotten. Although, once the inmates knew why we were there they were rather nice. Kieran always told me that other than serial killers and general sociopaths, most guys behind bars are major softies when it come to kids, puppy dogs and large animals who've been beaten every day since they were born."

"Did Kieran get you and your felonious buddies out?" Kieran, Johnny's Dad, is Deputy District Attorney in Manhattan.

"He made a call to a local judge he knew from Yale." Johnny beamed at me. "The judge happened to be president of the local animal shelter. So I—quote unquote— 'did time' for a whole week. What gripes my butt is why some dimwit bimbo like Lily Lowe is searching my background. I mean—why?"

I was silent for a moment, taking time to ingest this along with my coffee and kolaches.

"Because she's a bitch. I'm sorry, Johnny. Really."

"For what?"

"For not socking her in her overly-collagened lips, then pondering not-so-great things after Lily laid her little bombshell out last night."

"What not-so-great thoughts were you pondering?"

"Hmm. Now that you mention it, I wasn't even specific in those thoughts. My gosh, Shay comes up with scenarios to curl your hair, yet tells me to trust and I honestly couldn't imagine anything bad enough to have landed you behind bars. Uh. The word 'research' was my first thought as in, 'Johnny got himself behind bars to research something for *Endless Time*.'" I smiled. "I did wonder if robbery was your thing. Having seen your butt slide out of a tower window at the castle, I could just see you sliding out of other windows. You'll be happy to hear I didn't even consider murder, although by rights you should be listed with the other suspects around here for that piano tuner's demise."

Johnny smiled, then reached over and added another kolache to his plate from the dozen or so that had been placed in a basket in the middle of the table. He carefully took a bite, chewed and finished before he said another word. "Abby. It's okay. More than okay. You'd just been told by that saccharine-smiling, scheming—ah shit, words fail me when it comes to Lily Lowe—anyway, you'd just learned that I had a prison record thanks to her poisonous and mistaken mouth. Although, I guess I *am* an ex-con if you want to get literal. I should have told you ages ago, but honestly? It's not looming large in importance anymore. A week spent in what was actually a very nice jail space all for rescuing giant pussycats over ten years ago doesn't keep me awake nights."

"You're not mad at me?"

"For what? Going to breakfast and listening to my side of the story instead of giving me the silent treatment for the next week? There's nothing to be sorry about."

"Well, I'd like to go open up a big can of whup ass on Lily Lowe's bimbo-headed blonde curls though. Why the hell was she yakking about your past? And how did she find out anything anyway?"

"Are you serious? Join the 21st Century and learn to spy on your friends and neighbors. Hell, woman, you can get background checks of almost any kind on the Internet for a price. Type in your credit card number and pay your $39.95 and not only can you find out whether your new business partner or lover is a serial child molester, if you *'act today, the offer of information comes with steak knives, a bamboo steamer and a set of coasters!'*" His expression grew less cheerful. "Now, as to why the lovely Lily Lowe decided to check on me in the first place? That's a question I plan to ask the next time I see her. Which will hopefully be at the castle with a room full of people because I've never yet socked a woman and I don't want to start now. Well, unless you count Melissa Harrigan in first grade, who refused to let me release the fireflies she was keeping in a sealed jar."

"You're a worse softie than I, you macho actor, you.

Fireflies and lions. Next you'll be telling me you pick up stray dogs and—oh my—actually keep them!"

He looked sheepish. "You know I do. Except I can't keep them. Someday when you're Mrs. Gerard and we're sharing a big space to put the pups in, I'd love for us to have about ten. Sadly, 'til then, we're both gone so much it's not fair to the pups." His expression hardened again. "But Lily Lowe's efforts to entertain using the private life of Johnny Gerard make me feel anything but soft." He scowled. "Ah crap, I shouldn't have told you all this. I should have let you believe I was a three-strikes-you're-out arsonist or something even if it meant breaking up with you for a while."

"What! Why?"

"I mentioned this the other night but it bears repeating. Because I don't want you—or Shay—anywhere near *Kastle Kouzlo Noc*."

I straightened up. "Wait. I thought you were all set to acknowledge my place in your misbegotten life as your best beloved. What did I do now?"

"Don't be dense, gorgeous. You know you haven't done anything. It's what's *been* done."

"Ah. You mean murder."

SEVENTEEN

JOHNNY NODDED. "YEP. The big 'M.'"

"Wait. We talked about this before. Why run Shay and me off now?"

"Because I learned a bit more about the activities at the castle. Gustav was found by our favorite actor, Franz, on a spot on the grounds that fit perfectly with having been pushed out of the north tower window in the exact room where one Abby Fouchet has been ghost-hunting—and nearly everyone involved with *Kouzlo Noc* was nearby—including the latecomers to the north wing where that one Abby Fouchet was doing that ghost-hunting."

"What did the police say?"

"I didn't take the body to the little village, remember? Franz and Corbin did. I was a latecomer to the party. As to the police? From what Veronika has said, they're still holding the body, partly for identification since Veronika didn't have his last name and partly because they want the local coroner to make a determination."

"Well, that's something anyway. Look, Johnny, isn't it remotely possible that he was snooping in that room and really did lean too far out of that window and fell? I honestly didn't see anything in my vision other than—" I shuddered "—someone falling. No pitching beforehand."

"Sure. And it's possible that he decided to try a Superman routine and see if he could fly. Doubtful as hell but possible. Get real. Half the crowd here to do the movie isn't here to do the movie and the other half, which really isn't half since it's just one other person—Corbin—has one damn flimsy excuse for roaming the cemetery at all hours."

"Well, duh."

"Nicely stated." Johnny grimaced. "Interesting that out of the cast of characters assembled in Prague and associated with *Kouzlo Noc* in some way, the only people I'm sure did not come here to search for a certain dead musician's flute are you, me and Shay."

I stayed silent for a second. "Which begs the question, why are *you* really here? Did Yolanda talk to Madam Euphoria, sense trouble, then send Gregory Noble to scope things out?"

"*Moi?* Except for current murder, which I didn't expect, Yolanda really did just send me to the castle to do Veronika a favor by restoring her mural. Of course, now that I know about Ignatz and his flute, I think Yolanda had a little hidden agenda, as in—legends and ghosts would be great for ratings on the show. Hell, Yolanda knew with my natural curiosity—" he grinned "—which some might call nosiness, I'd hear about Ignatz within three minutes of knocking on those dragons at the castle. But, now, if I should happen across a magical, legendary flute while I'm—what's your word? 'muraling,' I can't say that I'd toss it into the nearest moat. I would hand it over to—well—I'd say Jozef Jezek is the logical choice."

"Definitely. Now—back to Gustav."

"Yes?"

"Who was he? Was he really here to tune the piano? Do you know?"

"Veronika told me he showed up at the door the other day, pulled the tapestry bell and charmed her into hiring him to tune the piano you probably haven't even seen since it's in the east wing. Apparently, he *did* do a bit of tinkering before wandering off to take a tour of the towers." He gave out sort of a chortled snort. "Veronika said she heard a few nice notes from the instrument before she and the girls went out to gather rosebuds or something. Of course, Veronika's ear for music is as good as my lions' ability to stand up for rescuer Johnny in court."

"Nice comparison." I squinted at him. "Is Veronika suspicious of Gustav's death?"

Johnny shook his head. "She's hiding any and all sad truths from herself. She's dealt with too much tragedy in her life and she's scared to admit violence is visiting *Kouzlo Noc* again. So she's convinced herself that a nearly anonymous piano tuner just happened to drop dead of a heart attack under the infamous north tower."

"An explanation you're obviously not wrapping up in a bow and taking home."

"Damn straight. I don't believe that any of the Duskovas climbed those stairs for a bit of pushing practice, but I damn well do believe that someone else was wandering *Kouzlo Noc,* and for whatever reason, helped the piano tuner meet an early demise."

I shivered. "Scary—and sad."

We fell silent for a few moments. Finally, I spoke up. "Gad. It just hit me. What you said about every one of us who ended up in that music room in the north tower that day. Anyone could easily have gotten in without being seen, couldn't they?"

"Ta-da! See why I'd like you to leave? You nailed it. Could be anyone. So, how to track down a killer? Unless your second sight kicks in with arrows pointing and DNA tested. Seriously, it's too easy to establish alibis and even if I could prove that Lily Lowe, for instance, was warbling arias in the trees across from the tower, it wouldn't mean she'd swung over on a branch and committed murder."

I couldn't restrain my laughter. "You don't like her much, do you?"

"I'm not fond of tellers of tales about others' peccadilloes, unless those peccadilloes include violent crime and warnings are necessary. Speaking of which, and I know I'm sounding like the proverbial broken record, but will you and Shay please heed my warning and find another castle to rent? Preferably in—oh—California?"

I didn't miss a beat. "If you believe that Shay Martin would forego the delicious opportunity to film in a castle that's not only haunted but is the scene of a very recent murder, well—let's just say your thought processes would be as out of tune as the Duskova harpsichord. She's already hip deep in atmosphere. Wouldn't surprise me to have her decide to write in a mad scene or something and pitch some stunt man out of the north tower. With a trampoline below so he could spring back up of course."

Johnny growled, "Well, what about you? You've found the damn castle—isn't your job over?"

"A—I wouldn't leave Shay to deal with all these crazies and possible murderers. B—My job isn't really done. I have to help her choreograph two dance sequences for the film and teach them to a dance captain who is currently, and wisely, not in Prague. In fact, he's on stage until next Friday—in *Oklahoma*. The show, not the state. C." I took a deep breath. "You're not going to like C."

"I'm sure I'm not. I didn't like A or B, either. But educate me as to C."

"I don't *want* to go. I want to find out what's going on with ghosts and flutes at *Kouzlo Noc*. And I'm not leaving you here to play hero by yourself, either." I gasped. "Oh my God!"

"What?"

"I bet it *wasn't* Ignatz Jezek."

"Who wasn't?"

"When I heard another snatch of music the other day up in the tower room. *"Night and Day."* I thought that was odd—I mean could a ghost learn other pieces of music after he's died? I guess they could, since they're fully capable of serenading and belting out various tunes and playing various instruments, but really, why would Ignatz be playing Cole Porter? That wouldn't be his style, would it?"

"Stop! You're making me crazy!"

"Sorry."

"What are you talking about? I mean, when?"

"Sorry," I repeated. "When fifty-gazillion people were exploring that part of the castle before Veronika chased us out the day of Gustav's death, I heard music. Thought Ignatz was performing for my benefit. Now I'm not so sure it was him. He. Whatever. It's possible the musician was your friend Gustav only hours after he died."

Johnny muttered, "Not my friend. Never met him—and am not likely to at this point." He closed his eyes.

"Yes?" I asked.

"Oh, nothing. Just—a thought. I'll let it ruminate before I open my mouth with theories."

"Oh. Fine. Be that way. I've just bared my ghost-listening ramblings and you're getting cryptic."

He smiled. "Yep. I'll try to tell you later when I won't sound like a lunatic, although you're the one who'd actually believe me. Something that happened the day I met you. Before the slide from the tree." Then he narrowed his eyes at me. "You're not leaving, are you." It was not a question. "Damn it, Abby, what happens when someone in this crowd figures out you're in concert with Ignatz Jezek—so to speak—and determines Jezek is telling his new best friend where to find the flute? Can we say danger?"

I paused, then dove in. "Johnny, while a murder is awful and frightening and just wrong, and you, me and Shay are doubtless in deep doo-doo from some villain-ous creep, do you realize it's possible we could find out what happened to not just Ignatz Jezek but to the recent victim of what seems to be the curse of *Kouzlo Noc?*"

Johnny looked grim. "I'm better with the 'we' but can you at least agree that you and Shay need to stay together—or around me—as much as possible when you're inside the castle? Or on the grounds for that matter."

I pondered this sensible suggestion. "Hell yeah. Shay and I aren't ready to meet The Almighty face to face. And while we can act tough, there's some major chicken bones within so I never have a problem wanting to stick close to you." I tried to smile. "Especially since I don't have the brothers Marricino and their ancient Sicilian friends from lower Manhattan here to play bodyguard. Nope. It's hip to hip—Abby and Johnny. But I do wish you'd let the rest of the *Kouzlo Noc* crowd in on impending vows so we could get those hips a bit closer."

He leaned over and kissed me. "You're a pain, but I love you. Sadly, with what's been happening it's safer for them to think we met the first day you were at *Kouzlo Noc*. Safer for you. I've been sure of that since the day I came sliding down the tree to see your perky little face staring up at me. Corbin and Franz are very aware I've been touring the castle and I'd prefer they didn't add you to their suspect list of fellow treasure hunters." His words mingled with the sounds of the Astronomical Clock—only blocks away from where we were sitting—announcing to all of Prague it was now nine.

"Oh nuts! Shay and I were supposed to meet at the hotel lobby at nine. We're off to the castle. She's Miss Punctuality to the minute. Talk about whuppin' ass."

"Relax. I told her I was going to talk to you if I had to kidnap you to make you listen."

I grabbed my bag from the floor under my feet. "All the same, I guess I'd better hunt her down. If I don't get back and give her the whole scoop on that dangerous criminal Johnny Gerard, and Fred and Ginger the lion twins, she'll never let me loose again to unearth truths of any consequence."

EIGHTEEN

THE PLEASANT BREEZE that had bathed Prague in a balmy glow last night when Shay and I came dragging in from the club, then remained this early morning when Johnny treated me to breakfast and confidences, had this late morning become demonic chilly winds forcing temperatures to fall at a rapid rate. Shay and I stood in front of the dragon doorknockers at *Kouzlo Noc* and shivered while we waited for someone to let us in.

"Why is Prague freezing in March? It's flippin' damn cold! Why didn't we turn back about an hour ago when we saw snow falling in cute little flakes? Why didn't Bambi choose someplace like Florida, which has never seen white flakes outside of dandruff?" Shay whined.

"Because Gothic novels do not lend themselves to Miami. That's why. Which reminds me. Did you ever settle on a real title?"

Her expression became impish. "What? You didn't buy the Naked Mistress of Whatever I threw out?"

"In a word—no. You won't sabotage what could be a terrific film by naming it something that will end up on online porn sites. And even if you were, Bambi would be flying in from India to whip your butt. Hopefully after sharing a fresh-made samosa with the location scout—*moi*."

"Good reasons all. Actually, I'm going with *Silhouette Tower*. Short, sweet. Has that Gothic feel. Doesn't scream 'chick flick'. Could be horror. Could be romance. Could be suspense. I like it."

"I do too. Now just don't name the damn heroine Kelsey, okay?"

"Little too modern for you?"

"Just a tad. Which reminds me, how are we supposed to have a boat chase down the Vltava in this epic film? I'm fairly certain recreational motorboats were invented back in 1860-something. A paddle-boat chase doesn't have quite the same quality of suspense—and that's all I see available for tourists."

Shay pulled the bell rope again. "They didn't have rock music either but Mitchell has some major crankin' tunes in mind. Be open-minded."

"When am I ever not?" I got brave and grabbed one of the demonic dragons then let its head rattle against the door. "Damn. What's the deal here? Freeze the poor movie people so they'll learn a lesson and not prowl around the castle hunting for the family ghost?"

As if she'd been waiting to hear me make that statement, Veronika suddenly yanked open the door and waved us in. "I am so sorry to leave you in the cold. But we were watching the tuning man with the harpsichord and we did not hear the door."

Both Shay and I stood in stunned silence. Tuning man? Was Gustav the ghost playing with tuning forks from beyond?

Veronika saw our expressions. "We haf good friend from Prague who tells us he hass boy who needs work. Many people not keep music instruments in repair yet he hass problem earning living because people not care. But we are happy to tell him that we haf money to pay him for making harpsichord sound pretty again. Thanks to Mees Martin." Her eyes clouded for a moment. "I only wish…"

"We know," I quickly interjected before my own eyes began churning out the tears.

Veronika led us to the ballroom where, sure enough, a pony-tailed young man wearing round-rimmed wire glasses was tinkering with the strings of the antique piece with an expression approaching ecstasy on his handsome face. The other *Headlights'* company members, namely Franz, Lily and Mitchell, watched him work with overly intense interest. Creepy.

Veronika made strained introductions. We were all reminded of the last young man who came to tune a Duskova keyboard and met a violent death. "Thees is Mr. Frederik Romberg. From Vienna but now living in Prague. He fixes harpsichord good for us. He arrives this morning early to help."

I'd relayed Johnny's warning to Shay about murderers roaming the castle, but from the way she reacted now, one would suppose she'd been kept completely in the dark about any danger at any time. She peered into the face of the man hiding under the harpsichord. "Yo! Fritz. Good to meet you. And you're saving our behinds here by making that old instrument sing. Did Veronika tell you about the movie?" Shay turned to the others. "That reminds me, did I tell you we settled on a name? Yep. *Silhouette Tower.* Now, Franz is still Count Zilania but Lily? You're neither Honoria nor Kelsey. I had to get creative here. So the new name for your character is Constanze."

I blinked. My musical biography knowledge isn't all that great but I could swear that Constanze was the name of Mozart's wife. Trust Shay to stir the pot just a bit.

I didn't want to make Shay preen any more than she already was, but I did love Constanze as the name for the heroine of *Silhouette Tower*. A touch of Bavaria mixed with sweetness. And no one was blanching, gasping or fainting at the sound, so either I was wrong and Constanze had nothing to do with Mozart, or people were acting casual about the coincidence, or maybe they knew and just couldn't see where it mattered in the scheme of flutes, treasure and death. I was going with the latter since I also wasn't sure if it meant anything at all.

"It's good, Shay." I pursed my lips. "Of course, after 'Kelsey' anything would make better sense for this period in history."

Fritz Romberg looked up from underneath the harpsichord. He held a tuning fork in one hand. "Madam Duskova tells me you are doing a film? With music?"

I let Shay answer. She loves sensitive, nerdy guys. Since she was still mad at Fuji, her boyfriend, who'd gone a bit star-crazy when he became the starting pitcher for the *Yankees* she was on the prowl for fresh meat. She now plopped down on the floor next to the piano tuner and stated, "Yes, indeed, we're shooting a film. The Duskovas have been kind enough to rent us the castle. It's a musical version of a Gothic romance. Mostly rock music but Mitchell does have some lighter, more classical pieces, too. It's going to be utterly marvelous."

Fritz's English was precise. He shyly asked, "Do you perhaps need a harpsichordist to play this wonderful old instrument once I am finished with tuning?"

I brightened and Shay looked like she was going to dance a gig on the harpsichord itself. I answered for our director. "Oh yell, yeah! That would be fantastic! A harpsichord is beyond perfect for this whole flick. Sash-ay, any comments?"

Shay's head nodded vigorously. "I love it. You're in, Mr. Romberg. Payment to be arranged later but I promise it will keep you in tuning forks for many years."

"Thank you. Sassh-ay? Is that right?"

I chuckled. "It's Shay, but I occasionally annoy her by reminding her it could be worse."

Shay took over without pausing to bash my head in. "Yes, it's Shay. I don't own *Headlights Productions* but I'm in control of this project. I've wanted to do something with this book since Abs and I read it a gazillion years ago before we even knew one another. You don't mind if I call you Fritz, do you?"

He bowed. As much as anyone could who was curled under a harpsichord plucking strings with a tuning fork glued to his ear.

"Fritz is fine." He looked at me with blatant curiosity. "Abs. That is not a common name, no?"

I shook my head. "It's Abby. Shay is being a toad."

"Ah. Well, nice to meet you, Abby. That is a prettier name than a nickname for body crunches. I like it. And I am very pleased that you and Shay will let me play for your film. It is hard to find work as a musician and as a tuner here in Prague, although it is a very musical city."

Shay had been waiting impatiently for a chance to chime in. "Sorry. About the work, that is—not the city. I love it. Great history of music. Like I'm telling you something new?"

They were in perfect sync. Within seconds, Shay

was under the durn harpsichord talking to Fritz like they'd been hooked up for years. I headed off to the sitting room to plunk in front of the fireplace and make notes as to where I thought various scenes for the film needed to be set.

The doorbell (or did Veronika call it a doorpull?) rang. Or sounded. Or chimed. Or...I had no words for a bell-pull that played *Kyria Eleison* from a master composer's *Requiem* Mass, other than "cool." I checked the clock on the mantle in the sitting room. Three in the afternoon. I'd been in this room for three hours. I had no idea where Shay was. Presumably she was following Fritz through the merry romp of twanging strings on instruments. I had ten pages worth of notes. A great start.

I got up to find out where the others were and what they were doing—and ran smack into an Abby-vision.

I could see Trina, draped in the patterned quilt I'd been so enamored with in that tiny bedroom Veronika had shown me my first day at *Kouzlo Noc*. Trina wasn't sleeping though. Trina looked cold. Trina looked white. Trina wasn't moving.

I nearly started screaming. I ran out of the sitting room in time to see Marta heading for the back door. Veronika was engaged in a heavy conversation with Franz. Shay and Fritz were still under the harpsichord. Three hours seemed a bit lengthy for master tuners and I had to bite back sarcastically inquiring as to whether work was actually getting done or they'd used the privacy for a long autumn nap or another pursuit more— in Shay's words—aerobic. Lily and Franz were in a far corner of the ballroom, heads deep in a script. I assumed it was for *Silhouette Tower*. Shay is extremely efficient even when she's going after a gorgeous male.

She'd had copies of the script made the minute she took on the project.

Trina was nowhere in sight, so Veronika and Marta were pulling double duty as hostesses and doorwomen. I prayed my vision was wrong. I knew it wasn't.

A minute later, Johnny and Corbin made a grand entrance into the ballroom with Marta. The men did not look happy. They were both shaking snow from bare heads and light jackets. Wet gloves were peeled off and tossed without formalities onto the marble coffin. Just looking at the pair was making me freeze. I tried to forget what had sailed into my mind.

Johnny took a few large strides to end up next to me and the harpsichord. I pounded on the top and Fritz and Shay poked their heads out. I performed the introductions bit for Fritz, then asked, quietly, if Johnny and Corbin had been arguing.

"No. Why?"

"Well, y'all looked less than pleased when you arrived."

"Oh. It's not him. It's Mother Nature. How long have you been here?"

"Four hours. What's up?"

"Not up. Down. As in falling. As in snow. Lots of snow. Can we say 'blizzard'?"

"You're kidding. It was just a few breezy flakes when Shay and I ventured out from Prague but not blizzard conditions. This is weird. But kinda cool."

"More than cool. Downright cold. The temperature has probably dropped a good sixty degrees since this morning. Corbin can't work outside anymore so he's ticked. I don't really care since the mural is upstairs, but he was suggesting that we form a grave-digging detail to help him today—which I'm extremely *not* into."

Fritz was following this with a rapt, but concerned, expression on his face. "Grave digging? Is that not against the law?"

Johnny leaned down to add, "Not positive but I hear it's okay if you're digging on your property and not opening the last homes of the departed—which he isn't—he's mainly looking at headstones and foot markers."

Fritz nodded, then ducked back underneath the musical instrument. So did Shay.

Johnny muttered. "No need to check graves—they've all been razed so many times in that cemetery I'm surprised they don't have WD-40 to make the hinges open more smoothly."

I winced. "Ouch. That's a gross thought."

"Sorry, hon. Hell. That cemetery is gross. I love the Duskova sisters, but the Duskovas from the last hundred years or so were not exactly shy when it came to unearthing the dead."

Johnny's volume dropped. "Who's the kid I've just been conversing with? Other than someone named Fritz who seems to be bonding rather nicely with Shay."

I kept mine low as well. "New piano tuner. Not to sound cynical but thankfully he's lasted longer than the last. I'm assuming he's a total innocent and no one has reason to pitch his body because he's clueless as to *Kouzlo Noc*'s history."

Wrong on that. Fritz ooched out from under the harpsichord again and stated, "The grave robbers are looking for the body of the flute player who lived here in the summer of 1792. He was murdered, you see, and his flute never found."

I sighed and appealed to Johnny. "Why are we trying to keep this a secret when it seems clear the legend of Ignatz Jezek and his flute has gotten more coverage in the world than a pop singer's sex change?"

Johnny nodded. "Someone needs to tell Veronika that everyone and his brother knows. Keep her from having a heart attack whenever the words 'Mozart' or 'flute' are mentioned."

"What did you say?"

Veronika stood behind Johnny. She looked like our friend Bambi in the headlights staring into the oncoming car. "Johnny? Iss this true? Who knows about Ignatz Jezek and his flute?"

He patted her shoulder. "Well, truth is—who doesn't? It's a given everyone here is well aware of the whole treasure hunting past of *Kouzlo Noc*."

She evenly stated, "Achh, perhaps that is best. If something iss not so secret perhaps truth will finally emerge and Ignatz will be at peace. But I feel evil, here in my heart." She pressed her hand to her chest. "Someone in this time wants to find the flute and use it for bad purpose. Jozef tells me this last night when he brings books and I believe this. I am ashamed to admit I now belief Gustav died because of this, although I do not understand how or why."

I took her hand in mine. "Perhaps if we work together to find out what happened to Ignatz and his flute we can prevent another century of grave robbing and despair here?"

She smiled. "You are nice. I am sorry I was cold to you when you want explore north wing. I was afraid you would not like us and not want to use *Kouzlo Noc* because of that mens haf been murdered there. And iss not safe."

Johnny inhaled. "Say what? Are you telling us that Ignatz was murdered there? In the north wing?"

She looked horrified. "Oh no! No. Iss not Ignatz I am speaking of, although I fear he too wass murdered. I am speaking off stories from centuries. Iss someone who came searching for the flute many many years ago. Before I was born. Before my mother was born. I hear story that soldier came looting through *Kouzlo Noc* for the treasure. He iss found here—found in north wing. So he destroys room and he was killed by being pushed down stairs. In north wing. But no one in my family says they did it. Iss mystery who kills him. But his body was buried in the old cemetery—the place Corbin works in. He wass given Christian burial by my great-grandfather even though the soldier had come to do evil." She paused. "And then of course, there was the tuning man—no—I hope, that is I thought, that was accident—but I am afraid."

Johnny and I exchanged a quick look. Shay was oblivious since she was too entranced watching Fritz play with a tuning fork. I tried to see if anyone else had noticed Veronika's comment about Gustav, but everyone seemed lost in thoughts of past centuries.

Any further revelations came to a quick halt when Jozef Jezek suddenly appeared in the ballroom dressed in a wool cape covered with snow.

Johnny checked his watch. It was close to four-thirty in the afternoon. "Durn. Jozef was supposed to be up at the castle no later than three today. The roads must be awful."

Jozef was clearly distressed. The man with the perfect English kept shouting in Czech, letting Veronika translate for him. "We are in snowstorm! That iss very bad." Her eyes widened in horror as she screamed the rest of his words. "But snow does not matter! There iss body in moat! He says he sees white on body—but moat is blackness! Hear me? There iss body!"

It was shaping up to be an interesting afternoon at the castle.

NINETEEN

JOZEF, HAVING SHOCKED everyone in the ballroom, immediately turned and ran toward the hallway, which led to the back entrance. Johnny and I took off after the bookseller. Fritz, pale behind his wire-rim specs, held onto the shaking Veronika. Shay, Franz, Corbin and Mitchell sprinted behind Johnny and me. Lily walked quickly over to a stunned Marta, who'd just come in from the kitchen with a huge plate of goodies. She calmly took the tray out of the woman's arms and placed it on the marble coffin. Not the best choice perhaps, but secure and the closest available piece of furniture.

Jozef had pushed open the huge doors. An incredible whiteness met our eyes. Those tiny flakes from this morning had indeed had become a blinding blizzard. Our coats had been placed neatly on a rack as each person had arrived at various times during the day, but it was obvious that the spring-weight hoodie I'd worn when Shay and I had first arrived this morning was no match for the elements outside. She'd been right. We should have headed back to Prague when we first saw the light fall of snow on our way to the castle.

Johnny barred Shay and me from trying to join the rescue—or recovery—group. I knew he was shielding us from both the cold and the sight that doubtless awaited outside, but I resented not being able to help. Completely illogical, since aside from dealing with blizzard conditions, I didn't really want to test my bravery—which currently felt non-existent.

"Guys, we don't need the girls to freeze to death. Jozef will guide us and Corbin and Franz and I are better equipped to deal with this—and better clothed too. Abby, Shay—just hang tough in here. We'll get back as fast as we can. Lily, you stay, too."

I lost any desire to argue. Shay and Lily nodded in agreement. If we forced our way into joining the guys we'd only end up frozen, useless and a hindrance to the whole operation. So we stayed huddled in our flimsy jackets by the open door and tried to see any movement other than swirls of snow and ice pellets. I kept quiet. I already knew what was about to happen.

It took them less than two minutes to follow Jozef to the moat and return with the cold lifeless body of Trina Duskova.

An agonized scream rang out behind us. "Oh, God, no! No! My baby sister. Trina. No! This iss wrong, so wrong!" Fritz hadn't managed to keep Veronika in the ballroom and she stood by the door staring as Franz and Johnny bullied their way through the snow and gently carried her sister into the castle. Corbin walked beside them, holding what appeared to be a frozen scarf of Trina's. Marta joined Veronika and the pair clung to each other and sobbed with such despair I felt daggers pierce my heart.

The men took Trina's body into the ballroom. The rest of us followed. I held my breath for a moment wondering if they would be crass enough to use the coffin for a resting place. For an instant in my awful imagination I could see teacups swept off in one motion to make room for Trina. I shut my eyes to the vision and was pleased to see that Johnny and Franz were carefully placing the corpse on the sofa. Veronika wouldn't care about snow melting onto the fragile fabric.

For a moment we all stood silent, unsure of what to say, or even where to look. I've never been around someone who's just died. Never seen a body that didn't pass away in a bed surrounded by loved ones. Trina had died, not from illness, but from—what? Drowning? Hypothermia? Alone and doubtless terrified.

Veronika, Marta and Jozef knelt by the sofa and began to pray. Johnny crossed the room to where Shay and I stood.

"Johnny? Any idea about what happened? Did she faint? Why on earth was she outside in this storm?"

He sounded tired. "No clue. She had a light coat on— like she went out much earlier today. Bet Veronika can tell us why. But how she ended up in the moat is anyone's guess right now." He gestured toward my bag, sitting snugly next to the harpsichord. "Do you have your cell? We need to call the Prague police."

"What's wrong with the landline? Is the power out?"

"Apparently. I tried making a call before Jozef came in and I got nothing."

I hurried over to my bag, took out the cell, turned the power on and handed it over. "Looks like the cell towers aren't working either. My battery is good but I'm not getting a signal."

"Great. A stinking snowstorm, a dead body and no communication. It's going to be a rough night."

Corbin and Franz joined us. Corbin pulled a cap off his head and dusted off the flakes of snow as though he were blaming them for Trina's death. "I'm at a loss here. Such a crazy, freak accident. I've known the Duskovas for five years and they're so close. What on earth was Trina doing outside in this mess?"

I tapped Johnny's shoulder. "Guys, I'm going to head up to one of the bedrooms and find something to cover her with. She just looks so…cold there. That can't be good for Veronika and Marta to see."

"I'll come with you." This from Shay.

We took off for the rooms Veronika had shown me only a few days ago. The sweet wedding-patterned quilt I'd seen in one of the bedrooms we'd planned to use for *Silhouette Tower* would be better served to lay over Trina than as a pretty background piece for the film. I stopped. I'd seen that quilt in my vision only hours before. The damn thing had come true.

Shay and I managed to stay silent until we hit the bedroom. Then the floodgates opened.

"Oh damn, Shay. Gothic atmosphere is one thing. Hearing a ghost is cool. But another murder?"

"Wait! You just jumped a damn large water hole there. Trina was *murdered?*"

"I'd give that a yes. With what happened to Gustav? I mean, what is a seventy-odd-year-old woman doing wandering out in a snowstorm, in less than warm clothes, near a moat that hasn't been utilized in the last hundred years or so?"

Shay tried to smile; failed. "Well, when you put it that way." She shivered. "Abby, that storm is bad. I wonder when Trina actually died? That's important."

"You're right. If she died after the blizzard started that's good indication that the only suspects are folks inhabiting *Kouzlo Noc* at this very moment since not even a chipmunk could navigate in that storm."

We stared at each other. I sat down on the quilted

spread and started to shake. "Shit. Can we not slide down that hill? At least not yet? My acting skills are not up to pretending to one and all that I'm not petrified to get snowbound in a castle with a killer. The other death didn't feel like this. I mean Gustav's. It seemed removed from all of us even though Johnny believed that someone here was involved. But this? It's close. Way too close."

She grimaced. "Are we rushing to conclusions? I mean, who's to say that Trina didn't go out to get the mail or something, and suddenly see a—uh—a stray cat. And try to get the kitty indoors before the cold hit. And wandered too far and couldn't see in the storm and just fell. It's a theory, right?"

I nodded. "I like it a hell of a lot better than imagining someone sneaking up behind her and tossing her into the moat. And for what reason?"

Shay sat down next to me. "I'm stunned. Trina. Sweet, fantastic chef Trina. Who had about three words of English on a good day. 'Hello', 'pretty', and 'do you want more pastries'?"

I tried to smile. "That's more than three words, but I get it. Why deliberately kill a nice woman like that?"

"For treasure."

We looked up. Johnny had entered the bedroom and made the pronouncement both Shay and I had not wanted to voice.

"She knew something about Ignatz and the flute," I stated flatly.

"I'd stake my life on it. Which isn't the smartest thing to say in these circumstances, but since I'm damn certain neither of you is a psychopathic killer, I'd say I'm safe."

"Wow. Okay."

The three of us fell silent and stayed that way until a weird thought hit me.

It was as good a time as any to ask. "Hey. This is totally off-topic but would you finally tell me and Shay why you were sliding down trees from the north wing the other day when I met you? Instead of using the stairs like a normal human being?"

He sighed. "It's so stupid. It's not even mysterious or in any way relating to something important. Well, possibly mysterious or eerie. But, really, it's more an embarrassing moment in Johnny Gerard's life."

Shay brightened. "Oh, go on. Embarrassing moments are some of the best sequences ever captured on film. And a helluva lot more fun than pondering the why of a sweet woman's death. So—do tell."

He took a seat in the ancient rocker in the corner of the bedroom. "I was being nosy. Working on the mural and decided to check out the other rooms, specifically the music room, and I heard voices coming from the window of the south wing. I didn't want to be caught in that music room since I didn't really have any business being there and I wanted to stay on Veronika's good side." He paused. "I started to leave—and then I heard laughter that wasn't coming from any person nearby— because there *wasn't* any person nearby. I knew the story of Ignatz Jezek and I didn't want to find myself going eyeball to eyeball with a possibly pissed-off ghost who was territorial about his space. To be honest? I was damn scared. And the stinkin' door was stuck so I couldn't make it back to the hall. I high-tailed it out the window and down the tree and met my charming

Abigail upon reaching the ground in a less than graceful manner."

Shay looked disappointed. "That's it? You were
spooked by a spook and you got locked in? Ah, I get
it. It's the guy thing. Chickened out of a close encounter and just not in lock-picking form that day? Shoot, I
was hoping for something juicy like you met a cham-
bermaid who'd been hiding in the castle from her jealous gatekeeper boyfriend and y'all had riotous sex for
an hour or so."

I blinked. "Shay, you've got to quit reading Gothics. It's time. Your mind has gone completely round the
bend with this stuff. That plot is straight out of *Keeper
of the Gazebo.* We read it the night I found out *Endless Time* was scrapping the Vanessa storyline and you
found out *Darien's Donuts* was stiffing everyone who'd
worked on the commercial because they were declaring bankruptcy."

"Oh yeah. Seems to me we inhaled a few gin and
tonics and at least three pizzas that night too. Well,
obviously it was a good plot since it stuck with me. In
fact, I foresee merging a few of the seamier elements
into *Silhouette Tower.* Hell, it's a heckuva better plot
than a wimpy wannabe burglar landing on his ass after
hearing—well—not much."

"Forgive her, Johnny. Hopelessly trapped in ado-
lescence."

The three of us started chuckling, then suddenly remembered we were in this room looking for an antique quilt to carry downstairs for use as a temporary
burial shroud.

I stood up. "I guess that's one mystery solved. Is that

why you got all shifty-eyed when you didn't want to share theories of ghosts in this castle?"

"Pretty much. I didn't want to join in the general atmosphere of ghost-hunting, although it hasn't seemed to have affected your brains, Ms. Fouchet. They're working at lightning speed even when you hear music when no one's there."

"Thanks. Sort of. Crap, I suppose we should be leaving our cozy nest here soon." I growled. "But, I'll be honest, guys. I have no desire to leave this room and join the group downstairs." My unspoken words rang in the room *with a murderer who's looking for the next target.*

TWENTY

SHAY, JOHNNY AND I hadn't been gone that long but major changes had occurred in the ballroom in our absence. Trina's body was no longer on the sofa. The food had been removed from the top of the coffin. And three guys in uniform had entered the scene. Prague police, I assumed.

I assumed right. Apparently, Jozef had managed to get a call through before he'd come back into the house to find help with Trina's body. So the cops were here and I felt much better. The fact that they didn't speak a word of English didn't bother me. The young trio looked solid and dependable and very reassuring.

I nudged Corbin, who was making his way from the ballroom to the kitchen. "How did they manage to negotiate through this mass of white? Or are we just imagining the blizzard of the century raging? Is this like New York where one block is ice and you walk down three more and it's sunshine and lollipops?"

"All these guys have done stints with winter Olympics. Honest. Two came gliding in on skis and the third drove a snowmobile like he was going for the gold in bobsled. I'm rather amazed he didn't take it directly into the parlor. I couldn't tell if the brakes worked at all."

Good. Levity. I was glad Veronika hadn't heard him but I needed cheery words. "Thanks," I whispered.

He shrugged. "I'm a historian. In my experience sometimes humor is the only way to deal with sadness."

"Yeah. I agree. My problem is I often don't know when to hold off."

"You do fine." He patted my hand and it hit me that he was an attractive man—in his own odd way. I turned just in time to see Mr. Gerard appear from the doorway of the sitting room where Trina's body was now reposing. Johnny raised an eyebrow my way. I squinched up my nose at him, slid my hand out from under Corbin's and marched over to ask what the procedure was in this situation. Sudden death, that is; not hand patting a definitely "only friends" friend in front of a secret fiancé.

"Corbin? You off to get tea for the mourners in the ballroom?" was Johnny's only comment.

"Yes. Veronika is hanging on by a thread and Marta is switching handkerchiefs by the fistful. All soaked through. She keeps chattering, but it's not coming out coherently. About the only words that make sense are 'Trina' and 'why?' Anyway, I figured if the Brits can use tea as the all-occasion comforter, who are we to argue with a proven remedy?"

"I'm with you. Can you boil a few more quarts? I'll come out in a second and help deliver."

Corbin stated stiffly, "Delighted. On both counts."

He took off.

"Johnny?"

"Hmm?"

"What did you see out there?"

"Nothing of importance. Really. Not that I was focused on being a crime scene investigator. I was busy. We were all busy trying to get to Trina just in case she was still alive. The wind was kicking up and the snow was getting heavy and if anyone or anything was out there that provided any clue as to what happened, I couldn't see it."

"Okay."

He gave me a sharp look. "Don't go there yet. Nothing has been determined as to Trina's death being anything but accidental."

"Okay."

"I agree with you. Someone decided Trina needed to leave the earth tonight, then decided to help her along. I just don't want you to be next if you decide to stick that cute little nose where someone doesn't want to be scented."

"You know what's scary?"

"Other than this castle and two deaths within days?"

"Well, let's say on par with that. What scares me is wondering if it even matters if I stick my nose where it doesn't belong. What if this killer decides some of us—like me—are more aware of the mystery of the flute than others of us? And that sounded convoluted and I'm sorry but I'm not thinking straight. Anyway, will he—or she—kill first and ask questions later?"

"Why have I been trying to get you away from here or stress that you, me and Shay need to stick together?" He flashed a brief smile. "If we can extract her body from its glued position next to Fritz the new tuner, that is."

"Yep. That's my roomie. Adaptable, comfortable, fearless and heading into faithless."

We lapsed into silence, waiting to see what would happen next. The trio of policemen emerged from the sitting room. Our quest for the quilt had been pointless. Not an inch of Trina Duskova could be seen. She was completely encased in a waterproof body bag. The zipper had been pulled up tight. Nausea swept over me.

"Are they taking her to Prague?" I asked, while trying to breathe normally.

Johnny nodded. "That's the plan. They've got to get out of here before the blizzard gets any worse. Safer for them traveling; easier on us here at the castle. I doubt they're going to get a lot of forensics done tonight anyway. Trina was found in a moat in the middle of a snowstorm. If there's a trace of evidence to explain why this happened, it can't be found until the winds and drifts die down."

Made sense. The police respectfully carried the body back through the ballroom toward the front door. Which didn't seem right. No one entered or exited *Kouzlo Noc* by the front. Trina wouldn't be comfortable leaving this way. I shook off the thought. Trina was gone.

That's when I heard her voice trilling a few notes. which bore a remarkable resemblance to the chorus of Eric Clapton's classic, *Layla*. Damn. I glanced over at the harpsichord, which bore those miniature busts of Mozart, Beethoven, and Haydn—and one more. It was indeed a replica of Eric Clapton. I hadn't merely imagined it the first time I'd seen those busts when I first entered *Kouzlo Noc* less than a week ago. Trina must have bought that little statue and placed it with loving care amongst the great composers from two centuries back. I'd envisioned this. Trina's spirit was singing her favorite song as she left her earthly home forever.

For the first time since her body had been recovered, I burst into tears.

TWENTY-ONE

THE POLICE HAD been gone for several hours. It was now late evening, tea had been served twice, dinner was being attended to by a weepy but determined Marta, helped by Jozef. Veronika had poignantly requested to be left alone to grieve in her room.

Which left Franz, Fritz, Lily, Corbin, Mitchell, Johnny, Shay and me. We sat in the parlor huddled near the fireplace and tried to make conversation that wasn't obsessively morbid or the reverse—inappropriately funny.

The best choice appeared to be to the "getting-to-know-you-so-tell-interesting-facts-about-yourself" game. Shay and I had started the proverbial rolling ball by regaling the others with tales about our roommate, the exotic dancer who was planning the wedding of the century with her beloved intended—a bodyguard straight out of a Nineteen-Fifties bad detective film.

"But, that bodyguard—all five-feet-three of him—saved my life one night so I am eternally grateful," I stated. "And if Cherry Ripe wants me to wear a leopard-print bikini as one of her bridesmaids I shall do it with pride."

Shay mumbled. "Not me. Nobody saved my life so I can dress like a normal woman during any and all weddings Ms. Ripe and Mr. Marricino engage in."

"Marricino?" asked Lily. "Like the jarred cherries?"

"Precisely."

Fritz got it first which further endeared him to Shay. "So your topless dancing roommate will soon be— Cherry Marricino?"

Shay and I both replied with a simple, "Yep." There wasn't really much more to say on the subject.

Once the laughs died down, Corbin decided he would share some tidbits about his life.

"Born in Germany to missionary parents who hauled us all over to China for ten years of my early life. I'm pretty fluent in various Cantonese dialects. Moved to Arizona during high school. My parents thought the re-tirees in Phoenix were more ungodly than the Chinese they'd been ministering to." He smiled. "Either that or they were really tired of spicy Kung Pao and General Tsao and various other Chinese delicacies. All of which, by the way, I can make without a recipe and are so de-licious that restaurants in Manhattan have begged me to come be chef."

I wasn't sure if the last statement was true but Shay had perked up at the mention of Chinese food. She's a confessed food hound (I am too) but Chinese is her ul-timate favorite. *Szchechaun Delight*—we call it *"Big Mama's Wok,"* a take-out and delivery joint way up near Inwood—is number one on our speed dial and Shay doesn't even bother to place an order. She just calls and they come even though it's supposedly out of their area. After Mr. Lerner's comments Shay would have Corbin's cell phone on speed dial for recipes. Whether he was digging in Albania or Alabama, that wouldn't stop Shay from asking for a quick way to make hot and sour soup.

She'd already started making nice. "So tell us more? School? Work? All that good stuff."

"Not much to tell. I moved to Munich about fifteen

years ago. I have a Doctorate in History. I teach at a university in Eastern Bavaria and I'm taking a sabbatical now to do some genealogical research." He paused. "What else? Um. I'm planning on turning some of those Cantonese recipes into a cookbook. I love racing."

Lily jumped in. "Racing? Horse, downhill skiing or what?"

Corbin smiled. "Cars, Ms. Lowe. My passion and hobby is racing."

"Ooh," she purred. "I love watching the car races. Very sexy! You'll have to take me to a track sometime and watch you race." She quickly smiled at Franz to reassure him she hadn't blown him off. "You are a ski racer, yes?"

Franz nodded but it was obvious that gliding over ice was dull next to Lily's desire for a fast car on a slick track.

Since Lily now had everyone's focus, she began to tell us about her background. It turned into a long monologue about her very artsy family. Apparently she'd arrived in London at the ripe old age of fourteen, enrolled in a drama school, then gone on to graduate from the Royal Shakespeare Academy.

I sat up. Lily came off as a bimbo, but Royal Shakespeare had a rep for disallowing dumb broads into the program. There was more to Lily Lowe than met the eye.

She continued. "I've done four major films—American, but shot in Prague. The last one was *Little Crystal*. It was a musical version of the Grimm fairy tale called *The Crystal Ball*. I was the star."

Rumor had it that *Little Crystal* had been a good movie. It had premiered at the Cannes Film Festival last year to fantastic reviews. Shay and Bambi, both astute businesswomen, had chosen the leading lady not only for her talent but for some durn good name recognition.

Lily wasn't finished with her parade of accomplishments. She giggled, "For my hobby, I collect Barbie dolls. I have models from the very first ones made. Over three hundred. And Ken dolls too." Her gaze was directed this time at Mitch, whose mouth had dropped at the staggering thought of all those Barbies. "And I'm single and I love cozy nights by a fireplace and walking across beaches on cool nights even when I'm caught in the rain."

That did it. I quickly focused on the embroidery work Marta had left in the room and simultaneously crammed a piece of chocolate cream pie (a Marta special she'd made before any of the tragic events of the day) into my mouth to keep from howling. The fact that I didn't give a rip about embroidery was irrelevant. I had to look anywhere except at Shay Martin. We both waited to hear Lily announce she loved *piña coladas*. If we made eye contact with each other anytime before, during or after that announcement we were positive was coming, we'd be on the floor sharing hysterics and in grave danger of offending our female star and we needed her for *Silhouette Tower*.

No use. Out it came. "Oh. And I love—what is that wonderful beverage with the rum and coconut and pineapple? I love those."

Shay got up, quickly muttered something about using the restroom and left. I intended on being right on her heels, but we'd look like a parade, so I held in all signs of bubbling hilarity and chewed pie crust, even when Mitchell nodded and responded, *"Piña coladas."*

Lily giggled again. "Yes! Well, I just love them."

Bless Mitchell. He took over by quickly saying, "Not hard to make. I've schlopped plenty of 'em into tall glasses during my stints as bartender all over New York."

I added, "Well, you'll only have to be making *piña coladas* at cast parties soon. No more relying on tending bar. This film is going to hit big and your big worry will be what part of Manhattan you want to move into while you sit back and let others bring those drinks to you."

He nodded. "Not sure about that. Not about the movie. I agree. It's going to be wonderful. But I kind of like my rat-hole down in SoHo. The rats and I are on a first name basis and I'd hate for them to have to find a new tenant to bond with."

Franz chuckled. "It sounds as though we have the same apartment but in different countries. My flat in Vienna is…what do the Americans say? A dead ringer? Yes. A dead ringer for your SoHo apartment. Even the same rats. I should make the little rodents pay the lease. So, Mitchell, I understand well that you are a composer. Yes. But you are also a studio musician, is that correct?"

"True. Composing is my passion but playing guitar for up-and-coming rap artists pays that lousy rent and buys groceries."

Shay returned in time to hear this remark. "Mitchell's an awesome guitarist, guys. And wait 'til you hear his stuff. I kidnapped him after hearing a musical he'd composed for some Indie theatre group down in the Village. He was skulking around the lobby trying not to notice the standing ovations every number was getting from extremely enthusiastic audiences. I grabbed him and shoved a contract in his face."

Mitch beamed. "And I was smart enough to sign it,

which is why I'm in Prague." An evil twinkle lit up his eyes as he stated, "I'm also single and love walks in the rain."

Lily inhaled and pushed her expansive bosom to its limit.

He added, "No Barbies though. Just Kens. In real life." Dramatic pause. "Did I mention I'm gay?"

If my lips hadn't been pressed together to stifle hee-hawing laughter, I'd've been on the floor clutching my sides. This time it was my turn to leave the room for the ever-popular restroom.

Johnny followed me. "I assume you don't really need to use the facilities?"

"You got that right. It was far too difficult being in silent communication with Shay back there. Or you. In case you hadn't noticed, I was studiously avoiding looking at either of you. And much as I'd've love to stay to watch Lily Lowe turn her charms away from Mitchell while pretending she'd never flirted with him…well, we don't need to alienate a cast member who has talent."

"Very diplomatic."

"So, dearest darling, what are you going to confess for this little show-and-tell session at the castle? The entertaining tale about how the lions now sleep well at night in their rescue habitat? Or are you going to discuss the multi-tasking Gregory Noble does in every damn episode of the soap?"

"Now, now, I'm too modest to talk about myself."

I snorted. "Or you just don't want to spend the next three hours answering questions about your possibly delinquent past."

"Well, there is that." He grinned. "Whacha think? I

could just tell everyone that I'm doing a mural for Veronika and leave them marveling at my artistic talent?"

I nudged him. "Only if we get to *see* that mural. I've been wondering for days if it's all a figment of your imagination. I hear talk but see no results. Gab. Gab. Gab. Put up or shut up, Gerard."

He grabbed my hand. "Want to take a trek to the east wing sitting room? That's where it is. I'm not sure we won't freeze on the way since this castle doesn't seem to be any guard against the cold but trust me, it's worth it. Oops. Sorry. That sounded pretty arrogant didn't it?"

"Since you multi-task as well as, if not better, than your noble alter ego, I'd imagine the mural is marvelous. If you're not confident about your various works, then I have a feeling you just don't do them at all."

He gave me a sharp look. "Hey, come on, Abigail. I'm not a perfectionist. I have numerous disasters in several endeavors attached to my name. You've witnessed more than one of them on more than one occasion." He stated, "But this mural is good. I think. And we won't stay long enough for your toes to turn to ice."

I kept my hand in his. "You're on."

He led me through the enormous kitchen (where I almost begged off from going further since it was the coziest room in the castle), then through a second back staircase I'd never be able to find again, through a room empty of furniture that rivaled the main ballroom in size and finally to the east wing sitting room. I'd missed this during my sneak-through of various areas of *Kouzlo Noc* the other day. I was almost glad now I had. Because seeing the mural with Johnny, its creator, was much better than stumbling into the room and wondering where this thing had come from.

I guess I'd expected a mural with images similar to the window seat with the tapestry depictions of knights and peasants engaged in the act of killing one another. Or perhaps one of those family portrait murals with the visages of Duskovas from centuries past smiling (or frowning) serenely down on all art lovers.

Instead, what greeted me was a backdrop for a comic opera. Specifically, one comic opera. *The Magic Flute*. Pillars of fire bordered a pyramid that stood in front of a dark forest. Three male figures in white robes floated in the air above the pyramid. In the opening to the pyramid stood three figures. A white robed male with a headpiece that screamed "Egyptian" held his hand up as those offering a marriage blessing to the other two figures, a male in the gold and red garb of an Oriental prince and a female similarly dressed in the trousers and tunic of a princess. On one side of the pyramid I could see the feathered covered shape of the birdman Papageno and his mate, Papagena. At the far end of the mural behind gates of fire three women huddled together in an attitude almost of terror as they stared down into what was obviously a hell pit. In that pit a woman dressed all in black stood with raised hands. The right held a sharp bladed weapon, like a scimitar.

There were other details, such as a flute in the hand of the prince and pipes in the hand of the bird catcher, Papageno. It sounds crowded and messy, but it wasn't. Each image was carefully crafted to force the eye to the next image so the overall effect was one of movement.

I turned to Johnny, who was holding his breath.

"This is amazing! Wow, I had no idea you could do this kind of work. Hell, you could quit the blasted soap and become the toast of Manhattan's artsy folk. Johnny, this is wasted at *Kouzlo Noc*. This should be in the museum along with the furniture Mozart used when he was in Prague and some of the props from the Estates Theatre. Damn. I'm just so impressed."

He exhaled. "Thanks. You love me, but you're also so bloody honest all the time, I knew you'd tell me if it stunk. I had to beg, bargain and promise tickets to a *Yankees* game to get Veronika to agree to this scene."

"She doesn't like it? You're kidding." Then it hit me. "Wait. *Yankees?*"

"Yep. Veronika loves baseball. The Yanks are her favorite team. Anyway, she now tells me she adores it. The mural. But she originally wanted me restore a very ruined mural of a landscape of the ground surrounding the castle. I told her that was boring. I'm surprised she didn't fire me then and there. And when I told her what I had in mind she turned ten shades of green and white but finally said to go ahead. She's afraid this could lead to suspicious characters searching for a certain flute."

"Oh, right, like that hasn't been happening on a daily basis for two hundred years?"

He ignored my comment and instead suddenly reached out and grabbed me. "Damn it. It's colder than that hell pit in the mural where I consigned the Queen of the Night for eternity but I've waited all day to do this." He stopped. "That's a lie. I've waited three months and nineteen days."

His lips met mine. His hands began wandering over portions of my anatomy that were rapidly changing from ice to steam. If there'd been anything other than cold hardwood under our feet we'd've been on the floor within seconds. But we had to stop. This wasn't the place and with the tragedy of what had happened this afternoon, it probably wasn't the time either.

I could see this thought mirrored in Johnny's eyes. We reluctantly drew apart, then clasped hands before heading back to join the other members of this house party.

Still, Shay would definitely have rated the last minutes as high-impact aerobics.

TWENTY-TWO

IF BY CHANCE no one had taken notice of our absence, Shay quickly shattered the hope that Johnny and I could slip back into the cozy little group without comment.

"Damn *long* bathroom break, kiddies. Where ya been hiding?" she asked with too much glee in her voice.

"We decided to baptize various rooms in the castle with a series of teeth-rattling sexual encounters. Happy?" I replied.

"Well, if I thought that were true, I'd at least be interested. Since I see 'I'm lying' stamped in huge letters on your forehead, tell us, where have you been? For real this time." Through the sweet sarcasm in her voice, I could detect a note of worry.

Johnny answered for both of us. "I wanted Abby to see the mural I've been working on here. And she needed to stretch her legs for a moment. Did we miss much?"

Franz shrugged. "I talked, but you already know who I am and all about Vienna."

I smiled at him. "We did get a fair amount of information from you the other day at the café."

He smiled back. "And Shay has told us of more exploits of 'Seven D' of the two of you. So we are all friends now. Yes? Except Frederick is new and Mr. Gerard's past does appear a bit of a mystery."

Johnny's show bounced off satellites around the

world daily but apparently Franz was not a fan of day-time drama. Johnny yawned as he oozed down onto a chair cushion that had been tossed on the floor. "I'm an open book. Musician. Muralist. Tour guide." Pause. "Actor."

"A damn good one," I stated.

Lily looked at Johnny with more interest than she'd previously displayed. I figured now that Mitchell's gender preferences had been aired she needed fresh meat on which to carve her considerable charms. Her eyes widened. It had taken our observant Ms. Lowe nearly a week to get it but this night finally the light dawned. "Oh my God! You're Gregory Noble, aren't you? I did not realize this since it has been a year or more since I've seen the show. You were in a coma a long time back then."

Johnny smiled. It was lovely and it was fake. "Gregory Noble. Supercop. That's me. Putting bad guys behind prison walls every damn day of the week."

Lily inched her way toward him, crooning about how much she had adored the show and his role on it before being forced to miss it while on location for *Little Crystal*. My fists clenched as I muttered, not quite inaudibly, "Lily-livered, loose-lipped, leeching, low-down trollopey, lackey-lacquered…"

Shay winked at me, then told Lily, "He's also Mister Animal Activist. Saves lions, tigers and bears. And puppies. He has a lot in common with Ms. Fouchet, who decided to douse a white fur with red wine once—while the owner was wearing it."

Not *quite* true, since I hadn't taken any out and out active steps to accomplish the dousing. That had only been a fantasy of mine one evening when I'd seen

Johnny in the company of a fur-clad lady, but Lily looked a bit startled anyway. Then her overly shadowed and mascared eyes opened even wider. "Wait. You are also on that soap opera! In a coma too for a while? What was that name?"

Nothing to do but admit it. "Yep. I played Vanessa Manilow. Who arrived on *Endless Time* after her hot-air balloon crashed and she ended up next to Gregory Noble in the coma ward of Saint Sympathy's Hospital in Sunset Park, Brooklyn, New York."

Franz stared at me. "I knew you were familiar. Didn't you and Johnny have something to do with corruption in theatre on Broadway?"

Johnny sighed. "We had something to do with *solving* corruption elsewhere in the city so that Broadway would retain its lovely, pure-as-Prague-snow status."

Franz looked at Johnny, then at me again. "Together?"

Shay chimed in, "They were both in *Boundaries*. Johnny won a Tony and Abby was nominated for best Featured Actress."

Miss Lowe didn't grasp yet that Johnny and I were more than soapy colleagues. From the looks thrown our way, everyone else got it. So much for keeping the relationship a secret. Lily purred. "You are a true Renaissance man, Johnny. That is very attractive."

He inclined his head. "Thank you. Um, didn't Franz say our tuning genius here hadn't gotten his life story aired?" He waved at Fritz, who was trying to look invisible by sitting alone on the dreadful window seat but failing miserably. "Fritz. You're on."

"Oh. What do you want to hear?"

I whispered to Shay, "Every damn detail, Fritzi-boy.

Especially—are you available? Can Shay be your sex slave for the next ten years or so?"

Shay poked me so hard in my ribs I considered asking for workmen's comp. "Ouch!"

All eyes turned to us. "Problems, children?" asked Johnny.

Shay batted her lashes. "Nope. Abby got a cramp in her foot. Probably because it's not accustomed to being out of her mouth. Please, Fritz, so sorry for the interruption. I'll keep Ms. Fouchet quiet here. You were saying?"

"Oh. Well, I grew up many years in Vienna, but I was born in East Germany. My family escaped to the West only months before the wall came down. We were afraid to leave because we are a big family and we were not certain we could do this without being caught—and without reprisals visited on the aunt and uncles and cousins who could not come. I was very, very young you understand. But when my oldest brother was to be entered, um, conscripted—is that the right word? Well, 'forced' is perhaps better—into the army, my father, also a musician, said, 'No. We go. Now.'"

He made it sound as if they'd just packed a few bags and driven their car across the barricaded borders like they'd been going for a day's outing at the circus. We all stayed silent, thinking about the painstaking planning that had doubtless occurred for many months. The constant fears about trusting someone who might ultimately betray the refugees. Living with total panic on a daily basis. The sheer terror of the entire escape was something none of us could begin to imagine.

But Fritz was smiling. "I love Vienna. I love the music and the museums and most of all I love the pastries and the sweet desserts that are to be found at every café. But of course, Prague has great music and museums and wonderful food at the *karvany* (cafés)."

That did it. Shay was already in attraction mode. She'd just met a fellow food hound who was sensitive and smart and cute in an artsy way and who had a great back story. The only question to be answered was when these two would be engaging in some high-impact aerobics themselves.

"Why did you move to Prague, Fritz?" asked Corbin.

"The Rombergs are originally from Czechoslovakia and my family felt it was right to return."

"Family?" was Shay's question. I knew she was praying that didn't include a Frau Frederick Romberg.

It didn't. He explained that five sisters, three brothers, an aunt and three nephews had all headed to Prague to commune with their ancestral roots. Every one of them was older than he and every one of them was a musician. Shay relaxed. I could see wheels turning in her head for the campaign to win the heart of this quiet man of music. *Watch out, Fuji.*

Fritz had finished telling us what he considered the pertinent parts of his life story. We all knew there was a lot more but we also knew that much of it doubtless wasn't pleasant. Fritz was looking a bit pale by the end of his saga. Time to move on.

Johnny stood, then crossed over to the fireplace and began poking logs to encourage the flame to burn hotter. "Anyone heard any weather reports?"

As if he'd been waiting for this cue, Jozef Jezek entered the room with a radio already tuned to an all news station. He raised the volume so we could all hear, although that was pretty useless for those of us with limited—or non-existent—skills in understanding Czech. Jozef politely waited until the newscaster had switched to the latest political scandal involving a Congressman and an evangelical preacher before giving the Americans the bad news. We didn't need for him to translate the juicy tale of sex the newscaster was delightedly sharing with listeners—the names had been all over the news for three weeks and I could just imagine the details had gotten juicier. The weather was the important topic.

Jozef frowned. "The announcer says we are snowbound. For this night, at least. It is the wind that is causing the trouble because it has ruined the visibility. They are warning people to stay inside." He added simply, if unnecessarily, "That is good advice. I have looked outside in the last half hour and there is nothing but white. We are having a full moon this night, yet it cannot even be seen because there is snow still falling."

Veronika had entered behind Jozef, so silently we barely noticed. Her tear-stained face was painful to see but her dignity was intact. "We haf plenty room at *Kouzlo Noc* so no one try to get back to Prague tonight. In those leettle cars that are like toys! Iss not safe. I find blankets but we must share rooms because not all of castle has good heat."

This was why Shay had requested a castle with "beyond modern heating." My friend wasn't dumb. I was sorry now I hadn't stressed this requirement.

Veronika whirled around and headed off, presumably to rummage through old hope chests and new linen closets and raid them for the best covers for her unexpected guests.

We were silent for a moment or two, then Shay took

charge. "Okay. As *Silhouette Tower*'s big bad director I feel like I'm entitled to be the one giving out room assignments. There's about four bedrooms that have heat so it's going to be a night of bundling, gang. Uh, Franz? Why don't you and Corbin and Jozef take that room that has the day bed settee thingee in it and those humongous stuffed chairs."

All three nodded. No argument.

"Fritz, Johnny and Mitch. Y'all are a bit more of a problem. Um, there's another bedroom down that hall, but it only has one bed. Who doesn't mind sharing?"

Mitchell grinned. "Here's the test of modern man and his homophobic worries. Gentlemen?"

Fritz stood. "I do not mind being in one bed. I grew up that way with brothers. And I do not snore so Mitchell will not have to worry about sleeping."

Shay shot me a glance that clearly stated, *"I love this guy already? That's a damn secure heterosexual. Of course, that supposes he had a clue what Mitchell was teasing about. But if I have my say Fritzie will be changing beds round about midnight anyway!"*

Since she hadn't said this out loud, I couldn't respond with a comment, although I had several completely inappropriate remarks I would have loved to spit out into the air. Johnny nodded. "Fine with me—sharing the room. I'll take the floor though, since I'm a toss n' turner."

Shay turned to me and to Lily. "Aside from the Duskovas' bedrooms, which I don't feel would be right in asking to invade after they just lost their sister today, there's just one bedroom left—and one bed. So I'm not sure how we want to go here."

I raised my hand. "Oh, cruise director lady? Howsabout I just stay in this room on the sofa. It's hard as a rock, which will probably be a wonderful thing for my back. And as long as I can keep the fire going I won't freeze my little footsies off."

"You sure?"

"Yep. You and Lily need a night of girl talk anyway. I've had more than my allotment for the week. I need a rest."

TWENTY-THREE

THE SITTING ROOM was quiet. All the little snow hostages were snug in their beds, sofas, and whatever other large pieces of furniture that could be used for sleeping. I'd fast decided it was in my best interest to simply pile a load of blankets on the rug close to the fireplace instead of trying to wrestle with the too-small sofa that rightfully should be called a settee.

I was warm. I was dry. I was embarrassingly comfortable. And I couldn't sleep. It was too still, too silent in *Kouzlo Noc*. I'd taken a look outside moments ago and seen a white world. Trees were covered, the artistically arranged leaves in the moat were covered, the ground was covered and cars were invisible. It was eerily beautiful but it gave me the feeling of being smothered. I quickly closed that window and returned to my makeshift bed. My thoughts were going ninety-to-nothing and that ninety was mainly visions of the cops with Trina. Of Jozef and Johnny and Corbin carrying Trina. Of me hearing Trina's spirit singing *Layla* as she left *Kouzlo Noc* for the last time.

This wasn't working. I got up, poked the fire a bit more, then turned on the brightest lamp the sitting room owned. I pulled out the book Jozef had given me (was it just yesterday?) about Mozart and Freemasonry. If I couldn't sleep at least I could dive into something that could help provide me a clue or two as to what powers

Ignatz's magical flute held that had caused so much distress in the last two hundred years.

The first thing I learned was that *The Magic Flute* was considered by many to be nothing *but* Masonic symbolism. The use of trios like the three boys who start out appearing to be working for the bad Queen of the Night only to be discovered by Kathyina, the prince and hero of the opera, as "good guys." (A character switch which has always baffled me.) This trio becomes aides for Sarastro, the mysterious, wise mentor who rules what the author of Jozef's book believed was most certainly a Masonic temple representing an entire kingdom. The other trio that was important was that of the ladies who served the Queen of the Night, who also switched sides in this opera more often than a politician in campaign mode.

All this trio stuff was fascinating but I didn't feel that the "power of three" had anything to do with Ignatz and the magic flute he'd crafted for buddy Mozart. I skipped over to the chapter where the author discussed the trial Tamino goes through to prove himself worthy, not only of Kathyina, his beloved, but to Sarastro and the members of the temple Tamino wishes to join.

I've personally always had a problem with these trials. Mainly the first one, the Test of Silence. I could almost imagine Mozart yelling at Schikaneder, the librettist of *The Magic Flute,* perhaps waving a conductor's wand at the man in rhythm with his words. "You did *what,* you twerp? You put a friggin' test of silence in my opera? This is not *mime,* you moron. We want mime, we go to Central Park and watch the kids in black and white pretend to get claustrophobic in a box. It's an opera. As in Op-Er-A. People sing, remember? Isn't the audience going to get a little confused—not to mention annoyed—when they're told the hero is about to shut up so he can ace this test, and then aren't they going to wonder how he aced it when he opens his trap and starts crooning to Papageno who hasn't shut his trap the whole first act? Give me an effin' break!"

Well, perhaps Mozart didn't use those exact phrases—but I'd wager his resistance and sheer ticked-off-ness could have been the same.

The only way I could see Ignatz Jezek making use of this silent treatment concept would be if he wanted to have people remember the adage "silence is golden" if his flute was really an alchemist's dream that turned metal to gold. Then again, I had no idea when that particular piece of wisdom hit the streets so it was pretty iffy as to whether Ignatz had even heard it.

Also, I instinctively felt the flute had nothing whatsoever to do with gold or even treasure that was "material" in nature. Ignatz wasn't greedy. I'd heard him play and you just can't coax music the way he did if you're focused on wealth, whether before or after death.

I moved on to the next trials. Fire and water. Tamino uses the flute in the opera to keep himself and Kathyina safe from the elements. Did Papageno have anything to do with elements? And in case anyone is wondering, yes, the use of the same durn name but in masculine and feminine forms was wearing on my nerves. Papageno and Papagena have that thoroughly fun duet using the cute name device but it still was annoying. Now I was confusing myself even bringing the birdcatcher and his bride-to-be into this whole question of trials and magic.

Back to the flute. At least a flute was finally mentioned in these trials, but as I kept reading I learned that Mozart doled out measures of music using a flute with the stinginess of an old miser. The flute is barely heard, even when Tamino is waving it in the air and telling the world how he and Kathyina are safe from falling water and ribbons of burning flames. So it wasn't very helpful. Now panpipes were something else. But since Ignatz hadn't crafted panpipes, I discarded their importance to my quest.

I read on. Interesting. The Freemasons weren't on good terms with the Roman Catholic Church in the 18th Century. A major power struggle had been started by Pope Clement XII in 1731 then gone so far and become so rigid that the Pope was excommunicating good and decent men for belonging to a Masonic lodge. The edict to ban Freemasonry from the Church had taken the extra step by Pope Benedict XIV in 1751, and the action was just reaching Austria when Mozart was composing his last works. The wisdom shown by the high priest Sarastro is not that of a bishop or cardinal—it's definitely that of a Masonic leader and spiritual mentor. It sounded like the Pope would not have been pleased with Mozart's *Die Zauberflote*. At least if he caught the nuances.

I wasn't sure what that meant in terms of Ignatz and power unless his flute was a symbol of defiance to a politically minded church. Sort of a raised middle finger and the promise that he wasn't going to be dictated to?

I was tired. None of this was really getting me anywhere closer to discovering the whereabouts of the flute or the magic within. Or who'd murdered Ignatz. Or Gustav. Or—I shuddered—Trina. I shut the book and turned out the light. Enough.

I shifted the blankets around me, closed my eyes and

told myself to "think black." Dad always used to tell me to use that technique when I couldn't sleep. It never worked. My mother, Minette, told me he would tell her the same thing and it never worked for her either. We decided it was a male quirk. Men have this little off switch they can manipulate to tune out stresses, worries, cravings for midnight snacks, and plans for the next day's activities. Women were not born with this. It's an entirely separate chromosome.

Instead of thinking black I was *thinking* about thinking black and that was just making me more wide awake. Consequently I wasn't terribly upset when I heard Mozart's *Requiem* come floating through the air. Surprised, but not upset. I first thought it was one of *Kouzlo Noc*'s ghosts out for a midnight jog or concert (I was pretty certain that more than just Ignatz Jezek, Gustav, and the nasty soldier Veronika had mentioned were haunting the place) but then my brain focused and I realized it was the bell-pull. Some maniac was at the door. At midnight. In the middle of the worst snowstorm in Prague's history. Shay was going to be thrilled since it doubtless meant a new lunatic character added to the cast of our little tale.

It appeared I was the official doorman for the castle. All the bedrooms were upstairs and by the time anyone made it into warm clothes and out to the back door, the night visitor would be frozen. I was *already* in warm clothes, having been smart enough not to remove a stitch earlier before collapsing on the floor that passed for my bed. I grabbed one of the blankets and wrapped it around my shoulders, then hurried to greet the midnight caller before either the dragon-headed knocker or the cold knocked him or her senseless.

I pulled open the heavy doors, then stared at the woman who sauntered inside as though she was out for a Sunday morning social call.

She was tiny, even smaller than my five-feet, two inches. I put her at about four-foot-ten. On a good day— in heels. She was wrapped in an ankle length red cape. Thick equestrian boots with those good-day heels at least three inches high hugged her feet. She could have been anywhere from fifty to eighty. She had wrapped a bright red muffler around her neck and it obscured the bottom half of her face but the turned up nose and blue eyes screamed "Imp" at me as though she were shouting the word itself.

A red Monica Lewinsky beret with a bow was perched on top of her head. Red Christmas earrings in the shape of poinsettias dangled and bounced as she led me through the house back to the sitting room with the air of someone who'd lived at *Kouzlo Noc* her entire life.

I followed. There wasn't much else I could do. As yet, she hadn't said a word.

By the time the night visitor and I reached the sitting room, every other person who was staying the night at the castle had arrived and was now sinking onto chairs and settees and window seats. It was as if they'd been drawn by an unseen force, told to leave their beds and come gather together.

Shay grabbed my arm as the mysterious woman took over the sitting room. "Who is this? Have you ever seen her before?" she whispered.

"Not a clue. She pulled the bell. I answered. And there she was, slap-dang in the middle of a snowstorm yet managing to be perfectly dry without a flake to be seen anywhere."

"Cool."

We waited.

The lady had taken off her cape and thrown it across a hat rack I'd never even noticed existed at the door of the sitting room. My mouth dropped open. Shay's mouth dropped open.

Our visitor was dressed in black jodhpurs. A white shirt peeked out from the neck atop a red vest which matched the red equestrian jacket buttoned at her waist. A jockey's outfit. At a guess—size 18 extremely petite. She looked like she was prepared to send Ol' *Running at the Bit* down the finish line at the Kentucky Derby. No, that wasn't right. More like lift the horn to send a dozen weekend guests at a Virginia plantation out to hunt down the fox. The red beret didn't really match the ensemble, but it neatly hid her hair, except for a jet-black gotta-be-fake ponytail flapping at the back of her neck.

She smiled at the assembled, blizzard-caused captives of *Kouzlo Noc*. In the honeyed drawled dialect only heard from ladies born and raised in the Deep South, she oozed, "Well, hai y'all! Ah'm so pleased to be here. Ma name is Auraliah Lee. From Atlanta. And we can start the séance any time y'all are ready."

TWENTY-FOUR

I POKED SHAY almost as hard in her ribs as she'd leveled me earlier that evening when I was bugging her about Fritz. "Did she say Atlantis?"

"Stop that!" she murmured. "What's this about a séance? Did your mother send her?"

"Minette has gone off to the wilds of Tibet for some annual Wiccan Catholics conference and she's not up on the latest comings and goings of her baby, which is such a shock to me I'm still processing the freedom. But there's no way Minette is going to be contacting Southern Belles to pop in during blizzards to commune with the departed. She'd be hijacking her to go to Tibet instead."

"Well then, where did Ms. Lee come from?"

"Atlantis."

"Oh shut up. You're hopeless."

We suddenly realized that our voices had been rising and our little discussion was now being intently followed by all the occupants of the sitting room. Auraliah Lee smiled at us.

"Ladies? Would y'all care to sit down? I can't staht the séance until ever'one is seated. Ever'one? Ah am Auraliah Lee. My friends call me Aura Lee." She winked at me. "Yes, Abby, just like the old Army theme song that sounds just lahk *Love Me Tender*."

How the heck did she know my name? Could it be my

mother wasn't in Tibet? Had Minette Dumas Fouchet flown back to Texas and had met Aura Lee during a connection in Atlanta (where all flights connect, including, I now strongly suspected, those of the newly dearly departed.) The only other plausible answer was that my buddy Jane Doe, aka Madam Euphoria, had run into Aura Lee at a psychics and mediums church social in New Orleans, then sent her to Prague to harass me since she herself didn't have the time.

The soft Southern tones were compelling. No way was I going to remain standing. Ms. Lee was bound to soon start explaining why she was here. And how in blazes she'd gotten here. I'd seen no car just outside the door. No snowmobile. Apparently she'd just transported her short frame through the snowy air and landed right at the nose of the dragons.

I sat, silent. Everyone sat, silent.

"Well, now, ever'one's here? Yes? Good. We don't need a big ol' table to have a lovely séance. But ah do ask that everyone hold hands because we must link to one another for the spirits to join us."

I raised my hand. "I'm sorry to interrupt. But it's been a really strange day and this is now becoming a really strange night. Uh, no offense, but why are you here? In words of one syllable, preferably."

She giggled like a girl half her age. "Oh, Honey, ah'm so sorry, didn't ah explain?"

I smiled. "No, not exactly, Ms. Lee."

"Well, now, ah'm here to conduct a séance so we can get at the truth and let a tortured spirit fahnd peace at last."

"Uh, what truth?"

She giggled again. "Well, now, that'll come out when the truth is revealed, won't it?"

I was getting a headache all over my body. And sadly, it appeared I was the only one in the group who had a problem with the circles I was chasing. Corbin and Jozef both looked a bit nonplussed but they stayed silent. Johnny appeared amused. Shay, my traitorous buddy, had already grabbed Fritz's hand and closed her eyes and seemed eager to commune with the spirits. I knew her. She was just glad she'd been given an opportunity to hold Fritz's hand. Lily, Franz, Mitchell, and the two remaining Duskova sisters all seemed tense, but ready to partake in whatever ritual Auraliah Lee from Atlanta/Atlantis had prepared.

What the hell. We were in a haunted castle where a dead body had been discovered less than twelve hours ago. A ghostly flautist had been entertaining me since I first arrived at *Kouzlo Noc*. The clone of Miss Hannah Hammerstein sat across from me in all her delicate glory. One piano tuner had died less than a week ago and the new one was being romanced by my best friend who would doubtless drop the poor kid the instant she returned to Manhattan and her baseball-pitching boyfriend. An elderly bookseller was gifting me with books on Masonic symbolism in the hopes I could solve a two-hundred-year-plus puzzle. Historians were digging through graves hoping to find a magic flute on a coffin. The man I loved was keeping our relationship secret out of some misguided knight-in-shining-armor attempt to keep me safe but was at least taking occasional time outs from creating murals and bringing in dead bodies to sneak in some aerobically-charged kisses. Circumstances kept going from bizarre to just plain weird. So a séance to learn the truth about a question no one had asked just seemed pretty normal for the week. *Rev it up.*

Johnny grabbed my left hand. Jozef grabbed my right. I looked around. Hands cozily encased by other hands with no break in the chain. Or circle.

In the midst of my inner monologue about various loony events experienced by Abby since first encountering *Kouzlo Noc,* someone had turned the lights off. The fireplace reflected the shadows of faces and added a nice scary touch to the whole event. We were ready.

Sideline: One could presume that with the rather odd abilities prevalent in Minette Dumas Fouchet's genetic make-up, séances had been like laundry day back home in El Paso. A normal occurrence. Not so. The first semi-séance I'd attended had been when I was ten and two friends from *Miss Anita's Dance Studio* and I had tried out a Ouija board older than we were to ask some questions to the great Nijinsky about what it had been like dancing for Mother Russia. He never responded and we tossed the board.

The only other séance had taken place in Manhattan over a year ago with one Madam Euphoria and had been a far different affair. In fact it had been a disaster filled with high drama and frightening revelations. I'd avoided the séance scene ever since.

Now I sat, with more than a little trepidation, and waited to discover how Aura Lee planned to ferret out "the truth."

"Well, now, y'all. Again, thank you for bein' willin' to allow me to guide y'all tonight. Such a cold naht too. But that's not relevant raht now, is it? Okey-dokey. So, movin' raht along heah, I'd lahk to ask the spirit of Baron Smetana to join us. Baron, are you theyah?"

A new voice boomed into the small space of the sitting room. It spoke in Czech. Jozef translated. "I am Baron Stanislav Smetana. Why do you bring me back to this house of torment where I died so badly?"

Ms. Lee never skipped a beat. "Stanislav? It's okay if ah just call you that, isn't it?"

There was no answer so I guessed ol' Stan didn't have a problem with dispensing with formalities. Aura Lee continued, "Now, you're a good Czech and always have been, but would y'all mahnd speakin' in English for those of us who just aren't up on our language skills?"

The next words by Stanislav Smetana were in English. I wasn't surprised. There wasn't a doubt in my mind that Aura Lee could talk the devil himself into opening a lemonade stand in the very bowels of Hades. The fact that Baron Smetana had doubtless never heard a syllable of English didn't faze a soul here. Aura Lee resumed her questioning of the man—spirit—whatever.

"Tell us wahy you need to speak to us tonight, Stanislav?"

"I want the truth revealed. I have watched through the centuries as the lies poisoned the Duskova family. It is time for truth and time for peace and time for me to be at rest."

The sentiments were nice but I was ready for the meat. Were we about to hear who had murdered Ignatz Jezek? Would Baron Smetana spill the beans as to where Ignatz had hidden the magic flute?

Apparently the answer was "no" to both questions. For the story the ghost had to tell had taken place in the 17th Century, long before Ignatz had even set eyes on

Kouzlo Noc, much less charmed the inhabitants with his musical talent.

I pulled my focus back to the sonorous tones of the dead man.

"I came to *Kouzlo Noc* in the year of our Lord 1621. I am a good soldier when my country needed me. I am also a good Catholic. An honorable man—or I was before I learned to hate. I was sent here by order of King Ferdinand to rule at the castle and be certain that the peasants returned to their Catholic beliefs."

I'm not exactly an expert in Czech history, but I did remember reading a long blurb in my guide book about King Ferdinand II, who took over in 1620 or so and knocked years of religious tolerance right out on its holy—uh—ear. Protestants who'd been worshipping for a century without fear of reprisal suddenly were forced to be part of the Vatican family again. Ferdinand even executed a group of something like thirty men who had fought to keep religious freedom a going concern. It had been a tough time of transition in Czechoslovakia.

But the Baron was telling his story, so I pulled my focus back, wondering when we'd get to flutes and Mozart—if ever.

"Ferdinand did not want the rich land destroyed." He paused. "I am a simple man and I do not always understand the ways of kings but I was not given a choice. I was to take control of the castle and the lands in the name of King Ferdinand the Second. I did. With no weapon used; no blood spilled. The Duskova family surrendered to me as a wise family ought when they see the outcome will be one of despair unless they choose peace."

Aura Lee gently prodded the spirit. "What hap-

pened? Wahy did dishonah fall upon you and yours?
Please tell those that ah gathered in this room on this
hallowed night."

The disembodied voice continued. In this last week,
I'd heard one ghost playing a flute, another playing
Cole Porter and finally a sweet old lady singing early
Eric Clapton as she left her ancestral home for the last
time. Musical spirits. I was comfortable with it. Music
was a genteel way to listen to those who'd passed into
that good night. I found I didn't like the chatter issuing
forth from—whomever. It was as though I was watching a piece of theatre. Aura Lee and Stanislav Smetana
were onstage and the rest of us were in the audience.
And even with my ghost-listening and ESP experiences
I couldn't help the phrase forming in my head: *"This
is one big crock."*

I focused hard on his next words.

"The Baron of *Kouzlo Noc* agreed to let me rule
over his lands and in return I asked his guidance in that
ruling. He agreed and for the first months of 1621, we
lived in harmony."

"And then?" Aura coaxed.

"Then his daughter, Marie, returned to the castle.
She had been away at the time of the invasion, visiting
family in Bohemia. We fell in love. Yes, she loved me
as deeply as I loved her, although she had been raised
Lutheran. She soon saw the truth of my faith and converted back."

Uh oh. I could see where this was headed already.
Heck, anyone who's ever stayed home with a cold and
watched daytime dramas while eating chicken soup and
ice cream and trashing tissue boxes could see where this
was headed. The makings of the *"yeah, you can have*

my lands but you can't have my daughter, you greedy, religiously arrogant sonovabitch" had begun at *Kouzlo Noc* the day the lovely Marie happened to catch the eye of Stan here.

I was right. And Stanislav—dead and from another century far removed from mine—apparently had a sense of humor, because he seemed to note the triteness of his story. With English getting more colloquial by the second, Baron Smetana continued. "It is an old tale and perhaps an all too familiar one. I recall a drama in my day by a poet of Britain that addressed very much this same feud, although he set his tale in Verona. Yes, my friends, Marie's father did not approve, but, unlike a man of honor, he did not let his feelings be shown. He waited until four months after our wedding night. Eduard Duskova, Marie's parent, came to our room in the north wing of *Kouzlo Noc* and stabbed me in the back as I lay sleeping with my beautiful wife. He then dragged my body to the window and threw me to the rocks below. Marie was screaming even as her father pushed her across the ledge of the window to her death."

The nasty father bit was certainly clichéd and the murders had happened four centuries ago, but I found myself suddenly blinking back tears. I could hear the screams of the young bride as she was pushed to an early death by someone she trusted with her whole heart. The man who'd provided his seed to give her life had taken it from her at an age far too young to die. No wonder Baron Stanislav Smetana was still haunting *Kouzlo Noc.* Royally pissed couldn't begin to nail the feelings he'd stored up for four centuries.

Auraliah Lee held up her hand for silence since several of the séance attendees were murmuring in shock and sympathy. She smiled. "Ah understand y'all's fee-lins, really I do, but Mr. Smetana needs to finish this, allrighty?"

No one spoke. The silence was so complete and solid that when the Baron spoke again it sounded huge and loud in the small space.

"My Baroness…my Marie…and I were to announce the arrival of our first child the next day. It is what drove him to murder us both. He would not let his lands forever go to the child of his Catholic enemy. Worse, after he murdered us, he spread the lie that I had taken his daughter by force, killed her, and he was glad I had had the grace to jump from that window and put an end to my life. The horror of this lie was that the priest believed I had killed myself. I was not allowed to be buried in consecrated ground. Three souls left this earth that night. My wife and unborn child remained together and I believe—I am certain—that they have reached heaven, but I was separated even in death by a man's lies and hatred. In my anguish and grief and pain over their loss, I cursed the Duskova family for the next twenty generations."

I tried to do a swift count in my head but my cousin Remy is the savant in mathematical disciplines in the Dumas family, so I wasn't sure whether Veronika and Marta were still living under that cloud or not. If a generation is considered twenty-five years, multiply that by twenty and if I was right, the Baron's curse was good until about 2121. Ouch.

Stanislav began to sob. "I have learned that hate destroys those who feel and speak that hate, as well as ruining those that he has cursed. I have existed in a limbo of despair for centuries, neither in hell nor in heaven. I miss my family. I want to rejoin them in eternal rest and peace and I want to tell the world that Eduard Duskova was a killer, but that his family, and the generations of family I blindly cursed, were innocent."

Veronika was sobbing. She broke the circle on the side holding Jozef's hand but pulled Marta up next to her as she stood and faced the pale presence of this tortured spirit. "I am so very sorry for wrong of my ancestor doing, and I am so sorry for child who never knew life. Stanislav, I forgive you for your curse if you forgive Duskovas that hass made you anguished soul."

Marta nodded in agreement with her sister. She probably hadn't even caught enough of the story in English to understand the Baron's words, but the emotion was the same in any language and I'd felt from the first day I met her that Marta was a gentle and kind woman.

With a voice that was fading and raspy, the Baron whispered, "I bless you. You and all of yours. I thank you. I have only one request more of you."

This could be interesting. Or dicey.

Veronika waited. We all waited.

"I wish to be buried in the cemetery with my wife and child with a headstone that tells the world my name and theirs so the truth will be out. I wish a priest to say a Requiem Mass for my soul."

Veronika nodded. "I will see that this is done. God bless you."

Aura Lee got in the last word. "Good-bye, Baron. *Requiescat in Pacem*."

He vanished as quickly as he'd appeared. It was so ridiculously fast that for a moment I wondered if the whole thing had been a mass hallucination brought on by too much snow and grief, but when I looked around

I saw that everyone was accepting the Baron's story and subsequent dispellation of his curse as though they'd just attended a pleasant tea party.

Aura Lee reached over and clicked on the lamp she'd doused what seemed like hours ago. I checked the clock on the mantle over the fireplace. Twelve-thirty. The séance had lasted less than half an hour. Aura Lee calmly headed for the rack, donned her coat, her hat then wrapped the muffler around her neck three times.

"Ah'm goin' now. It was real nice to meetcha'll and I hope we have occasion to get togethah in the future."

She was out of the room and at the back door almost before any of us had snapped out of the trance or shock or whatever we'd been in for thirty minutes. Shay and I took off after her then politely held the heavy door open for her as she stepped out into the frigid night.

The blizzard was still raging. I couldn't even tell if the snow was sticking with the fierce winds blowing. The visibility was nil.

"Aura Lee. You can't go out in this. You can't even see. Where's your car? There's room here. Please stay the night."

Aura Lee stopped for a second in the doorway, turned and smiled. "I'm fine, darlin'. Really ah am. Don't y'all worry about me. Bah-bah, now."

I had the strangest urge to call, "Y'all come back now, ya hear?" as she stepped out into the snow but I stifled it. Although I'm sure Auraliah Lee would have appreciated the sentiment. So much so that she might be so inclined as to take me up on that, show up tomorrow and haul in another family ghost the next visit. With the way my luck was going in solving the flute mystery, it probably would not be Ignatz—again.

Auraliah Lee turned once before walking in the direction of the old cemetery where the Baron would now be buried. I knew she'd turned because I could see the red muffler blowing and the red bow on the beret facing Shay and me.

"Requiescat in Pace," she called.

Within seconds, she was swallowed up into the night.

TWENTY-FIVE

I PUNCHED SHAY'S shoulder.

"Would you close the damn door?"

"Oh. Yeah. Sure. Sorry."

She complied. We stared at each other for a full minute. Finally, I took the initiative.

"What just happened?"

"Huh?"

"What. Just. Happened."

Shay's eyes widened but she remained silent.

I shook the shoulder I'd just punched. "Shay, a very strange stranger just showed up unannounced and conducted an even stranger séance to grant pardon and absolution to a really strange ghost none of us knew was hanging around *Kouzlo Noc.* Does any of this seem slightly—oh—*strange*—to you?"

Her normal sense of irony was gradually being restored. She smiled. "Just a tad. But aren't you thrilled? Shit. A real live talking ghost spills a tale that's extremely Shakespearean in nature and you were right there with front row seats. Can't ask for more than that on a dark and stormy night in Czechoslovakia."

"Czech Republic. You add Slovakia and there's liable to be two American ghosts floating around the Vltava with the Baron." I thought for a second. "What's bizarre is that he had nothing to do with Ignatz Jezek. Or with Trina for that matter, unless you consider her untimely demise part of the curse he laid down a while back there."

"And your point?"

"I'm not sure. I guess I didn't imagine anyone like Aura Lee zipping in for a brief séance and zipping out without getting some answers to the questions that keep nagging me, subsequently keeping me awake. And, excuse me—how did the woman zip in? And zip out? Was she real?" I paused. "Wait. She's real. Has to be. No self-respecting witch or ghost or goddess would be caught in that awful red beret by anyone living. Aside from former congressional interns."

Shay burst out laughing. I joined in and felt the tension from the last thirty minutes—heck, from the last entire day—begin to slide away from the knot in my back.

Shay nudged me. "Let's get back to the sitting room. It's far too cold here and I have no desire to stay at the door. It's my guess that Auraliah Lee—and, by the way, is that her whole name or her first name? Anyway, she's not coming back to *Kouzlo Noc*. At least not tonight."

"Agreed. Just wish she'd given some sort of hint or clue or pass code that helped with the main mystery. And don't tell me she couldn't point her little red beret right to it 'cause I'll bet you a week's salary that she could."

We'd made it to the sitting room by this time. Johnny heard my last comment and sailed right in. "Who could what?"

The group of enthralled séance-goers were still littered around what had been my bedroom for an hour before it had undergone renovations as a pit stop on the highway to eternity.

I ignored them. I kept my volume low and muttered, "Shay believes what just happened here—happened."

"Gotcha. Want to talk later?"

"Oh sure, why not?"

Jozef joined us. "That was an unexpected event, was it not?"

"I'd give that a yes." I raised my voice. "Hey, gang, anyone here have any idea of who called Ms. Auraliah Lee?" I turned back to Johnny. "Is she an old buddy from early and endless days of *Endless Time?* Or from the Montana circus? A fortune teller gone off the reservation so to speak?"

His green eyes sparkled in sheer delight. "Never saw, heard or met the woman until just now. Loved the performance, though."

"Yeah, well, okay. Shay and I are clueless as to where she came from. We thought she was a trip and a half and that was a pretty amazing show she put on, but I'd love the name of whoever told her we had a snowbound party going on so this'd be a good time to set spirits free."

Veronika quietly crossed to me and took my hand. "I do not tink anyone called dis woman. I tink Baron Smetana chose her for her kindness and he iss the one who decide that he must be free of his rage and his pain and his name must be made whole. Why tonight?" Her eyes suddenly grew moist. "Perhaps Trina hass passed him as she passed into the light and hass told him that we are now wanting the rid of curses and this is good time to get forgiveness for all?"

It was the longest speech I'd ever heard come from Veronika Duskova and it also made great sense—inasmuch as anything around this castle made sense. I suddenly felt exhausted, as though I'd personally conducted the séance and aided the Baron in achieving his new peaceful dwelling place in the hereafter.

I waved at the crowd in the sitting room. "Hey, troops. It's been really fun but I for one am more than ready to call it a day. And a night. Tomorrow was supposedly going to be a workday and I'd love to get some sleep. So, ungracious as this sounds can everyone go tippy-tappy off to their respective rooms and let me crash for a couple of hours?"

They left. No argument. The adrenalin high of channeling spirits was over. I'd started punching pillows into shape for my bed on the floor but stopped when I noticed one person hadn't left with the others. Johnny.

"I'll go if you want, Abby, but I have the feeling you'd really rather I stayed. I won't try to engage you in scintillating conversation or scintillating exercises in passion—" he hugged me "—unless you get some wild aerobic energy back—but if you'd like, I'll stoke up the fire and lie down on those blankets and just hold you until you believe you're safe enough to fall asleep."

I shivered. That word—"safe." I was anything but. I'd hidden my own thoughts from myself with comical comments and scholarly pursuits into what did and did not constitute symbols in *The Magic Flute*. I'd pushed any whisper of that word to the back of my brain. But it had snuck up on me about three minutes ago and I was shaking and freezing because Johnny Gerard had it pegged. I was anything *but* safe. And I was damn scared. I didn't know where the flute was. I didn't know who'd murdered Ignatz. Or Gustav. Or Trina. What I did know was that there was a menace surrounding this castle—and it was aimed at me.

I looked up at Johnny, who'd turned his face away to

let me deal with my realizations. He was adding newspapers to the fire and the last logs that had been brought in this morning when the weather started changing.

"Thanks, Johnny."

He didn't say anything for a few seconds, just continued his task of keeping the room warm for the hours left this night. Finally, he sat down on the floor next to me and took my hands in his. "It hit me today that you hear music when spirits sing it. I understand that even though I'm getting nothing but silence. Abby, I hear the music in your soul because I can feel it. I have since the day I first met you. Whether that music is light and airy or dark and heavy. Today, that music is edgy, and not in a heavy-metal rock band crashing boundaries kind of way. I've personally been getting more and more edgy and instinctively knowing that edginess isn't coming from the events—awful as they've been. It's coming from you because you're absolutely terrified and you're trying not to let yourself even become aware of it."

I couldn't say anything for a few minutes. I closed my eyes and focused on my feelings—hard as that was. I'm not the greatest with tuning in to my emotions. It's easier for me to shrug off problems, easier for me to ignore them than to confront them. But tonight those feelings were pouring through me. They weren't pleasant. But Johnny felt them right along with me.

I laid my hand over his. "You're right. I'm absolutely terrified. There. I've said it. Do I feel better? Hell, no."

He hugged me. "Would you like to hear the fact that I'm not exactly oozing with manly manliness and mucho macho toughness right now either? There are really strange things going on at this castle. I'm feeling—uh— *zamzodden*."

"Say what? *Zamzodden?* What the hell is that?"

"Literally, 'half-boiled.' It's a perfectly lovely, very old Anglo-Saxon term pulled from Latin verbiage that I only yank out of my thesaurus when I have no other words. And it's a great description. Me. Like a soggy pudding."

"How do you know this stuff?"

His turn to tease. "I taught school, remember? I picked up all sorts of marvelously useless trivia that has stuck with me ever since, not to mention I had a marvelous education."

"Yes, but Old English terminology is not a required course, if I remember correctly from my days with nuns who blanched when they hear the name Chaucer."

"It is."

"What is?"

"Required."

"It isn't—wait—we're doing it again." I took a deep breath. "Where is it required?"

"I went to an all boys' school in Massachusetts for exactly one year of my secondary education. Long story about how and why and not relevant. Anyway, we learned art history, English Literature, and when and how words that are now common dropped into the English language. We learned ballroom dance, lacrosse, and curling. Very eclectic education. Sadly, no decent theatre program so I wasn't thrilled."

"Curling? You learned curling? You've got to be kidding."

"I'm not."

"Dang. Johnny Gerard knows curling. Holy Caledonia! I only thought drunken Scotsmen and intense Canadians even knew of the sport. Although, recently, it has crept into the regular way-into-late-night broadcasts of the Sports Channel. Shay and I placed bets on the winner last Olympics. You'd just taken off for Kenya so you didn't get to participate in the TV parties that were more lively than the events. Very entertaining. We sip tea and munch scones with cream cheese pretending it's clotted cream and we speak in thick brogues yelling, *'Verra gude! Ye nailed that shot, ye wee bastard!'*"

He smiled. "So, we're avoiding the real subject? We're not going to talk about being scared?"

"No. We're not. We're tabling that discussion until at least tomorrow. I have faced my fear and I know it exists. That's enough angst for one night."

I snuggled down into the wealth of blankets and added, "But if you care to curl up with the terrified lady, she won't object 'e'en a wee bit.'"

TWENTY-SIX

I AWOKE TO the sound of screaming. For a moment I thought I was reliving yesterday's events, then realized this was real and not a playback. Johnny sat up beside me.

"What the hell?"

"It's Veronika. Sounds like it's coming from the kitchen. Let's haul."

He stood, then tossed a jacket to me. The fire had burned down to ashes only and it was now chilly in the sitting room. Especially since I was now separated from the nice hot body that had been snuggled up against mine. We'd stayed wrapped in each other's arms for the few hours of night that had been left by the time Aura Lee had traipsed off into the blizzard. Oh, nothing I couldn't tell Sister Mary Matrimony at my old high school. No high-impact aerobic activities. Unfortunately. Just sharing warmth and comfort and a badly needed feeling of safety. Very nice indeed. I'd missed him more than I cared to admit those rotten few months he'd been out of the country.

We raced through the ballroom and on into the kitchen. No one was there. The screams morphed into keening. The sound was coming from the back staircase; the same stairs that we'd taken yesterday when Johnny had shown me the mural. We quickly headed that way.

Veronika knelt on the floor, rocking and sobbing and moaning as she stared at the body of her sister, Marta, who lay in a crumpled heap at the very bottom of the stairs.

We heard voices and fast footsteps. The rest of the group who'd spent the night in the castle had followed the sounds of Veronika's distress and were now crowding in just behind me. Johnny immediately turned around and held up his hand in a classic "Halt" pose.

"Don't anyone touch her. Stay back for a second."

Everyone obeyed. The tone of his voice would allow for nothing else. He walked over to Veronika and Marta and knelt on the floor, reaching his hand out and placing it on Marta's neck. He breathed out a big "Whew."

"Sweet Jesus. She's alive. I've got a pulse here. It's not terrific and she's definitely not conscious, but she's alive."

Utterances of "Oh, thank God!" were heard from Jozef and Fritz. Lily continued to stare in silence while Franz and Mitchell and Shay stepped forward toward Johnny. Corbin turned and walked back into the kitchen yelling, "Are the phones back up? I'll try the one in here."

Fritz helped Veronika to her feet. Her face was set in horror and her eyes were glassy. He murmured, "Veronika. Marta's alive. Do you understand that? We've got to get help but she's not dead. Do you hear me? She is not dead. Not like Trina. Not like my brother."

"Help," Veronika whispered. "Yes. There must be help." She looked at me. "Is *polici* still here?" Then the import of Fritz's words hit. "Brother?" Veronika began to cry again. "Iss brother the piano tuner? Ach, no."

Fritz nodded while every last man and woman gathered in the hall stared at him. "Yes. Gustav. The brother closest to me in age. And he came to *Kouzlo Noc* and he died."

Veronika buried her face in her hands. "I am so, so very sorry. He should not have died. He worked good and he wass in north tower to look for a book for me. I now am of belief he did not fall. He was pushed. Like Trina was pushed into moat. Like Marta pushed down stairs."

For a moment no one knew what to say. The only thought spinning through my brain was *"Someone here is a killer."* It was vital to discover who. It was also vital to get help for Marta.

I turned my focus back to Veronika's question about the police. "Madam D, the police left early last night. Um. You had already gone upstairs and you didn't hear them leave." *With Trina's body carried out in a bag,* my mind screamed, but I didn't say those words. "Corbin has gone to see if any of the landline phones work. Everybody? We need to focus here and figure out how to get Marta to a hospital. We can deal with the who, how and whys later."

Johnny nodded with me, then added, in a tone of pure steel, "And we will."

I turned to Shay, who began to gently lead Veronika away from her sister's pale frame. "Shay? Were you able to recharge your cell last night? I wonder if we can call out if the regular phones aren't back on line?"

She shook her head. "There was a major power outage from about one in the morning on. I was going to plug the cell in after Auraliah Lee left but I forgot and then when I remembered there was no power for the adaptor."

I glanced around. No power was still the rule of the day. I'd thought the blizzard had stopped and assumed we now had electricity, but I'd been wrong on both counts. The short break we'd experienced in the snow last night had only served to recharge the strength of the blizzard this morning. No cheery lights blazed in *Kouzlo Noc.*

Corbin came back inside the stairwell. "Kitchen power is out, too, so the kitchen phone is not on."

"Let's check the rest of the house…I mean, castle," I suggested. "Even if none of the phones work, there could be one power source to plug in a cell." My mind suddenly flashed on Jozef's arrival early yesterday. "Wait! Duh. There are cars outside. One of them's bound to have a charger somewhere."

Franz, Mitchell and Corbin all headed back through the kitchen toward the door that led closest to what passed for a garage. The boathouse. Johnny was still kneeling next to Marta, cautiously feeling for broken bones while trying not to move her. He looked up at me. "She needs a blanket, Abby. Or two or more. She's really cold and I'm sure she's in shock."

Shay and I raced back toward the sitting room and gathered up the bedding I'd used last night. Lily stayed in the kitchen with Veronika, asking where the cups were for tea and coffee, since it was apparent we were all going to need something hot soon. Bless gas stoves.

We'd barely made it back to the stairwell when the guys who'd gone to check the cars joined us.

Franz looked disgusted. "The cars are dead. The batteries are too. In Corbin's Jeep. In the car that Lily's friends loaned to her. She and I were in that one. But even in the motorcycle that Fritz was riding there is no power."

Shay brightened. "Fritz drives a cycle? Cool."

"Hush," I told her quietly. "You can drool later. And remember, this is a man who lost his brother a few days ago. Not to mention there's a certain baseball player back in Manhattan who may be acting like an ass but as far as I know has been nothing less than faithful."

She nodded serenely and ignored my less-than-subtle chiding. She addressed Franz. "So you're saying the car chargers not only are too dead for a cell phone charge but the cars themselves won't start? Did I get that right?"

"Yes."

I stood. "Wait. How did Jozef get here yesterday? Didn't he have a car? Johnny, what about you?"

"I came out on the tram, then walked, although it was getting pretty nasty. I'm pretty sure that's how Jozef got here. He doesn't own a car. So that's a bust. Damn. Marta's got to get some help. I'm no doctor but I'm scared she could have internal injuries. We can't just wait around for the power to come back on or for the roads to clear."

For a second I had to force back a rising fit of hysterical giggles. Johnny had said, "Not a doctor." Someone had once made the comment that everyone on a soap is either a cop or a doctor. Johnny had dived into more occupations as Gregory Noble than a reincarnation trainee except the one we needed.

I was wrong. Johnny glanced up and caught my eye. "However, the character you love so well did do a stint as a medic in the Navy and I *did* do my research. So I'm not totally useless."

I nearly rolled my eyes in sheer disbelief over the myriad of junk Johnny'd learned on *Endless Time*. But this was good. Any kind of medical training should help.

Franz added, "I can ski. Downhill, not cross-country, but that should make no difference. If Veronika has skis?"

Veronika had entered the now crowded stairwell to hear Franz's question. "No. No skis."

She surveyed the people who were helpless to aid her sister. And her eyes fell on me. A curious gleam of hope appeared. "Abb-ee?"

I put my arms around her. "What can I do?"

"You can ride. Horses."

"What?"

"Yes. You are from Texas, no? I overhear you talk last night about El Paso when you try to cheer everyone up so no one cries too much."

"Uh—yeah, I'm from Texas but not everyone from Texas rides." I pursed my lips. "I did learn a bit during my short stint on the soap opera and ages ago one summer. But I mean 'a bit.' Nothing like—well—Johnny. *(Who needed to stay with Marta.)* And I haven't noticed any horses around here. Not to mention there's a major blizzard, which is lousy visibility for rider and horse."

"But there iss horse at neighbor down the hill. He iss gone for months and Marta and Trina," her voice paused then she continued with a definite catch in her throat, "my sisters and I—we take care of horse for him. Did you pass by barn on way up here yesterday?"

I tried to recall seeing anything resembling a barn. Veronika took my hand. "I tell you how to reach barn. You ride to Prague and you bring back help for Marta, yes?"

The fact that snow was still falling at a furious pace didn't seem to bother Veronika. The fact that Prague was a good forty-minute trip in nice weather in a great car didn't seem to have penetrated her thoughts. The fact that I'd never ridden a horse through a snowstorm didn't faze her. Abby the Super Equestrian. So, naturally, I agreed to try.

At least six different voices—all from real human sources—began bitching at me not to attempt such a crazy stunt. I'd never make it. The horse would bolt in the storm and the two of us would be lost. Even if I did manage to find my way to Prague, it would be too late to help Marta.

They were all doubtless right. It was insane, foolhardy, and just damn stupid. But faith shone through Veronika's eyes as though she'd just witnessed St. Agnes personally conduct the beginning of the Velvet Revolution. Shay gave me a thumbs up. I looked at Johnny, who could do everything, including ride a horse far better than I could even imagine, but had to stay here for many reasons, not the least being he had some medical training and could help Marta—and guard her. It was up to me and for once in my life I was going to do something brave.

It was funny. Once I'd made that decision, the fear that had been smothering me for the last two days or more disappeared. It could well come back in a day, an hour, or a heartbeat, but for now that fear had been replaced by a tense excitement that told me, "yes," I needed to stay cautious, but I also needed to get on that horse and ride.

TWENTY-SEVEN

VERONIKA AND JOZEF managed to walk with me the half-mile or so to the barn where a horse named *Yankee Doodle* was standing up taking a nap. At first the entire crowd had asked to make the trip, but someone needed to stay with Marta. I'd stared at Johnny and tried a little silent communication. He and Shay were the anointed bodyguards. They had to keep her warm and dry and be there when—if—she awoke. Keep her safe and secure.

I knew and he knew and Shay knew and damn well everyone knew that Marta hadn't gotten up in the night for an after-séance snack, then tumbled down those stairs. To begin with, her bedroom was in another wing and the kitchen was on the main floor. There was no reason for her to go gallivanting around in either the east or north wings. Someone had pushed her. Or coshed her at the bottom of the stairs then made it look as though she'd fallen.

Shay needed to stay to guard Johnny. His attention had to be focused on Marta, which cast Shay in the role of watcher. Just in case someone decided to come sneaking in and cosh Johnny.

I wanted to scream, *"Look, one of you is a stinking murderer so it's best that everyone stay to keep an eye on everyone else"* but I kept quiet for fear my words would just make the situation worse.

I went the diplomacy route. "There's no need for y'all

to have to go tromping out in this snow to provide me an escort service. If Veronika can just show me the barn, I'll be fine. Stay inside. Drink coffee. Keep warm."

Jozef offered to walk with us and that I agreed to. His warm and reassuring presence would help me quell the rising terror that was just at the surface of my emotions. *Yankee Doodle* would not be happy to meet a new rider who was quaking in her sneakers. A very new rider. The five or so lessons in Colorado six years ago when I did the show *Will Rogers Follies* for summer stock had not exactly produced a champion Abby and the three extra lessons for "Vanessa Manilow" had mainly been trotting around Central Park at a pace of about two miles per hour. I smiled to myself, musing that I could have used Aura Lee's nice equestrian gear today to reassure the horse I knew what I was doing. Horses sense fear and they don't react well to it. They damn sure don't bond with a spooked rider. If I jumped on the saddle without calming down, *Yankee Doodle* would have every right to toss me on my butt before we left the barn.

I was provided with a new outfit for my undertaking, dredged up from various closets and suitcases in *Kouzlo Noc*. An oversized black turtleneck, my own black jeans and sneakers, a black woolen scarf and black cap. I now looked like one of the *Klezmer Volny Rabin* nursing a sore throat.

The walk, which should have taken about ten minutes, stretched to forty. The blizzard conditions had subsided, but snow was still falling and the ground was icy, so the three of us were forced to tread slowly and carefully in order to stay upright. And the wind striking against us had other ideas about that position. Skis were a nice option, but if the Duskovas had owned a pair then Franz or Fritz, who'd also volunteered the information that he was a racer, would now be out here schussing and slaloming or double poling or shoveling. Heck, Johnny, as Gregory Noble, had gone undercover for a few episodes to play one of those athletes in the Winter Olympics who ski and shoot. If provided with the correct gear, he'd've been to Prague and back with the cavalry by now.

These last thoughts brought me up against the barn. Veronika opened the doors with a key bigger than the dragonheads at *Kouzlo Noc*. The place was enormous, but only housed the one valiant steed, *Yankee Doodle*. Mr. Cohan "who owns the house and the horse, loves Americans," Veronika had informed me as we'd made the trek to his house. Apparently, Mr. Cohan was currently soaking up the American culture in California at Disneyland, which was why the Duskovas had been "horsesitting." I cautiously approached *Yankee Doodle,* and gave him the fat carrot provided from the Duskova kitchen, rubbed his neck and tried to establish a unified relationship as best as I could within the limited time I had before he and I sallied forth on our rescue mission.

Jozef handed me a compass, explained the directions for the fifth time (I did mention I'm not the world's greatest navigator, didn't I?) then hugged me. "Be safe, Abby. We shall pray for your journey to be a successful one. God go with you."

Veronika didn't say anything. She just hugged me, tears in her eyes. That was enough. I knew how important it was that I not fail in bringing back help for Marta. One Duskova had died yesterday; there needed to be joy brought back to this family. If Marta died, I would call upon the colorful vocabulary that hits me in times of real anger and spew out a few choice words for Aura Lee and the Baron. His curse was supposed to have been lifted sometime after midnight but so far I wasn't seeing a lot of evidence of peace and harmony restored.

I was helped to the top of the horse by Jozef, who then held the heavy barn doors open so I could take off in the storm while continuing to lean down and chat with *Yankee Doodle*. I'm neither a real rider nor a horse whisperer, but everybody who ever read *Black Beauty* or watched *National Velvet* knows you and the horse have to have a rapport, especially in times of crisis, so the more *Yankee Doodle* and I bonded, the better the chances of both horsey and girl actually making it to Prague in one piece. It took me at least ten minutes to get any kind of "feel" for riding again but *Yankee Doodle* didn't try to throw me or tease me by racing off toward a cliff so it appeared I had a chance to survive this adventure somewhat intact.

We had to go through a patch of forest before we could get onto the main road leading back to the city. The snow was blinding, the ground slushy and it was just damn cold out as well. But the compass showed me I was headed in the right direction, the snow had turned to simply snow, not sleet, and I was wearing more layers than a Texas Seven-Tier Nacho Dip so I wasn't completely chilled. The horse understood that we had to weave between the trees and not hit them head on and for a few minutes I felt like I was a rodeo rider, zooming in and out of barrels, dead-set on grabbing the ribbons off the tops of each one.

What comfort I'd felt for a few moments oddly disappeared when we were well away from the trees and on open ground. We'd even made it to what was normally a fast-moving highway when all the fear and lack of confidence came wailing back at me. The storm had picked up again. Snow wasn't coming down in nice heavy drifts as it had for the first half-hour of this jaunt. Ice pellets were stinging both the horse and me, and the wind had kicked up again to an extent where it was no longer safe to go any faster than a walk. No trotting and definitely no galloping. At the rate of movement, we'd be lucky to reach Prague for *Yankee Doodle* to celebrate the Fourth of July.

I jumped off his back to lead him for a while. It was too dangerous to try to ride with the visibility as bad as it was and neither the horse nor I needed an injury. I kept the compass out and figured at least I wasn't lost. Just covered in ice, snow and desperation. Every bad thing that could happen flooded through my mind.

Marta could already be dead. *Yankee Doodle* could slip and fall and we'd both be frozen by the time anyone was able to find us. Then we'd be dead. We'd actually get to Prague and find a police station but it would have been hit by an avalanche and they'd be dead. Or the one man left would have a car that wouldn't start. The car would be dead. Or it would start, but that one man would be dead and telling me that the ambulances were all in use for a crowd of vampires who'd bitten all the patrons of *Club Krev.* And gotten sick because of the drink called Teeth of Blood.

Okay. It was really friggin' cold because I'd started hallucinating—assuming these weren't Dumas premonitions. I got back on the horse, then screamed. I'd dropped the compass. I jumped back down and spent a few futile moments digging through snow and ice.

And, then, miraculously, I found it. It was lying next to the large rock that had coincidentally managed to completely smash it.

I buried my head in the horse's sodden mane and debated the merits of just sobbing for a few moments, but decided that would not be a good plan since all those tears would merely freeze and I'd still be lost, cold, wet and frightened, plus have chunks of ice nailed to my cheeks. Painful as well as plain unattractive. And then I'd be dead.

I shouted to the universe, "That's it! This is just nuts! Why is nothing going right in this scene? For that matter, who's *directing* this scene? Do you *want* Marta to die? Do you want *me* to die? And is it fair to kill the horse just because Marta and I are goners? You can't kill a horse, dammit! It's like bumping off a cat or worse—a dog—in a cozy mystery. It's just not kosher! So, enough! I need help and I need it now!"

The snow stopped. The ice stopped. The wind stopped. The sun suddenly appeared. The frigid air became—well—not warm, but not freezing either. It was as if the temperature had risen thirty degrees in thirty seconds. This was all good.

But the compass remained broken and I still had no idea which way to go. I looked every direction hoping to at least see a spire from one of the cathedrals in Prague. I saw various towering monuments, but shoot, I saw them everywhere. This area was crawling with castles with high turrets. No clue as to which turret was in Prague—or over the mountains in Bavaria.

Then I heard a flute sounding the notes used in the scene in *The Magic Flute* where the trio of young boys guide Tamino and Papageno toward Sarastro's temple.

Bless him. My favorite ghost, Ignatz Jezek, had snuck
out of the castle to provide music for the trip and I was
going to follow it. I was still on *Yankee Doodle*'s back.
I nudged him gently with my knee encouraging him
to go the way I wanted to go. The lovely notes continued for the next fifteen minutes or so, leading us to a
small town I hadn't known existed. It wasn't Prague; I
doubted it was even on a map. It didn't matter. It was
a town and a town meant people. A town meant hope.

The music stopped right as the horse and I reached
a small building that looked surprisingly official. I
jumped off *Yankee Doodle,* wound his reins around
an ancient lamppost outside the building, rather in the
manner of a cowboy in a Western movie heading for
the saloon, then staggered into the very solid warmth
of what turned out to be a police station.

Far from being the empty room filled with dead people like my sad vision on the road, this place was more
crowded than the Duskovas sitting room had been last
night for Aura Lee's séance.

"Anyone speak English?" I gasped.

A middle-aged man who reminded me a lot of my
dad hastened to my side and threw a dry blanket over
my shoulders. "We all speak English, young lady." He
didn't waste time. "What has happened? Where do we
need to go?"

I also didn't waste time. No one needed the details
of my trip, or even my very real suspicions that a murderer lurked at *Kouzlo Noc.* The important thing was
that Marta get help.

"The castle up on the hill? Um—about eight miles
from here? *Kouzlo Noc?*"

Nods all around.

"Well, there's an injured woman there who needs medical attention. It's Marta Duskova. Is there an ambulance available anywhere close by or do we need to get someone to come up from Prague?"

The gentleman looked almost offended. "Of course we have an ambulance. My brother is finest doctor in the village. We go now."

He was on the phone within one second, calling numbers and rattling off instructions in Czech. I dried my hair and my clothes as much as I could, then turned to leave to help guide the villagers to the castle.

The gentleman handed me another dry blanket.

"No, no. You are soaked and cold. You stay here. I am the *Chief of Polici* and I know the castle well. Do not worry. All shall be attended to. You may trust us."

Trust. That word again. And without analyzing why or how or whether I should—I knew I could—and I did.

TWENTY-EIGHT

ANIMAL LOVERS EVERYWHERE will be pleased to hear that I did not let the sweating, shivering horse just hang out by the parking meter to flirt with any of the cute little fillies—*aka* tiny European autos—that were parked close to the police station. A boy who looked about twelve years old and did not speak English engaged me in a nice pantomime which clearly indicated he would see to the horse's needs. He smiled at my mispronunciations of "stable" and "feedbag" but I figured *Yankee Doodle* was in good hands.

I looked and felt like a refugee in a bad 1950s horror movie. As soon as the police chief and five of his deputies left on the rescue mission, three women popped their heads in from the back entrance and motioned for me to join them. I was afraid that the area held the jail cells for the tiny station, and I'd be tossed into the slammer for my own good (keep the crazy American from rushing out into the snow) but was pleasantly surprised to discover a dining room, and two den areas behind the front offices. The ladies ushered me into one of the dens, then pointed to a restroom.

"You change in there, yes?" stated the tallest of the trio, a plump, red-faced lady who was clearly the leader of this pack, probably because she spoke English.

I smiled. "I can definitely use the facilities and I'd love to wash some of the grime of the road off, but as for changing, I guess that's going to wait until I'm either back in Prague or up at the castle. I didn't exactly bring a suitcase on this trip."

"Oh, we haf see that," she exclaimed. "But we haf brought for you dry clothes and warm. Katya! Quickly, give to the young miss before she becomes chilled."

Too late. I was already chilled, but the prospect of clean clothes was heating me up in a hurry.

Katya, a tiny woman who looked like she'd passed her ninety-fifth birthday about ten years ago handed me a bundle, bowed, then backed away, flashing a toothless grin as she picked at her long black woolen skirt, then smoothed her nondescript, colorless scarf. Central Casting would have trotted her out for every World War II "peasants-sheltering-Resistance" movie ever made. If I didn't get her signature on a Features Extra contract for Shay before I left, there'd be another ghost at the castle because Shay would make sure I joined all the recently deceased.

"Dekuji" I said in my very best (and limited Czech). I bowed too. The ladies all seemed thrilled that I'd managed the one big word of "thanks."

I'd left the now-soaked coat Veronika had given me in the main office of the station, so I just headed for the restroom and tore off my wet jeans and turtleneck. My socks were so damp they'd almost frozen to my feet, and my sneakers were two lumps of fake leather ice, so I hoped whatever garments the good ladies of this nameless town had procured included some sort of dry footwear. Within minutes I'd changed into what had to be the town festival outfit for some local Saint's Day.

The blouse was a simple white peasant top that laced at the neck. A red vest, also laced, hugged my torso. The skirt was made of black wool with red and white embroidered flowers stitched into cute scenes every four inches or so of a skirt that stuck out as wide as a ballerina's tutu. The ladies had neatly folded socks, which I found under the skirt. They were also made of wool and fit nicely into black boots which were the warmest footgear I'd ever had on in my life. I wanted these suckers for those days in Manhattan when the wind chill drops to minus nine and the sidewalks inhale the cold and then send darts of ice through unsuspecting New York feet.

I emerged from the restroom to the sound of "ooh" and "ah'" and *"hezky"* from my trio of dressers. The only one of the group who hadn't said anything, nor provided me with clothing, now stepped forward with a woolen cape, complete with metal hasps in the front. The last part of this outfit was a white scarf tied through a bonnet that had little red flowers bursting out all over.

I could have joined the Von Trapp family singers on the spot. Call me the foxy chestnut-and-green-haired one on the left.

I loved it. I thanked the ladies again, then we all trooped back into the offices where a divine little electric heater was keeping things cozy. Apparently, this village had been spared the power outage we'd been hit with up at *Kouzlo Noc.* I sank into a huge leather chair on the "wrong" side of the chief's desk (obviously tough love for criminals was a non-existent concept here) and closed my eyes, intending merely to soothe the feeling of cold from the stinging pellets of ice that had assailed my face on my ride.

I woke up several hours later. Only one of my trio of dressers was still there, Katya, the ancient, and she was still smiling that toothless smile at me. I had the strangest feeling that she hadn't moved the entire time. My guardian angel.

My eyes traveled from Katya to the figures standing behind her. Johnny Gerard and Shay Martin.

"Am I hallucinating again?"

"When were you hallucinating before?" The sound of Shay's voice flowed over me.

"On the road coming here. Had the damndest visions of dead vampires. Must have been because of that night club we went to last night. No, wait. The séance was last night. Damn, I'm tired. What time is it?"

"Noon," was the answer from Johnny. "The cops and medical team reached *Kouzlo Noc* over three hours ago. They're good. Checked out Marta and determined that she got a huge bump on her head and a concussion to prove it, but no internal injuries and amazingly, nothing broken except for one wrist. She's resting comfortably in her own bedroom. Apparently it took you about ninety minutes to reach this village, but they were able to get back up to the castle in only twenty."

"Well, they had cars with big stinkin' chains and snow tires. I was at a bit of a disadvantage doing my Paul Revere ride thing. Oh, shoot!" I sat upright.

"What?" Johnny asked.

"*Yankee Doodle*. The horse. Some teenager took him off to get him dry but I have no idea where he is now. Kid could have been a horse rustler and Mr. Cohan's prize stallion—or only stallion for that matter—could be in Russia by now."

Shay shook her head. "The horse is fine. He's currently chowing down oats and hay and probably *gulas* and potato pancakes while we speak. That kid is the son

of the police chief or captain—whatever they call him—
here and he's going to be very good to *Yankee Doodle*
and take him back home when the roads are better for
riding. Some friend of his who was doing translations
did mention something about adopting him since Mr.
Cohan was never home but nothing criminal was discussed in our presence."

I smiled. "Okay. Guilt lessened. So, Marta's okay?
That's fantastic. Did she say what happened?"

Johnny replied. "As much as she knew. Jozef translated for her but all we got was that she'd gotten up to
go start breakfast for all the *Kouzlo Noc* guests and
heard a noise upstairs in the north wing so she thought
a bird had flown in and couldn't get out. She headed
upstairs and tried to determine which room the noise
was coming from. Next thing she remembers she's in
her bedroom and there's a doctor holding her hand and
telling her she's fine. Her head has a lump the size of
Cleveland and she's chugging down aspirin like they're
candy, but that's the extent of her memory."

"Which means she was undoubtedly pushed down
those stairs. Or bonked over the head and dumped at
the bottom of them."

The three of us stared at each other.

Johnny muttered, "*Kouzlo Noc* should have been on
the Czech Tour of Murders over the years. Guess it was
too much to hope that would change overnight."

"I thought that was supposed to be fixed by Aura
Lee's little routine last night?"

Shay snorted. "For the big bad Baron—yeah. He's
off to do the rest-in-peace gig for all eternity, but—
well—how long does it take a big honkin' curse to get
uncursed?"

"That's not a word."

"What? Honkin'? Or uncursed."

"Either. Neither."

"So, what now?" I asked. "Hey, could be the curse really *was* lifted. After all, Marta's okay and she's not dead and neither am I, nor the horse I rode in on. So those are all good omens."

Johnny held his hand out to me, then helped me out of the all too comfortable chair. "Well, Marta is being guarded by about fifteen people, including several law enforcement types and one very pissed-off sister, so now I get you both back to Prague and Abby takes a long nap."

"Me too! Me too! I made soup and I'm tired," Shay wheedled and whined.

"Fine. You too."

I tried to look through the window at the white world behind. "By the way, how did y'all get here anyway? I thought the cars were all dead."

"They were. But the police kindly gave us a ride and even more kindly found a man who has a car to rent here in the village, and I rented it and we're on our way."

"Good. I feel sort of bad not going back to the castle, but I can assuage my guilt with a nice hot bath and a nice long sleep." I let my breath out.

Johnny helped me with the red woolen coat, then he, Shay and I headed for the door. I turned around and, using my best bad Czech thanked Katya once again as I gestured toward my new outfit. "I'll bring it back tomorrow. Thank you so much," I repeated, then I looked at Johnny. "Can you tell her what I said?"

He could. She shook her head several times after Gerard explained that we were leaving but would get the clothes back to her and the other ladies. She rattled off a few sentences and Johnny smiled.

"What did she say?"

"*It's yours, little flower of the Czech Republic.*' Really. I gather this costume was hers back in the day and she's not exactly wearing it for dances anymore and you look lovely and she wants you to keep it."

It was all I could do not to start crying. Her kindness had just made up for a hell of a bad start to this day. I thanked her again, then ran over and hugged her as hard as I could without breaking the brittle old bones.

We left her standing by the electric heater warming those bones and blessing us and our children and children's children and on and on. *Kouzlo Noc* was still struggling to shove off the effects of murders and curses from the ungodly but in this little village, it was obvious that saints ruled.

TWENTY-NINE

THE DESK CLERK at the hotel didn't even blink when I waltzed through the lobby in my folk dance apparel looking like I'd been at a modeling gig on a cuckoo clock. A few of the hotel's guests stared. I debated breaking into a few choruses of *"My Favorite Things"* for them.

Shay and I parted by the elevator (the stairs were just too much effort) and I was barely in the room for ten seconds before I removed the Czech folk ballet regalia. Next up was diving into a shower so hot I was nearly scalded, then collapsing, towel wrapped around me, on the comfy bed.

I wasn't sleepy anymore, just exhausted. I stared at the ceiling for about thirty minutes before getting dressed and roaming around the room tidying up the clothes and books and junk I'd left the day before. The hotel's maids had replaced linens and made the bed, but wisely left my stuff where I'd tossed it. I'm not one of those folks who minds having someone clean for me, but I was rather glad the maids hadn't gotten obsessive and put things where I'd never find them.

I grabbed the bag I'd been carrying all over Prague, including all the times I'd been up at *Kouzlo Noc*. Shay had had a fit of efficiency and brought it to me at the police station. I was sure it needed cleaning out of old tissues and receipts and crumpled notes and all those items that reproduce asexually in suitcases, carry-alls and purses if one does not attack one's luggage with a vengeance at least once a month.

This bag had all that clutter and more. My new clock was still inside; wrapped in its original box. The pink suede organizer I thought I'd lost at *Club Krev* was wedged between my wallet, keys and a package of black-cherry-flavored cough drops. Three bags of cheese doodles (ill-gotten gains from a vending machine in Manhattan, unopened but at least four weeks old), the *Magic Flute* playbill from a few nights ago, *Louie's Lingo* translations, and two guidebooks filled up the rest of the space.

The bottom of the bag produced a surprise. The book I'd borrowed—okay—snatched from the room in the north wing of *Kouzlo Noc* where I'd found the music stand and the modern-era flute the day Shay had arrived, was lying alone and unwanted on top of three crumpled tissues. If I remembered correctly after the insanity of the last couple of days, I'd grabbed the book because it had a title about Mozart prominently displayed on the dust jacket. I was right. I pulled it out of my bag and read the words, *"Mozart—A Man Ahead of His Time."* I didn't see a sub-title like, *"How Ignatz Jezek created a Flute for the Maestro and Imbued it With Magic then Hid the Flute before He Was Murdered by Baron Smetana's Father-in-Law in the Bathroom with the Golden Towel Rack"* but that didn't mean I wouldn't find some interesting insights into possible hiding places and/or murder weapons.

I got my second surprise when the dust jacket came off and I discovered a plain leather binder with no title. I opened the book. Czech. Nuts. The dust jacket title with Mozart's name had been in English. Why didn't the contents match? I took another look and realized that not only was this Czech but it was handwritten. I slowly began turning pages. This was not a published work. This was someone's journal.

"Johnny. Holy crap. I need to call him and tell him to get his denim-clad burgling butt over here to try to translate."

I was at the phone before it hit me that I didn't have Johnny's number. I wasn't even sure where Johnny was staying. He'd never told me. For all I knew, he'd dropped Shay and me off at the hotel and gone back to *Kouzlo Noc* to make sure nothing else happened to Marta. Either that or headed for the *National Marionette Theatre* to do another command performance as Macduff.

I called Shay. "Guess what?"

She growled. "'What' had better be damn stinkin' good, because otherwise I'm breaking your other ankle. I was finally getting some sleep—something that wasn't possible last night with Lily Lowe and her stream of consciousness monologues about how wonderful she was as Little Crystal. As Ophelia. As Portia. As Titania. If she'd told me how wonderful she'd been in a one-woman show of *The Tempest,* I'd've just thrown her out of the window and accepted the twenty-generation Duskova curse on my head."

"Will you hush? This is important."

"Fine. What?"

"I found a journal."

Silence.

"And your point?"

"Shay, this journal is handwritten in Czech and I

found it in the north wing where I first heard the
flute music."

Silence.

"And your point?"

"Gad, you are being pissy, aren't you? This could
be a major clue in finding out where Ignatz's flute is."

"Yo. Abb-ess. Hold up there. This was just lying
around in a room in the north wing, right?"

"Right. I sort of filched it when I was there the day
you and the rest of the wandering hordes arrived."

"I did not wander in with whores, thank you. Lily's
a slut, but as to charging for her services? Now, now.
Be charitable."

"Oh, shush. Anyway, I thought it was a book about
Mozart and I grabbed it before y'all came in and then I
forgot about it. The dust jacket wasn't the same."

She didn't bother to ask me what the dust jacket had
to do with anything. It's nice to have a friend who understands your dumbest statements without asking for
explanations. Instead she jumped back to the point she'd
been trying to make.

"Okay. Book is there. You pick up book. Let me repeat. Book is there in plain sight. No warrant needed.
Now, why, if this book, journal, diary, whatever, contains vital clues as to the mystery surrounding a two-
hundred-year-old flute—why, I repeat—is that journal
just lying around waiting to be picked up by any old
bum who drops in. Not that I'm calling you an old bum,
of course, but you get my drift."

Silence while I pouted. "Shoot. You're right. It's too
easy. Even if by some loopy stretch of the imagination
it happens to be Jezek's journal, with my luck it'll just

contain notes on how many potato pancakes he consumed the night before with his in-laws. Nuts."

"Now, Abby, don't sulk. It could well bear more fruit than you or I are giving it credit for. Let's get the bloody thing translated and see what it's about."

I brightened. "Okay. Who, what, where, and when?"

"Well, not now, you nag. I'm sleepy and the durn book has been untranslated by the American geniuses for many years, so it can wait at least a couple of hours to let me regain my lively and lovely self."

"Oh. Okay. Who do we want to trust with this thing, though? Or is it whom?"

"Jozef," was the prompt response. "He told you about Ignatz, he's related to Ignatz, he was marvelous with the whole tragedy about Trina and marvelous helping with Marta and he's a nice guy."

"He also looks like God."

"I beg your pardon." I could see Shay's eyes widening even over the phone.

"You heard me."

"Go to sleep, Abby. We shall contact the bookshop Deity later today. Right now the only god I want to meet is the Sandman."

She hung up. I knew she was right but it didn't help. I wanted to know whose journal I held in my hands and whether it had anything at all to do with Jezek. Or what had been the murder of Trina Duskova and the attempted murder of her sister Marta. Jozef was still out at *Kouzlo Noc*. If he'd been in Prague, I'd've trotted down to his bookstore and politely forced him to read the thing to me. I wondered if any of the hotel staff would accept a substantial tip for translating, but decided that wasn't a great plan in case some startling revelations were—well—revealed.

If I got desperate, I could rent a car and head back to the police station and ask one of my Czech folk dancing dressers to read it. The one who spoke English seemed pretty trustworthy. Or I could rent that car and drive it all the way to *Kouzlo Noc.* Yeah. Over what were still wintery conditions outside. Not a good plan. Either trip.

I began to pace around the hotel room. Crazy. I was impatient and frustrated and I didn't even have an inkling of whether this book had been written by Ignatz Jezek, Baron Smetana, his bride Marie, Wolfgang Amadeus Mozart or some guest of the Duskovas named Johann Schmidt.

The phone rang. I grabbed it. "Shay? Change your mind? Want to go back to the castle?"

"Johnny, not Shay. My mind is made up. And I'm willing to go back to the castle, but I called to see if you'd like to go to *Bertramka* with me. I'm down in the lobby."

"Do they have good *gulas* and wine?"

He howled. "Wine? Possible. *Gulas?* Not so much. Don't you remember your music history, darlin'? *Bertramka* is the Mozart Museum."

"Meet you in ten minutes."

THIRTY

LATE AFTERNOON ON a day that had started with a blizzard, and now the sun was out and I was almost too warm in a light jacket over my knit jersey top and jeans. I'm used to the Texas quick changes in temperature— the old joke is that if you don't like the weather in Texas just wait five minutes—but this was bizarre for Prague. I wasn't complaining about the difference from below-freezing-with-ice-pellets that I'd so enjoyed during this morning's ride; I was just rather astonished by them. Aside from a few dismal dirty snow piles, most of the ground was merely slushy, and it felt like it was in the fifties now. As it should be on a fine early spring day in the Czech Republic.

We took the metro to the museum, which gave me a little time to tell Johnny about the journal. I'd dropped it back inside my now somewhat-cleaner bag before hauling downstairs to meet him.

"You stole it?"

I was indignant. "I didn't steal it. I borrowed it."

"Right. And you accuse *me* of felonious activities?"

"Only every now and then. And you must admit that you deserve the accusations. Sliding out of trees at unsuspecting women who are just out for a peaceful walk around castle grounds."

"Peaceful walk? You, love, were so involved in searching for the source of flute music I'm surprised you weren't sniffing like a bloodhound leading the fox hunt."

"Well, I wasn't so intent on my quest that I failed to notice your butt hanging out the window."

He chuckled. "That's because I have such a fine derrière."

He did. It looked damn nice in ripped denim. Out of ripped denim too. He changed the topic before we started an anatomical discussion that could only lead to trouble on public transportation. "Where is it? The manuscript that'll get you five-to-ten in a Prague pokey."

"Would you stop that? I'm taking it back. I promise. After you take a look since that's why I brought it." My hand dove into the bag. Naturally the journal was down at the bottom again. "How good are your Czech reading skills? Really."

"Not terrific. I've got menus and tourist sites down to a fine art but that's about it."

"What? The great Gregory Noble who will doubtless win a Nobel Prize along with creating a cure for cancer while simultaneously solving global warming can't zip through a lousy book in Czech in five minutes or less? And you got hired as a tour guide?"

"Hush. Since you obviously didn't notice the other day the bus said *Tokyo Tours*. It's a company that caters to Japanese tourists. I do speak some Japanese. Spent four months in Gamagori which sounds like a shape-shifting monster in a horror flick but is actually a coastal town with a cool amusement park and before you ask—yes—*Endless Time*. It was a stupid storyline and I've been trying to blot it out. So did our producers since it was never aired."

I groaned. "Why do I even bring up topics which can

only lead to soap episodes?" I smiled. "I do feel better
that you don't read Czech that well. It's so durn hard to
try to outdo you and I was really reaching for any hidden talents I possess to shock you."

He gave me one of those green-eyed, melt-my-bones
stares but kept silent.

I handed him the journal. "Here."

"Thanks." He studied it for a few minutes. "Okay.
I've admitted to not being an authority on manuscripts
written in Czech, but I can tell you this much. It's not
the journal of Ignatz Jezek."

"Durn. I'm disappointed. I guess I thought the first
page would say something like *'Hi. I'm Ignatz Jezek
and this is my diary and I'm going to lead you right to
where I hid the flute I wanted to give to my good buddy,
Mozart. And by the way, future treasure seekers—here's
the scoop on what the flute really does—now wait for
it. Here it comes.'* Something basic and concise along
those lines."

"Sorry. The first page doesn't even say, *'Yo. My name
is John Duskova and I killed Ignatz for his flute but I
was too stupid to find out where the bloody thing was
before I conked Ignatz over the head with the dragon
poker in the parlor. Oops! My bad. Now I'm cursed
and sharing space with Eduard Duskova, murderer extraordinaire of the Sixteen-Hundreds and I wish he'd
bathe more often.'*"

"We're having far too much fun with this."

"Better than weeping and wailing, Ms. Fouchet."

"True. Plus, I have no great stake in even finding the
flute, although I have this nagging suspicion that I'm
supposed to help Ignatz Jezek find peace not on this
earth. Why else would he be serenading me?"

"Uh…he likes your looks? Which is easy since you're cute. He's hot for you and wants to take you out but can't cross the great divide between worlds so he's going to entertain you or drive you insane wondering about him?"

"Hmm. It's a concept."

We smiled at one another. Johnny tapped the book, which he'd closed moments before. "Well, I'm jealous. Since I also like your looks and would be more than happy to help you cross any divides that keep you from me."

We were still on the metro. It was populated by small children, little old ladies, and mamas with strollers. Not the time for serious romance.

I grinned at Johnny. "Save that thought for a starlit night, would you? Preferably *not* at *Kouzlo Noc*."

He grinned too, then gave me a chaste kiss on my cheek. "Promise. Okay, back to business. Sadly, I'm sure this is *not* Ignatz's journal. For one thing, on page three there are references to political events happening that seem pretty obvious the writer is referring to the beginning of the Nazi invasion of Czechoslovakia and unless Ignatz was adept at spirit writing, I doubt he was forecasting the future. Now, don't get morose. No, there aren't any startling revelations on the few pages I've managed to decipher, and admittedly I zipped through this in a hurry, but…"

"Yes?" I tensed.

"You'll be very pleased to hear there are references to Jezek on the last page."

I held my breath. "Really? Anything pertinent to the investigation? Or just *'There was another murder at my castle this morning and now I have to go buy flour, butter, and cheese for the next batch of dumplings.'"*

"No clue. My skills aren't up to this. There are words. I simply can't translate and let's face it—this was not printed out on a laser jet color copier. It's handwritten and the penmanship is so bad that your favorite nun, Sister Mary Manuscript would have had this bad boy in the principal's office after school on a daily basis writing, *'I will learn to loop my O's and cross my T's'* fifty times. Anyway, I can't decipher this enough to tell just *what* the guy is saying. But I *can* tell you it seems to have been written by a member of the Duskova family. Perhaps someone who did discover a few things about his family's often sordid past? And yes, there is that intriguing reference to Ignatz right at the end." He inhaled. "Oh my God. It's more than intriguing. Abby, this could explain some of the past day's events."

"What do you mean?"

"Trina. And Marta."

"Okay. You can't name drop and then clam up. Give."

"Unless my Czech is really flat-out wrong, this guy mentions both Ignatz and the boathouse at the edge of the Duskova property in the same sentence."

"And Trina was found in the moat about three feet away from the boathouse, wasn't she? At least that's what Jozef said last night."

"He's right. So, that begs a question."

I chimed in before he had a chance to beg. "What was Trina doing that close to the boathouse on a snowy day and did what she was doing relate to Ignatz Jezek and his flute and did someone else figure that out and if so, did that someone follow her, hit her and shove her into the moat?"

"That's about it. Tangled way of stating it—no offense, love—but that's exactly what I surmised."

"What about Marta? Theories?"

He sat back on the bench of the metro train. "Let's pretend that Trina had finished reading this journal. Looking for clues about Ignatz? Picked it up in a fit of housecleaning and browsed through it one evening in front of the fire. Anyway, she reads about the boathouse. Decides to investigate to see if something is hidden there. Now, why she didn't just go out immediately after reading this instead of leaving the book, then waiting until a houseful of suspicious people were hanging around to trek down there, I have no idea, but let's say that that's exactly what she did."

"Could be that she thought she'd be safer at the boathouse when she knew she had a houseful of people at the castle. I'll bet she's the one who put the different dust jacket on the journal so anyone who casually wandered into the music room in the north wing with sinister motives would just take one look and sneer, *'Oh, great—another book on Mozart—big help.'*"

"Abby, I'll bet that wasn't Trina. Probably Veronika. You told me how antsy she was about the north wing, and she was pretty tense when I was painting up there, but I guess she thought even if I wandered into that room I'd look at a textbook about ol' Wolfie and say *'Not my choice of light reading today.'* So whoever was following the Duskovas could have assumed Trina had it?"

"Whomever."

"Whoever."

"Whomever."

"Whatever."

"Oh, hush." I smiled, then grew instantly somber. "So, someone kills Trina, but doesn't find the book since I pinched it and also he or she doesn't find what Trina was after at the boathouse, I'll bet. But why conk Marta over the head or push her down the stairs?"

"Hypothesis number two. Our mysterious killer is in the north wing looking for other clues, like another manuscript with the words, *'Flute-seekers—read me now!'* Marta hears him but thinks there's a bird trapped in one of the rooms. The killer, not wanting to take a chance at being caught where he doesn't really belong, says *'One Duskova out of the way, why not another?'* and gives her a shove."

"Sounds probable. Nasty, but probable."

We didn't talk for a minute or two.

Then Johnny quietly stated, "What scares me is that our killer also knows Abby Fouchet now has this book."

I gulped. "Yeah, well, I'm a step ahead. Thought the same thing the instant you mentioned Ignatz's name in the thing. After all, I found it the day Gustav's body was discovered on the grounds and all you guys came trooping in just after I'd plopped the book into my bag. Who knows who saw what?"

"Wish I could help. I was the last one in so I didn't see who was first and I didn't notice any major furtive looks cast your way in the room. Damn. I was worried before but now I'm pretty damn terrified. I am now official bodyguard for my girl." He added, "And would like to do a few more bodily things that don't involve waiting for someone to sneak in with harmful intent."

He leaned down, still holding the book, and gently kissed me on the lips. Nothing that those small children and little old ladies couldn't see but it quickly turned me into a *gulas* noodle. Just as quietly, he released me, then handed me the book. I swapped the dust jacket that had Mozart's name for the gothic romance dust jacket Jozef had had over the book on Freemasonry he'd lent me. Just in case someone got snoopy. *Seduction of Countess Marissa* didn't sound like a book with clues to flute treasures.

"Bad time and place for your high-impact sexual aerobics."

"Where did you hear...? Never mind. Shay has teased you as much as she has me about those activities."

He nodded. I cleared my throat. "So, Gerard, can we go up to *Kouzlo Noc* after paying tribute to Mozart at the museum and bug Jozef into translating for us?"

"Honey, can we say 'risking your life'?"

The thought of leaving my comfy hotel room for a place that had given shelter to a killer warred with curiosity and the distinct feeling that time was running out. I needed to be around Ignatz's spirit to prevent another tragedy and perhaps put an end to more pain and disaster for future residents of *Kouzlo Noc*. I bit my lip, then responded, "I'm a wimp and I don't like the idea of life-risking any more than you do. But, Johnny? If it'll help stop the doom and gloom and death and destruction? I don't see that I have a choice."

THIRTY-ONE

BERTRAMKA, THE HOUSE where Mozart had stayed when he wrote *Don Giovanni* and parts of the coronation piece he'd been working on just before writing *The Magic Flute,* started life as an estate on a vineyard but became a summer home for the Duseks, eminent Prague musicians and good buddies of Wolfgang. The lady of the house, one Josepha Dusek (also referred to as Duskova—no direct relation to the *Kouzlo Noc* sisters) was an amazing singer. Mozart had even written several arias for the lady. Whether or not Constanze Mozart had been jealous of this woman in her spouse's life was iffy, but I can imagine Connie being just a bit wary of Amadeus staying at the house of a reputed "babe". Then again, Mozart's kids stayed here at various times after their dad had died, so the relationship between the Duseks and Constanze must have been pretty solid.

The museum could have been some stuffy, boxy—well—museum. But it truly was a home. At first glance, it reminded me of an Italian-style villa plunked down into the middle of the Czech Republic, gardens and all. Perhaps that was due to the outside coloring. Gold and cream intermingled into what I'd call "Tuscany" yellow. Seven rooms on the main floor had been converted to a museum.

I fell in love with *Bertramka* about ten seconds after entering. The décor was 18th Century. Letters,

documents, pictures, and musical scores all written
by Wolfgang Amadeus had been carefully preserved
for the curious and the rabid fans. Mozart's bedroom
was really impressive, with the wooden ceiling that
had been painted with a floral grape design. Not just a
bunch of grapes on one teeny rafter. Nope. The whole
ceiling was covered with vines and grapes and had me
craving a glass of wine within seconds of entering. I
read in the little tourist brochure we'd been given that
the ceiling had been restored to the glory of its con-
struction from 1700.

The music room held a huge painting that resembled several scenes akin to the Duskova window seat.
Horses fighting. People dying. The usual light-hearted
wall décor. A poster for *Don Giovanni,* dated 1788,
was displayed on one wall. There were musical instruments behind glass in the large salon: harps, strings,
and an oboe.

But the room that stole my attention was the one
holding documents and posters relating to *The Magic
Flute* and its performances in Prague. Mozart's keyboard, used by the Maestro himself, sat proudly underneath a wall full of framed letters and pictures. For a
moment I nearly went into cardiac arrest as I entertained
the loony possibility that Jezek dropped his flute off
here in an insane hope it'd be safer than at *Kouzlo Noc.*

Johnny nudged me. "Forget it."

"What do you mean?"

"Ignatz's magic flute. Not here."

"How did you know what I was thinking?"

"Other than our soul-matedness to each other—don't
say it—not a word—I considered the hiding place issue
the first time I came here, about two weeks ago."

"Ah. Well, it would've solved a lot of problems if bright boy Ignatz had just wrapped it in a box and sent it C.O.D. to the Duseks with a courteous note stating, *'Do not open until Christmas and then be damned careful what you do with it.'*"

"Makes sense to me. Ignatz just wasn't on the ball, was he? Perhaps too busy worrying about murderers lurking and skulking about his presence?"

We smiled at each other, in perfect "soul-matedness" sync with our inane musings. Then my eyes widened. "Oh my God."

"Problem?"

"Do we have G.P.S. tracking devices installed in our butts or something? Take a look."

He turned. A group of five intently listened to a leader who read one of Mozart's letters, then translated it into English. Franz Hart, Lily Lowe, Mitchell Romberg, Fritz Herbert and Corbin Lerner. Corbin was the speaker.

Johnny grimaced. "That particular crowd does seem to show up wherever we go, don't they?"

"Well, they have to."

"Why?"

"Jeez, Johnny, get with it! They're all dubious and questionable. Don't you read or watch mysteries? Or your own bloody soap opera? You have to have your suspects in on the same clues your sleuths do and you have to have your suspects all lumped together so no one will guess who the villain is until the climax."

"So what about Veronika, Jozef and Shay, who are the other *Kouzlo Noc* crowd? I guess we can rule out Marta. At least she should be okay today since this particular crew of dubious questionables is roaming *Bertramka* instead of surrounding her."

"Probably rule out all four of that last group. Veronika has no reason to kill her sisters that I can see. And if she wasn't in the most gut-wrenching grief I've ever witnessed from another living soul when Trina's body was brought in, then the woman should win the Academy Award for Best Actress for the next fifty years. Ms. Shay Martin is *definitely* not a suspect. Aside from being my closest friend and bosom pal and a woman with an absolute inability to keep a secret, she was clueless about the secrets at *Kouzlo Noc* until I told her, and besides, she's a total pacifist and she's currently sleeping like Ignatz has for two hundred years and therefore she's not part of the suspect pool. Aside from all that, she's my comic sidekick."

Johnny snickered.

I ignored him. "Jozef is just a good guy." Johnny started to say something but I held my hand up and continued. "He is, dammit. I can just tell. He told me all about Ignatz Jezek, which he wouldn't have done if he wanted to go skulking about looking for the flute—which incidentally, he could have been doing for forty years before we all showed up and besides that…"

"Yes? Mind—I agree with you on all counts, which is what I intended to tell you before you rudely intimated I should stay silent but what's your last point?"

"He looks like God."

I shouldn't have said it. Not because, in my opinion, it wasn't true, but because Johnny Gerard started belly laughing so hard he attracted the attention of the real suspects, along with every one else in the museum. I'm surprised the guards didn't come over and toss him out for disrespectful behavior. Of course, from everything I've read about Mozart, the composer had had a wicked sense of humor and would have been delighted that his old quarters hadn't completely turned into a staid old shrine.

That said, we had indeed caught the eye of our friends and possible enemies. All five trotted outside to the garden to join us at the table that held the bust of Mozart and where Johnny was now trying to contain his merriment.

"How are you feeling?" asked Fritz.

"Huh?"

"You had a ride in snow this morning. How are you feeling? You did not catch the cold?"

I'd almost forgotten. Amazing.

"No, I'm fine. Warm, dry, somewhat rested and extremely relieved and happy that Marta is okay."

Nods all around.

Johnny asked, "When did y'all leave the castle?"

Franz answered. "Not long after the police and doctor showed up. One of the *polici* was a good mechanic and he was able to get our cars started again. Do you want to hear something very strange? The batteries were fine. The distributor cap had been twisted on every vehicle so they wouldn't start but wouldn't be permanently disabled."

Johnny didn't even blink, so I tried to keep my face somewhat expressionless except for mild surprise. It wouldn't do to start screaming, *"Well of course the cars were sabotaged! Can we say 'bad slasher movie'? Some rotten scoundrel was terrified for Marta to be seen by a cop or a doctor because that particular suspect wanted her dead. He just hadn't counted on the*

*intrepid Abby Fouchet being nuts enough to go charg-
ing into the snow for help."*

Instead, I played dumb and innocent. "Probably a
snowy prank by some smart-ass village kid from the
Town With No Name where I found the police station."

Lily beamed at me. "I never thought of that. That's
a very good explanation."

It was a damn stupid explanation but I was pleased
Lily was pleased. Yeah. Right. It appeared that the fact
I'd played "Vanessa Manilow," daytime drama inge-
nue, had placed me into Lily's top echelon of folks to
fawn over.

I changed topics. "Did y'all like Mozart's Museum?
Pretty cool, huh?"

Fritz bobbed his head in agreement. "These keyboard
instruments are worth everything." His tone turned to
pure reverence. "Mozart actually sat at these and composed arias for *Don Giovanni.* They hold special magic
for anyone who loves his music, but for a 'piano tuner'
such as I? I am in heaven."

"I like the letters," said Lily. "They are romantic
and truly give one a glimpse into the mind of Mozart
and his family."

The letters Lily was talking about included epistles
from some of Mozart's sons, especially Karl, who'd
stayed at Bertramka for several years of his childhood
after his father died. I wondered if any of those letters
also mentioned good hidey-holes for mysterious musical instruments Karl or one of the other kids had played
with, not knowing the magic within, but I discarded
that idea almost before it fully appeared in my head. If
decent clues were to be found, they would have been
found a hundred years ago—or more. Then the thought

hit me that just such a thing could have happened. Who knew if Ignatz's flute had been discovered two days after his death, and all the suspects and sleuths were chasing our respective tails, along with other treasure-seekers over the centuries?

That idea got tossed out of my brain as well. If the flute had been found, the world would know about it. Also, why would Ignatz Jezek still be hanging out at the castle playing pretty tunes, which could hopefully lead someone—not a villain—to find the answers and the treasure?

I must have been muttering under my breath to myself. Six pairs of eyes were staring at me. Johnny's were the only pair that twinkled with humor. The others were looking at me as though I was demented.

"Sorry. Talking to myself. Bad habit. Works great on the subway in Manhattan when you want others to ignore you because people assume you're nuts so they go to the next car. I should learn not to do this in polite society."

The polite society smiled all around at crazy Abby Fouchet.

Johnny took my arm. "Well, it's been lovely seeing my housemates from last night, but we're on our way to dinner so you guys have a great time exploring and we'll see ya later."

"Where are you dining?" asked Franz.

"Not sure."

"We'll go with you. There's a marvelous restaurant back in downtown Prague that serves Indian food and by now I'm sure all you Americans are tired of nothing but Czech delicacies."

I didn't particularly want to dine with five other

people—any of whom could be a killer—and I knew Johnny didn't either, but I didn't want to appear rude and, in all honesty, a little curry and chicken briana sounded like a nice change after potato pancakes three days running, so I glanced at Johnny to see if he could come up with an objections that didn't sound pissy. He shrugged. I nodded yes. Indian it was.

"I do, however, want Abby to get a chance to buy one of those clocks with the bust of Mozart though. Isn't there a gift shop right outside the museum?" Johnny asked.

"There is," was the response from Corbin. "But that's a very expensive one. There's a better souvenir shop that carries museum replicas not far from the bus stop."

"Then we're on."

The seven of us trooped out of the museum bound for souvenirs and samosas. I made a mental note to return to *Bertramka* when I wasn't accompanied by a crowd and when I could just enjoy the memorabilia of Wolfgang Amadeus Mozart without looking for hidden meanings or trying to unearth hidden flutes beneath the strings of two-hundred-fifty-year-old harpsichords.

THIRTY-TWO

THE CAFÉ FRANZ had suggested turned out to serve food as good as places I've eaten down on New York's Sixth Street, which is home to quite a few very authentic Indian restaurants, so I couldn't stay mad at the *Kouzlo Noc* crowd for messing up my outing with Mr. Gerard.

I'd called Shay from my cell while Johnny had been buying one of the Mozart busts complete with a little clock as its base. "A gift to my lovely Abigail for being heroic," he'd said. I'd told Shay the name of the café and mentioned they had a rep for really spicy *samosas,* her favorite Indian appetizer. She'd made one simple statement, "Order before I get there and you die," then hung up.

Shay was already waiting at a table when the seven of us marched in. She'd even graciously been holding that table for us. She'd barely refrained from already ordering for everyone, although I did notice that a basket of garlic *nan,* the flat Indian bread, was suspiciously empty.

The food was fantastic and a nice change from the heavy, but not spicy-hot Czech dishes we'd been diving into for nearly a week. I inwardly groaned when the vision of a scale flashed through my head considering the amount of high-caloric goodies I'd been consuming during my days in Prague but brightened when I

convinced myself the ride through the snowstorm had
knocked off a pound or two.

The conversation stayed general throughout dinner,
which was fine with me. Neither Johnny nor I desired
to get into any discussions about the Duskovas, *Kouzlo Noc,* Mozart, flutes, séances, dead Barons or live
curses. Shay, intuitively understanding our reticence,
took over.

Shay told everyone about the *Klezmer Volny Rabin*
band, who'd be joining the cast of *Silhouette Tower.*
Apparently she'd neglected to mention this to Mitchell,
because he was rather annoyed at having music brought
in he hadn't composed, nor knew anything about, but
I assured him that I could choreograph one whale of a
wedding number to the Klezmer sound and he'd love
it so much he'd immediately want to start composing
for the band, which they would also love. He wasn't
pleased, but he did settle down and quit arguing.

Shay told everyone about the new names for characters in *Silhouette Tower.* Since Franz and Lily had been
put wise to this yesterday, and the others didn't really
care, there was no great angst over that particular topic.

Shay told everyone she was indeed going to find a
way to use *Club Krev* in one of the scenes. (Getting
the picture that this had become Shay's pre-production
meeting?) Lily was thrilled. Visions of vampires suck-
ing her neck while loud music played were definitely
dancing through her head. Mitch was glad to hear this
gave him another number to compose in a really heavy
metal sound. Fritz asked if he could play an old pipe
organ for part of that scene, to give it the feeling of a
1920s black and white horror film. Shay agreed. She
didn't ask where the pipe organ was coming from or

how much it would cost to rent or buy. It was clear that he could ask for the renowned instrument from St. Stephan's Cathedral in Passau, Bavaria (the world's largest pipe organ) and she'd have it delivered to his room gift-wrapped.

Shay finally told everyone she was tired of tossing the conversation ball and she was going to just shut up and enjoy her *samosas* and curry.

After that people broke into duos and trios and talked about whatever the heck they wanted. I stayed quiet (I don't like talking with my mouth full). Shay stayed quiet because she was eating so much and so fast she didn't have a chance to talk with her mouth full, and Johnny stayed quiet because he was busy with inner thoughts. I didn't ask. I had a pretty fair idea what those thoughts were since they were identical to mine: *translate that journal, find out what the boathouse had to do with Ignatz Jezek—if anything—and determine the identity of someone—sitting with us right now—who happened to be a killer.*

My appetite fled the instant that concept tapped into my brain. A killer. It wasn't Shay. It wasn't Johnny.

If one discounted Veronika and Jozef—and while I was pretty sure neither had gone into a murderous rage and dumped Trina in the moat—I hadn't taken a final faithfilled *jeté* all the way their direction, although I really did have to rule out Jozef since one cannot be suspicious of God—that narrowed the killer down to Franz, Fritz, Mitchell, Corbin and Lily. My dinner companions.

I'd stopped eating but hadn't stopped drinking the excellent beer which cooled down the curry, so I took another sip and pondered the possibilities.

Franz. From Vienna, spoke German and Czech. Displayed more interest in Mozart than one would have imagined coming from a good-looking actor primarily concerned about his latest movie project. Did he know about the flute that was rumored to possess magic powers? Did he have the temperament to coldly shove an elderly woman who had kindness oozing from her very person into a frozen moat of dirty water? Then push another frail lady down a set of stairs? Had he snuck into *Kouzlo Noc* before meeting me the other day and dispatched Fritz's brother?

Fritz. From East Germany; spoke German and Czech. Loved music, so not surprising he'd be interested in Mozart and had heard the rumors about Ignatz's flute through various musicians over the years. Heck, it's a great legend. He had that "nerdy" appearance that captivated Shay, and Shay is normally a surprisingly good judge of character. A plus for Fritz. Again, did he possess the traits of a killer? Would he have killed his own sibling over a legend?

Mitch. From the U.S. Could he speak anything other than English? Probably. As a composer who had degrees in music cluttering his garret in SoHo, he was bound to have studied German, Italian, French, and who knows what else as part of his studies in classical music. Was it out of the realm of possibilities that he'd picked up a little Czech along the way? Like Fritz, since he traveled in musical circles, he could have heard the stories about the flute anywhere at anytime. He had a temper and he was argumentative, but that didn't mean he would ever dispatch another human being to the next plane of existence.

Corbin. From everywhere. A linguist. Veronika had told him about the flute so he could search. Or, was that wrong? Had Veronika let him dig through St. John's cemetery without giving him the correct information? He had occasional flashes of humor which endeared me to him but was also pretty damn stuffy at times. Which had nothing to do with murder. He had that scholarly air that exuded professionalism and "I'm above all this", but there are plenty of college professors who've gotten rid of rival academics through lethal means.

Lily. I really wished it were Lily. Charge her with murder, clap her in irons and cart her off to a women's prison where she could perform Lady Macbeth for inmates every night at chowtime. But I was charitable and realistic enough to know that I felt this way because she was the spitting image of Hannah Hammerstein. Plus, I hadn't liked her slander of Johnny, which had shifted to drooling over him when she found out he had a "name" in theatrical circles. I went through my very short list of reasons to label Lily the killer. She spoke Czech like a native. Duh. She was a native. She was a good actress so her weeping and wailing over Trina could have simply been one whale of a good performance. She might have wheedled the story of Ignatz Jezek out of any of the male suspects and non-suspects (except Johnny. Mr. Gerard was not normally susceptible to wheedling—even from me.) The last question—was Lily capable of murder—netted the same answer as I'd determined from the others. Anything was possible.

I forced myself to perk up again and join the light-hearted conversation. Dessert had been served. That helped. It was a rice pudding with unidentifiable spices and I mentally added it to my list of *"Where can I get this when I'm back in Manhattan?"* food choices. So I ate, I had coffee, I chatted about tourist attractions throughout Europe. Once dinner was over, Johnny, Shay and I said our good-byes and walked back to the hotel together.

"Abby, I'll wait for you to pack a few things," Johnny stated.

"Pack?" Shay's jaw dropped.

"Yes, Ms. Martin," I responded, "the man said pack. I told Johnny we're going back to *Kouzlo Noc* tonight. This time I'm bringing at least two changes of clothes, a coat, a ton of make-up, boots—and dust jackets from Gothic romances I can substitute for any other *'Aha! the truth'* journals I find lying around."

"Well, I'm coming, too. And while all that shifting of dust jackets and journals and packing of boots and cosmetics is well and good," she stated, "hell. The way this script is headed, what we really need to pack is one damn big gun."

Trust Shay the pacifist to suggest it.

THIRTY-THREE

JOHNNY, SHAY AND I stood outside the back entrance of *Kouzlo Noc.* We'd made the trip from the hotel in under forty minutes, thanks to the nifty little rental Johnny had picked up. It flew, without a single skid, over what was left of icy roads. Nonetheless, it was close to eleven-thirty by the time we'd parked, then walked up the hill to the castle.

I was about to pull the *"Requiem"* tapestry chimes when it hit me. "Won't Veronika think it's odd that we've shown up with our jammies and toothbrushes for another sleep-over? At a not-so-social hour to come calling?"

Johnny was amused. "She'll be fine with it. Hey, we have reasons. Excuses. Whatever you want to call them. We're guarding Marta. I need to work on the mural since I haven't been able to do much on it with all the rather intense events unfolding. You ladies never got to do your room-to-room surveillance to decide which scene goes where, so you figured why not just do it at night and get a feel for each room without a ton of people around?"

"I like it," I pronounced. "Simple. Clean. Enough truth to satisfy Sister Mary Mendacity."

Shay groaned. "All except for the last statement."

"Huh?"

"Take a look. The crowd has arrived. Or as you so eloquently put it the other day—the wandering whores."

They had. Our dinner companions were spilling out of two different vehicles. Corbin's Jeep and a cute little sports number that made me immediately consider taking up car-jacking. I wondered to whom it belonged. Then I realized that the wanderers were all hauling luggage out of that Jeep and cute little sports car and were obviously planning on staying at *Kouzlo Noc* along with the three of us. Lily led the way.

"Oh, hell. Shay? Can I use my little quip about 'hordes' and…"

"No! So far you and Lily have not come to blows, but if you make a crack using that not-so-nice term being a word that is *way* too phonetically similar, she'll walk and I have no idea who'd replace her. Unless you want to play Constanze and then Mitchell will kill me since you're an alto and he's composed all these songs for her that are in coloratura soprano land. Plus the costumes won't fit since you're a foot shorter than she is."

"You're no fun." I pouted.

"Oh, hush."

By this time, Lily, Franz, Fritz, Mitchell and Corbin were at the door with us. All were smiling and being very chummy. I considered wiping a smile or two off a few faces by tossing in the grenade that someone in this group killed Trina Duskova. And why the hell they didn't know that? Or they did know that, suspected one and all, and were wandering in hordes to be safe?

"Anyone pulled the, uh, pull yet?" asked Mitchell.

No one had. So he tugged and we were rewarded by hearing Mozart and his *Kyrie*.

As if the man had been waiting for hours for just this event, the door opened to reveal Jozef Jezek. For a second he seemed slightly overwhelmed at the sight of eight people, all bearing overnight bags of one sort or another, calmly waiting underneath dragonheads to be given shelter at the castle. I prayed he'd ask why in *Amadeus* we were descending on *Kouzlo Noc* at this hour. I was primed and ready to hear the outrageous excuses. But Jozef simply smiled. I transferred my hope that Veronika would direct a tough inquiry to the group. The lies had to be delicious. At least Shay and Johnny and I had plausible reasons for spending the night. Well, they'd sounded that way when Johnny had outlined them for us.

Jozef did shoot a sharp look at me. He'd been expecting the original trio of Gerard, Martin and Fouchet to show up and was welcoming a chance to exchange information. I was dying to ask him about the journal (now safely tucked back in my bag with the dust jacket to *Seduction of Countess Marissa* snugly wrapped around it) and whether the references to Ignatz was a major clue. We just needed some alone time.

Jozef politely ushered one and all inside then led us to the sitting room like a proper family butler keeping silent about family misdeeds. The room had been straightened up since I'd made my mad dash out of it this morning leaving my clothes strewn over the sofa and fireplace poker. The blankets had been neatly folded at some point and placed on a fragile chair near the fireplace. Relief. I had no plans to share a room (unless with Johnny) and the makeshift bed I'd put together last night had been very comfortable. Shay tossed her bag into a far corner then sank down on the sofa.

"I'm bunking with you, Abby," she declared. "Lily and I had a marvelous time last night," she smiled at Miss Lowe, "but I need to sleep and Abby needs to sleep so I figure we won't keep each other up all night with scintillating conversation. We've been roommates for long enough now that we're not scintillating much anymore."

Sister Mary Mendacity would have chased Shay up, down and sideways and whapped her with a ruler a foot wide for all those fibs, but Lily didn't seem to take offense.

"That's just as well. I enjoyed talking with you too, Shay, but I need my sleep, and it will be nice to have the bedroom alone."

She'd emphasized the word "alone" just enough to make it obvious that that was the last thing Miss Lowe desired, but I wasn't sure who'd be the first male to challenge the statement by knocking on her door at midnight. The only men I could rule out with absolute certainty were Mitchell, unless he'd suddenly turned bi-sexual overnight, and Johnny, who'd hopefully be sleeping with me albeit as a part of a platonic threesome since Shay'd made her plans to do the roommate thing.

I glared at both Lily and Shay. Staking out claims to bedrooms before we'd even been invited—hell— just barely given permission—to spend the night at all was really pretty rude. Shay winced and I knew she'd been too tired to realize what she was saying. She was now struggling to find a way to repair that particular *faux pas* so I spoke for her. "How is Marta? Shay and I have been so worried about her all day. Has she had a chance to eat anything? And is her head hurting less?"

Veronika beamed. Shay's fall from grace and lack of courtesy was forgiven. Probably wasn't even noticed. "Marta iss so much better this night. She hass taken soup and bread. She says her head does not hurt like before. She iss sleeping now. Doctor from village gave her drops to rest. I tell her tomorrow how you ask. Oh! Abb-ee! She says early today how much grateful she iss for you riding to village to bring help." She grabbed both of my hands and squeezed. "I am most grateful also. You haf save her life."

The savior bit was kind of pushing my contribution to Marta's recovery since she'd only suffered a broken wrist and a concussion but it was still nice to be appreciated for my bravery. I hugged Veronika, who made her "good-nights" then left, escorted by Jozef.

I started wondering about the Village of No Name. Did it really exist? Had it sprung up out of need in the blizzard and then disappeared like a Czech *Brigadoon,* only to reappear a hundred years from now when another desperate rider came dragging in begging for help for someone else injured at *Kouzlo Noc?*

Veronika didn't even ask why all her houseguests from the horrible previous night had arrived on her doorstep to camp at the castle again. *"Well, gee, Madam D., we all came for the great chow and even better séances."* She merely smiled at everyone and announced that it was late and she was heading off to bed and if everyone wanted to take the same beds they'd had last night they were most welcome. Bless the woman; she'd even found time, while Marta lay recovering, to put clean sheets on the beds. I'm lucky if I get to mine once a month.

Shay and I were the only folks who remained in the sitting room once Veronika had graciously issued that polite invitation to stay. No one seemed very interested in chatting, which was fine with me. I'd had enough chat for the last couple of days with these same people and I wasn't up for any further life revelations, no matter how juicy and scandalous. I wasn't thrilled when Johnny left, stating he needed to try to sleep for a change.

We'd barely changed into sweats (I'd been kidding about the pajamas) and arranged the bedding to our mutual satisfaction when the mantel clock struck midnight and we heard knocking.

"I'm getting a bad feeling of déjà vu," I muttered. "Are the dragons outside the door yapping or is someone tap, tap, tapping at the chamber door?"

"I hate to say it, but we have another guest," Shay growled.

"Who the heck is left to pop into this scene? The *Klezmer Volny Rabin?* The operatic troupe we saw doing *Magic Flute?* The *Marionette Theater Company?* Katya, the No Name Village eldress, wanting her folk dance costume back? Well, I left it in my hotel room in Prague so she can't have it. Besides, she said I could keep it. I plan to wear it to my next audition."

"Will you shut up? Come on, Abby, roust yourself out of bed—or floor. I'm not going alone."

We threw blankets over our shoulders and headed for the back door. We opened it cautiously. And stood in sheer silent disbelief as Auraliah Lee stepped inside.

THIRTY-FOUR

I SIGHED. "I hate to ask this, but are we about to be witness to another evening of resurrecting the dead, lifting curses and blessing the tormented souls of the Duskova lineage? Because, honestly, if that's the case, I'd just as soon opt out and, oh, scrub the floor in the north wing."

"Oh, darlin'. No! Of course not. No more dead people tonight. Ah can't do more than one big séance every couple of days. Just wears ma bones out."

Aura Lee breezed in and headed straight to the sitting room. Shay and I followed like sleep-deprived sheep. Once inside this makeshift bedroom, our soul-saving psychic dropped the long black trench coat she'd favored this night over last night's cape. I blinked. Shay blinked. My breathing began to come in spurts and sweat poured down my spine in an effort not to imitate signature lines of email posts and "roll on the floor laughing".

Tonight's ensemble was a fairy costume. Pink tutu over a white leotard with a pink bolero vest attempting—and failing—to hide Aura Lee's ample bosom. Her wig was a multi-colored 'fro topped by a silver tiara so huge it blocked any vision behind it. Her feet were encased in dark brown combat boots with pink bows at the tops. Her cosmetics looked like a cross between Nineteen Sixties Carnaby street models and Seattle Goth bands. The silver tiara resting between the bangs and the top of her head was so huge it blocked any vision behind it. I'd've had a migraine within seconds of attaching that thing. The fact that the tiara was bejeweled with rhinestones that encased twinkling lights was a plus. Great way to see at night without having to hold a flashlight. She kept waving a wand that had to be two feet in length, with an added six inch star at its peak, in every direction.

Aura Lee resembled a—no—make that *all* three fairies in *Sleeping Beauty* after the gals had spent a day at the mall and a dancewear store going out of business.

The happy medium was oblivious to the effect she was having on a stunned and hysterical Abby Fouchet. Which is to say she ignored any trace of snickers emanating from my mouth and nose.

She pulled a cigarette holder longer than one of the fireplace pokers (okay, that's slightly exaggerated) out of an enormous tote bag, found a crumpled pack of cigarettes, pushed the only one that appeared intact into the holder, lit the cigarette, coughed and choked for three seconds, then threw the entire holder and cigarette into the fireplace. She giggled. "Ah just shouldn't try ta smoke these nasty things. Ah keep hopin' it'll help me slim down some, but it just doesn't seem to work. Perhaps I should try ta inhale?"

There was no reasonable answer to this. Aura Lee didn't expect one. She went right on. "So, did y'all have a good time at last night's séance? Wasn't it fun?"

"Fun" would not have been my first choice of words. "Hell" and "emotional exhaustion" would have come closer to describing that little party. And now she was back to torment me.

Aura Lee sat down on one of the embroidered chairs

and gracefully tugged her skirt over her knees. "Well, let's get on with it."

I ground my teeth and said, less than politely, "Auraliah? Miz Lee. Beg pardon, but get on with what? You said we're not going to have to endure, I mean enjoy, a repeat of last night's dip into the world of the undead. So, no offense, but why in hell are you here?"

Her overly arched and dyed black eyebrows shot into her forehead. "Oh my. Don't tell me ah haven't said?"

Shay finally found her voice. "We hate to tell you, but it's a mystery to us."

"Well, dahlin', that's exactly why ah've come. Mystery." Her smile dimmed. "No, that's puttin' it pohly. Sadly, there's not just mystery, but danger. Terrible danger. Ah couldn't make it yesterday in time to help that poor Trina, but then, sometimes ah'm not supposed to save the innocent. But tonight ah'm here to give a warning."

"Who exactly is in danger?" I asked, stilling my breathing and willing my voice to talk without cracking. I knew damn well who was in danger but somehow needed this bizarre godmother to state it before I'd truly believe it.

"Oh, hon, I thought that was cleeah. You are. Bad danger. You'all be all right if you can work out the details about the flute, but if not, well, ah guess ah'll just be chattin' with you in this room again sometime in the future, but you won't be with me, or anyone else, except in spirit."

I let my breath out in a huge whoosh. Yep. Abby Fouchet's name was next on the hit list. Even though I hadn't figured out where the flute was or where Ignatz was buried. It didn't matter. Even if I somehow divined the whereabouts of the flute, if the killer assumed I was as greedy as he or she and that I'd keep this treasure for myself, I was looking at a quick dip in an icy moat without a paddle. I was most definitely in danger no matter what I knew—or didn't know—at this point.

All the fear I'd managed to squooch way inside me this past day came barrelling back. Shay had gone white. Our psychic wanderer was a great eccentric and fun for a character actress to play in a movie, but she'd also proven last night that she could work magic. I didn't know if that was good or bad news.

Cards on the table time. "Okay. Aura Lee? Where is Ignatz buried? And where is his flute?"

She made no effort to deny that she knew exactly what I was talking about. "Ah cain't tell you, hon. Y'all have to work those l'il details out for yourself."

Shay's face became grim. She yelled, "You come waltzing in here at midnight in your incredible pink fairy costume to scare Abby and make pronouncements, but you can't give her one stinkin', fantastic clue so she'll be safe? What kind of nutcase tease are you?"

Aura Lee wasn't offended. She patted Shay's hand, then turned and patted mine. "Now, girls, ah know this is difficult at this moment, but please try to look on me as Cinderella's godmother. With Abby as Cinderella." She giggled again. "As you noticed, ah'm kind of dressed like her, aren't ah? Well, parts of me are. Sorry you're scared, darlin', but I'm in hidin'. Shoot, that reminds me, this tiara is borrowed. Ah'd best remember to return it before the police come runnin' after me. And after ah replace the batteries. Some of these l'il lights just keep blinkin' out." She struggled to get her giggles under control. "Where was I? Oh, yes. Cinderella. Shoh nuff, it's true, her sweet godmother waved that pretty wand around and did marvelously lovely things with mice and pumpkins and fashion design, but Cinderella had to do her part, too. She was not some pampered l'il ol' Southern Belle wannabe lyin' around before the Wo-ah of Northern Aggression who let everyone else do the work. No, no. Cinderella, like a true Southern lady, cleaned and she got that house spiffied up. Then she used every ounce of bravery she possessed to go to the ball when what she really wanted to do was shout to the rooftops, *'Ah found ma prince!'* Why, she had to keep her mouth closed and silent around her nasty family. But in the end, she won. Y'all understand?"

"Not really. But since you and your wand do bear a striking resemblance tonight to at least fifteen fictional fairy godmothers, I'm going to just flow with this and not bitch too much about the fact that you're withholding vital information about musical instruments and murdered flautists and probably who the killer is now roaming around this castle with me in his or her sights."

Shay jumped in, teeth bared. "Well, I'm sure as shootin' going to bitch! You're telling my best friend she's in danger and then—what? Planning to step out into your pumpkin carriage and take off for a nice dinner in Oz?"

"Ooh, I love Australia!" she exclaimed. "Y'all just have to go there sometime. The beaches are marvelous. Almost as pretty as South Carolina."

Shay shouted, "Not *that* Oz!"

Aura Lee sighed. "Oh, ah see, you're avoiding the subject and trying to be cute. Jivin' me. Well, that's fahn."

I held up my hand for peace and tried not to look at the bouncing tutu. "Shay, you calm down. Aura Lee,

you, you…oh, blast it. Can you help at all? At least give
me some teensy small hint?"

"Hon, you have all the information you need. You
jes' need to put it together. And no, Ignatz Jezek is not
gonna play that flute and lead you to the location like
he's some sort of dead Pied Piper. He's got his pride,
shugah."

"Well, what about at least telling me *who* I'm in danger from? Is that breaking some sort of cosmic rule?"

Aura Lee glanced at the clock over the mantel. It was
like a complete repeat of last night after she'd let the
Baron chew the scenery in his pivotal scene. "Look at
the time! Ah have to get goin'. Oh! Ah almost forgot.
Shay? Robby said to thank ya for the enchilada recipe.
That l'il pinch of basil in the sauce jes' made *all* the
difference."

"Robby? As in my cousin, Rob? You're friends with
Rob? Is he still playing bagpipes? Where is he?"

Aura Lee ignored the questions. "Ah'm goin' now.
Ah'm glad there's no snow tonight. Ah'd hate to get ma
pretty boots all soaked in bad weather."

In a daze, Shay and I walked her to the back door.
Déjà vu indeed. Once again, Aura Lee opened it,
stepped outside, waved as she walked toward the cemetery, then called out *"Requiescat in pacem."* Shay and
I made the mistake of glancing at each other and shaking our heads in wonder. Mistake, because in the time
it took to shake our heads just once, when we looked
outside again, Aura Lee had disappeared.

THIRTY-FIVE

"WELL, THAT WAS just too flippin' annoying," Shay stated in a flat tone.

"Oh? And why would you say that? Because a short, zaftig, flaming pink Nutcracker Sugar Plum reject sailed in for ten minutes and tossed loaded missiles around using the 'D' word—as in danger—and then took off in her non-existent horse and carriage?"

Shay snickered. "No, that was merely frustrating. Annoying is having the fairy drop my cousin's name and then take off without telling me where he is or what he's doing or how they're acquainted. She's right about the basil though. Just a pinch. Amazing."

"When did you last talk to Cousin Rob?"

Shay closed her eyes. "Uh, the day you called about *Kouzlo Noc*. He was in Mexico somewhere and I was still in Paris and I told him I was on my way to Prague to film at a haunted castle."

I groaned. "You actually said 'haunted'?"

"I did."

"Well, now the only surprise is that Rob didn't skate in along with Aura Lee, his enchilada-eating buddy, for the séance last night."

Shay howled. "I'd wager any amount of money he's the one who found the tiara for our Southern Belle psychic. In a flea market in Juarez or someplace. Left-over from a Miss Hot Tamale contest in El Paso after a bender."

I brightened. "I want one. Exactly like it for my next audition. Preferably one that has the little flashing lights on it. A perfect replica of Aura Lee's. It would look really cute with my Von Trapp outfit from Katya the Ancient. Although, using a lit tiara here in the Czech Republic would be better used for those times when one needs to find one's way through blinding snowstorms."

We tried to smile at each other, but my lips had started to tremble and I could see that Shay was holding back shouting obscene curses into a night which had apparently swallowed Auraliah Lee up whole.

"Let's go back in. It's not snowing anymore but I'm feeling colder than I did during my wild ride on *Yankee Doodle*…oh my gosh, that was just yesterday morning."

We shut the massive door and hurried back to the relative safety of the sitting room.

"Damn. Damn. Damn."

"Well, that's descriptive," I said.

"I don't like it, Abby. This crazy medium, ghost-chattering, clairvoyant loon scares you into nearly having a heart attack, drops some one-liners about how you're in danger, doesn't seem to give a Yankee Doodle Doo about helping you, then leaves us here at Spook Station and goes off to dine with her fellow tiaraed minions."

"*You* don't like it? What about Danger Girl here?" I stared at my friend. "I've been kind of anxious or nervy these last few days, but it seemed almost a joke. Then Trina died and I felt all that horror and sadness but it didn't seem to be touching me—I mean as far as the idea of Abby Fouchet in someone's sights. Then Marta gets hurt and again, I'm worried and terrified for her but it still doesn't penetrate that I could be next in line for a stair push even though I'm pretty damn sure everyone in this castle knows I'm in sync with a ghost and I'm the one who might find that flute. Then—tonight. Doorbell rings and in bounces Flora, Fauna and Meriwether all in one, and I'm now scared out of my wits because she's right. I'm a target. Put a big red marker on my butt and call the hunters."

"Get out. Now. I'll drive you back to Prague."

Johnny stood in the doorway of the sitting room, fully dressed and with as grim an expression as I'd only seen on those dragon doorknockers. Shay and I turned to face him as he urged me to make tracks for the city.

"What? I can't leave."

He took a long stride into the room. "Yes, you can and yes, you will. No stupid treasure is worth your life and I heard enough from Auraliah Lee—yes—I was sneaking around the ballroom and eavesdropping during her little diva scene—but what she said was enough to convince me that you do not need to be at *Kouzlo Noc* anymore."

"Sounds good, Johnny, except I have this suspicion that it won't help now if I'm in Prague at my hotel or in Vienna drinking coffee and downing *sachertortes* by the plateful or in Manhattan in Times Square watching the New Year's Eve ball drop. This killer is not going to stop merely because my geography changes. He wants that flute. He believes I can get it for them—and that's the bottom line."

Johnny stared at me. "Shit."

"Precisely."

Johnny sat down on the sofa and pulled me down next to him. "I hate it when you're right about death and doom and killers. And where are the Marricino brothers when they're needed?"

Shay dropped her bottom onto the hearth of the fireplace and growled. "So, lady and gent, what can we do? We must protect the innocent Abby Fouchet from whomever," she paused, "say 'who' and I'm throwing pokers at you both—and we must find the flute too."

I'd actually started to chortle over the "who/whom" comment but when Shay mentioned the flute I sat straight up on the edge of the sofa.

"Flute. Okay. That's the answer."

"The flute? Definitely the objective, but why is it the answer?" Shay inquired.

"Because it *is* the objective. Look. The killer wants the flute which he—or she—oh heck let's just say 'he' for sake of argument and for the fact that I really can't see Lily or Veronika skulking about pushing anyone into a moat or down a flight of stairs and the only other female around here is Shay and if she kills me I'll haunt her mercilessly while she's in the midst of kinky sexual activities and she'll be too embarrassed to continue them. Where was I?"

"Objective," Johnny murmured.

"Right. He, as in the killer, wants the flute. He probably has convinced himself that the flute is the answer to all his troubles in life. I'll bet anything this guy thinks it will make him rich. Greed. I'm tellin' ya, of the seven deadlies out there, greed is one of the worst."

"A-greed," quipped my best friend.

"Oh, hush."

"Well, I thought it was a nice pun—or something along those lines. Go on. I'll try to refrain from humorous interjections."

"Yeah, right," I snorted. "Okay. Logically, it seems to me that if I find the flute or at least put on a good show of leading him to it, then the killer will pop out from wherever because he has to get his hands on the flute and then we can grab him and I'll be out of danger. Yes?"

Johnny pursed his lips. "I'm thinking. And I'm not thrilled with what I think you're thinking."

I looked over at Shay. "Yes?"

"It's way too simple, which means it probably is the answer."

"It's also a good way to get yourself killed by this sicko," Johnny uttered quite tersely.

"Got any other ideas?"

"Not at the moment. Other than shipping you off to an igloo in Alaska to be guarded by Inuit ice dwellers where you'd be less likely to be found—no."

I stifled my laugh. Mainly because I was afraid if I let it loose it would become hysterical. I didn't need hysteria. I needed to stay focused. "Well, gang, this 'draw out the killer' plan does have one other little drawback."

"And that would be? And excuse me, but like we needed another drawback?" griped Shay.

"I don't bloody well know where the flute is! And while I'm positive Ignatz was the one flaunting his flauting to me yesterday when I rode the horse to Anonymity Town, I'm not so sure his ghost is going to drop any more hints than our Deep Southern-fried-fairy godmother."

"Yep. Drawback. But descriptive."

Johnny rose and began to pace. "Okay. I'd say the first order of business is to figure out where the flute is. Aura Lee said you had the clues, right?"

"Yeah, but she wasn't too forthcoming about what those clues were, nor was she generous in hinting where to even start to look for those clues. Damn, damn, doo-doo! That's the least she could have done before she went tippy-tapping out to fly back to Atlanta—probably without benefit of a plane. Anyway, it would have been nice of the woman to at least drop some giant breadcrumbs. I'd still have to put them together to make toast, so to speak."

"Then it's time to do some major deducting."

"As Shay has said, a-greed."

All three of us got up and started pacing. We were all too active even on normal days to be able to get creative without a good deal of movement. So we criss-crossed one another and circled one another and miraculously didn't bump into one another and barely noticed we were looking like hamsters on crack at a miniature rodent "rave."

I halted and put my hand up like one of the Supremes doing the chorus of *"Stop in the Name of Love."*

"Yes?"

"We need Jozef." I tapped Johnny's shoulder. "Did you get a chance to talk to him about translating the book?"

"He did."

We turned. Jozef stepped inside the sitting room. He was holding a book with a dust jacket that read *The Whispering Ravens of Naked Rock.* Another very cheesy gothic novel. I just hoped Shay hadn't seen it because "naked" would be right back in the title of *Silhouette Tower*.

"I told Johnny that I had already gone through the journal you found in the north wing, Abby. The one that now has the jacket cover of *Seduction of Countess Marissa*. It belonged to Eduard Duskova—not the Eduard from Baron Smetana's time, but a man who lived at *Kouzlo Noc* during the Mid-20th Century. He was quite a scholarly man who became very interested in the legend of Ignatz Jezek. My father knew him and liked him very much. He always told me that Eduard wanted to find Ignatz Jezek to give him a Christian burial because he felt that someone in the family had done great wrong and murdered the musician soon after he had moved to *Kouzlo Noc*. Eduard did not really care about finding the flute; in truth he did not believe the flute held any special powers. He wrote in his journal that he believed that Ignatz had been thrown from the window of the north wing."

"Isn't everyone?" Shay muttered.

We stared at her. "Sorry. Trying to be funny to lighten a very tense moment. Failing miserably. Go on, Mr. Jezek, I'll stay quiet."

"Yeah, like that's going to happen," I grumbled. "She'll be good, Jozef. Please, continue."

"There is not much more to say. He wrote something about wanting to search the boathouse because he felt that Ignatz's body had been dragged there and dropped in the water beneath, but only days later the Nazi army entered and they took over *Kouzlo Noc*. Eduard was arrested and thrown into a concentration camp."

"Did he ever return to *Kouzlo Noc?*" I asked.

"Yes, he did. He was the grandfather of Veronika

and Trina and Marta. Their parents were killed when the Communists took over and Eduard raised them. He never again wrote in the journal and his injuries from the camp were so severe there was no physical possibility for him to search the boathouse alone. I believe he gave up trying."

I was getting frustrated. "So we're kind of back to where we started—at least as far as the flute is concerned. I'll bet that Ignatz's body is buried under the boathouse but I'd really be amazed if the flute was with him. And if it was—were—whichever—I doubt it would be intact." I looked over at Johnny. "Wasn't there another journal though? Didn't you tell me that the part of Eduard's diary you read mentioned that someone else had written down some of their theories as to where the flute could be?"

"I did, but I have no idea where that other book went. Trina probably didn't have it, although it seems pretty obvious that she read Eduard's journal and decided to take a chance and do a look-see around the boathouse."

Shay added, "Which was when some s.o.b. killed her. And she probably thought she was safe since she had a full house—excuse me—castle—that morning."

Jozef shut his eyes and thought for a moment. "I have an idea where that other journal could have been hidden. Miss Martin, would you accompany me through the rooms in the north wing? There is a small library in one of the bedrooms and it is very possible that the journal is in what you Americans call 'plain sight'... simply stacked with the other books." He smiled. "If you are not frightened to go into the north wing where so many bad things have happened."

Shay's chin jutted out. "Me? Scared? Never."

Jozef turned and left the room. Shay followed but whirled around before she stepped through the doorway and winked at me, making sure first that Jozef didn't hear her. "After all, I'm with the man who looks like God!"

I bit my lower lip as Shay and Jozef disappeared into the ballroom. "I'm *so* sorry I ever said that. Shay will never let me forget."

Johnny laughed. "As long as no one tells Jozef, you'll be fine. He's a man of great faith and it would seem sacrilegious to him."

"I'm not talking."

"Well. So, they're off in the north wing and we're left to cool our heels and pray for divine inspiration. Shall we sing a bit of the *Kyrie* and ask mercy for all the various sins of *Kouzlo Noc?*"

"Couldn't hurt. Ignatz will hear us and decide it's time to make a command performance. Where the heck is he when I need him?"

"Not to be totally skeptical, but I can't really see this ghost blasting out tunes for you on cue, hon."

"Well, he does. Unfortunately I can't ask him straight out for an answer to where he hid the damn flute and I have to use my imagination to figure out any clues." Something nagged at me. "Wait. I do hear something."

"What?"

"Hush. I can't believe you can't hear it too."

"I can't. Sorry. My ghost-communing skills don't match yours. Okay. What is it?"

I closed my eyes and concentrated and Johnny remained silent. Ignatz had chosen something I couldn't grasp for his concert. Partly because it was a damn short concert. Only about four measures in, the ghost stopped.

"Johnny. This song. It's not a classical piece. And it's not one I'd've expected from Jezek since he died way before it was written. Durn. Right now it's failing me. And there's something you said a minute ago that's kind of poking at the tip of my mind and it goes along with the song. It's important for some reason."

"Want to talk it through? Or would you prefer that I not chime in with a hundred dumb thoughts?"

I laughed. "You couldn't have a dumb though if you emptied your brain into a garbage disposal. Oh! Wait. That poke is back. Only this time it's more like a thwack in my brain going 'you dimwit it's all there in front of you.' What the heck am I trying to get at?"

"Would it help to go back and remember what we've been saying?"

"Yeah. Although, I have this feeling that it's not what should be important that *is* important. It's more like bits and pieces of random words we've thrown out."

"Okay. Um. We were talking about God. We were talking about garbage disposals. Uh. We were…"

"Asking for help only you said something about singing the *Kyrie*." I inhaled. "That's it."

"What?"

"*Kyrie*. That's what I'm hearing. Only not Mozart's. Remember the rock group called *Mister Mister* from the 1980s? Had a great song called *Kyrie*. Really good to do chaineé turns in dance class. Which is beside the point. You were talking about chiming in." I paused. "Hang on. I'm hearing Auraliah Lee yelling '*Requiescat in Pacem*' every stinkin' time she leaves the castle."

He got it. "*Kyrie. Requiescat.* As in Mozart's *Requiem Mass.*"

"As in the wind chimes at the bottom of the bell-pull, which rings out the notes of the *Kyrie* portion of Mozart's *Requiem.*"

THIRTY-SIX

JOHNNY AND I raced to the back entrance where the tap-estried bell-pull had nestled quite cozily next to the dragon-headed doorknockers for several centuries.

"It's *got* to be in the wind chimes. Aura Lee said I had all the information and she was right. I hope."

Johnny carefully removed the pull, then began to untie the wind chimes from the rest of the fabric. "Makes sense. Three chimes. No more, no less, just like all the various uses of three in *The Magic Flute*. Ignatz was no dummy. He was being hounded for his flute by crazy fortune hunters even in his own time. He knew future treasure seekers would destroy every section of the north wing. I'm sure that's where he lived his last days. And he probably reasoned that people would even turn to grave robbing in that old cemetery. The one that held the remains mostly of the members of his generation. So that was out."

"Hurry," I urged him. "Let's find that thing and split—now."

There was a cold chill between my shoulder blades. Something wicked was wafting this way.

Johnny suddenly dropped the ground. The man be-hind him calmly leaned over and grabbed the wind chimes out of Johnny's limp hands. His other hand held a sock which appeared loaded with something which created a great blackjack. He dropped it on Johnny's chest, then reached into his coat pocket and pulled out the dagger I'd seen him use in the crypt the first day I met him. He calmly removed it from his belt and waved it at me.

"Thank you, Abby. Very kind of you and amazingly smart to finally figure out the answer to this centuries old puzzle. I was afraid I'd be stuck here for the entire time you were filming your stupid movie, waiting until you solved the mystery."

"Glad to oblige, Corbin," I stated in a monotone. Then that serene countenance disappeared and Abby with the temper popped out. "So, you're the slimey, slinking, scummy, sordid, sonuvobitchin' snake who's been causing all the hurt and sorrow over the last few days!"

"Snake? Fine alliteration, Ms. Fouchet, but I don't accept the slur. But then, you're deep into *Magic Flute,* aren't you, so perhaps the serpent in the first scene has stuck in your pretty frivolous head?" He paused, then thrust the wind chimes at me. "Here. You open whichever damn one holds the flute, you little fool."

"Why should I help you find it?" I asked with as much calm as I could muster in my voice. It still shook harder than twenty tumbleweeds in a Texas dust storm. And squeaked. Not a pretty sound.

Corbin shrugged. "You'll find it because otherwise I shall not only use this extremely sharp antique dagger to slit Johnny's throat, but you'll feel it thrusting into your ribs very soon thereafter. Not enough to kill you, dear, just enough to cause some pain."

"Oh-kay. Good reason." With trembling hands, I was able to find the tip of the first chime and twist it open. It was a heavy metal material and it was old and rusted and not inclined to move but after a few desperate wrenches I got it loose.

Nothing. I tried the second one. Same process and the same result. If the third chime didn't yield one major magical flute, I was in big trouble. Of course I was already in big trouble. But, if I'd been wrong about the flute's hiding place, I'd be in *less* trouble while Corbin Lerner debated whether he needed to kill me and Johnny or keep us alive in hopes that my deductions would be spot on for the next possible theory on where this treasure lay.

Tamino in *The Magic Flute* undergoes three trials. I prayed that's what Ignatz had tried to recreate with the wind chimes. I tugged and twisted and panted and twisted and finally, finally, the third chime was open.

Buried inside was an old wooden flute. I drew it out of the wind chimes and held it out to Corbin, while anxiously looking at Johnny, still lying at his feet. He hadn't moved.

Corbin grabbed the flute and began to scream. He dropped the instrument onto the dirt below us. His face became distorted with pain and anger. "Bitch! You burned me!"

"What?"

"That damn flute is blazing hot! It's like grabbing a fry pan that's been cooking on high flame! Damn you!"

I leaned down and touched the flute. It hadn't been hot to the touch when I'd drawn it out of the wind chime. It wasn't hot now. What the hell was going on?

"There's nothing wrong with this, Corbin. Actually, it's very cold for a flute that's wooden, not metal. You're imagining things. Your senses are tricking you."

I held the flute out again. This time he only touched

it with one finger, then quickly drew that finger away while screaming again. Part of the screams were pain and part were curses I'd never heard before but was sure were damning me, Ignatz, and all our relatives to everlasting hell. Since some of the curses were in German, I was kind of guessing at the actual suggestion.

He switched to English again and moaned. "It's supposed to turn to *gold*. That's the legend. The alchemists of the Masonic Lodge that Jezek belonged to were turning metals to gold. The flute was supposed to be magic because it is made of wood, yet turns to gold and then turns other materials to gold. What the hell is wrong with this damnable instrument?"

Johnny tried to sit up. His voice was weak but determined. "It's not the flute, Corbin. It's you and your greed and evil. You took more than one innocent life. You bastard, you killed Trina and Fritz's brother, didn't you?"

"Those were accidents. The kid was in the north wing, leaning out of the window and reaching for something above it. He was so excited I thought for sure he'd found the flute. So I reached around him to grab it and he toppled out. He'd been looking at a bird's nest outside the sill. Idiocy. And Trina? The old broad was digging through all this junk in the boathouse and she found a set of panpipes and held them up like they had been gold. I grabbed her and told her I wanted the flute. She ran away toward the moat. I grabbed her again and she started screaming. She wouldn't tell me anything I needed to hear. I pushed her and she fell into the moat."

A cry that would make a banshee's hair curl arose from behind Corbin, in the doorway of the back entrance. Veronika Duskova was yelling and calling

Corbin names that I tried to remember so I could ask Johnny, if we all lived through this, exactly what they meant. They sounded pretty rough even in Czech.

Veronika threw herself on Corbin and began pounding at him with her fists. He still had the dagger in his left hand, the one not scalded by the flute. He quickly raised it to her neck and pulled her in front of him.

"Shut up, you hag! I've had enough of screaming women and false hopes. Much as I do not want to take Ms. Duskova traveling with me, it's best I do for the reassurance that you—" he pointed to Johnny "—and you," he pointed to a horrified Jozef who'd appeared from the outside of the house with Shay, "won't be tempted to do something dumb. Back off."

He turned, shifting the knife to touch Veronika's back. Jozef didn't waste a second. He threw a leather-bound object at Corbin's hand. The knife dropped. Veronika immediately ran to the safety of Jozef's arms. I noted, with the interest of an eternal romantic, that he held her with more than a little tenderness. I foresaw a nice merger between the Duskovas and the Jezeks.

I shouldn't have gotten so involved in watching the pair, because Corbin, deprived of one hostage, decided he'd better get another. I was the closest—and the smallest. Corbin's arm was around me and the knife was at my neck and I was being pulled toward the Jeep that was quietly parked by the edge of the cemetery.

Johnny managed to get up but stopped when Corbin pricked the edge of my throat with the knife. "Want to see your girlfriend dead, Gerard? I have no qualms about spilling blood all over this damn place. It's not like no one's done it before." He smiled. "Or I'll just drag our ghost detective up to the north wing for a nice fling right out the window like all the other losers who've been tossed for the last ten centuries."

Johnny was shaking with rage and frustration and fear. For me. I was in deep trouble here. Shay was edging closer to Corbin and me and I knew she was planning to throw herself on his back but I silently pleaded with her to hold off. That particular attack could get us both very dead. I stared back at Johnny while Corbin moved the knife directly toward my chest.

"Don't go feeling secure, Miss Fouchet. It's more comfortable than holding the damn thing at your neck. In case you thought I was in danger of dropping it."

I didn't answer. I kept staring at Johnny, then, since Corbin hadn't moved, I sang the last few notes of the *Queen of the Night* aria. True, it wasn't in Mozart's original key, since I lowered it to one more comfortable to my alto range, but Johnny caught it. This aria is sung when the Queen of the Night is trying to persuade her daughter to kill the priest Sarastro with a dagger. It's a series of very light notes that scale up and down in a staccato rhythm. Rather like a flute.

Johnny moaned and sank back to the ground. Corbin laughed. Johnny quickly grabbed the flute and threw it at Corbin. It bounced off the hand that held the dagger. Apparently Corbin was still fixated about the heat because he howled as though he'd been scalded by boiling oil. His hand came away from my chest although he still gripped the knife. I rammed my elbow into his chest, turned and gouged my fingers into his eyes, then ran to the safety of Johnny. Shay galloped over to Corbin and delivered a nice kick to his head as he lay on the ground, whining and cursing.

Johnny kissed me until I turned to jelly. "Are you all right?"

"I'm fine. What about you? You looked down for the count. But you got up and you knew what I needed. I'm damn impressed."

"Well, it was a decently hard head blow, but not as bad as Mr. Lerner thought. I was faking about thirty seconds after he coshed me. Excuse me a second."

He ran to Corbin and held him down. "Shay? You can quit kicking him now. Anyone got a cell to call the cops?"

Shay offered hers. "Is there a nine-one-one number here in the wilds of the Czech Republic that hits the Prague police?" she asked.

Johnny shook his head. "Doesn't matter. I'd rather call the police chief who gave me his card yesterday when he came with the doc to help Marta. From Abby's favorite village. Abby? It's in my shirt pocket if you'd care to do the honors so I won't have to let go of Corbin here."

I carefully reached into the pocket and got the card, quickly handed it to Shay, then smiled. "I'll do you one better, Mr. Gerard. In the interest of absolute security for this bastard." I grabbed the long bell-pull, now lying limply on the ground, then neatly tied both Corbin's hands and feet together behind his back.

Johnny looked at me with sheer admiration. "Wow. That's a better move than Gregory Noble ever imagined. Where'd you learn that?"

"Remember I did that summer stock season in Colorado? The big show was *Will Rogers Follies* and our 'Will' was an ex-rodeo star. Taught me a dozen tricks during scene changes. You just saw my favorite. It's called a 'tie-down rope' and it requires a dummy. So I used the biggest dummy at hand."

THIRTY-SEVEN

IF ANYONE IS wondering where the rest of the house-guests had been during all the commotion, let me answer with a simple explanation. Trite, unimaginative, but simple. They'd all been snoring in their respective bedrooms because Corbin had spiked their cocoa with sleeping pills when he'd kindly offered to help Lily in the kitchen making midnight drinks only hours ago.

I didn't hear about this until late that morning because Franz, Fritz, Mitchell and Lily didn't make an appearance before well after ten. Which was fine with me. Being taken hostage, however briefly, with a knife aimed at one's tender body parts, is very wearing on the psyche—not to mention the actual body that owns those tender parts.

My police buddy, whose name I'd discovered only after seeing the card was *Polici* Captain Wolfgang Bernstein, arrived promptly after Johnny called him. He took a snarling and slightly bruised Corbin Lerner into custody to the village I'd at last discovered the name of—St. Agnes Crossing. Perfect.

Corbin hadn't been a good sport during his exit scene from *Kouzlo Noc*. He yelled, screamed and used language ill-befitting a University professor and scholar. Then he whined again and again about how he'd been tricked and destroyed. The man just unraveled. Not pretty.

"That blankety-blank flute holds no magic!" I leave it to those possessing lurid imaginations or teenagers to fill in those blankety-blanks.

After several minutes and different phrasings but the same intent of Corbin's theme song, I'd walked over to the now-handcuffed Mr. Lerner (Captain Bernstein had admired my roping skills but exchanged the bell-pull for a set of steel handcuffs) and stared the killer in the eye.

"You're very wrong, Corbin. Ignatz's flute holds infinite magic. I believe it can change sorrow into happiness and protect those who hear it. Turn night into day, figuratively that is, if you see night as evil and sorrow and day as goodness. Study your *Die Zauberflote* libretto while you rot in prison, Corbin. The Ladies who attend the Queen of the Night are quite specific in their explanations as to what the flute represents and Ignatz Jezek miraculously instilled those powers into this instrument."

I held up Ignatz's flute before the eyes of the angry Corbin Lerner, then swept my free arm around and pointed at Veronika and Jozef. "Sorrow into happiness. Right there. And when I heard Ignatz play I was protected. Shay and Johnny were protected. You touched it and you got burned. Enough said."

Corbin had been led away muttering about sacrificing everything looking for the fortune he'd been certain he'd possess when the flute magically turned everything he owned into gold. I guess he thought it would evoke sympathy but instead, his word choices reminded me of the song by the classic rock band, Foreigner, *"Cold as Ice"* when they sang about greed. I gleefully made Corbin even more furious by belting it out, every durn chorus and verse.

Veronika, Jozef, Shay, Johnny and I returned to the house. We didn't even bother to conduct post mortems on what had happened. Exhaustion overwhelmed us. We'd been struck down in our prime. The next—the only—order of business had been sleep.

So this morning, Shay took center stage and recounted the night's events to a captive audience in the sitting room, who rather warily sipped hot chocolate and munched on cinnamon rolls. I had no idea when the pastries had been made. They take some time to prepare and they were fresh. I could only assume Veronika and Marta had gotten about two hours sleep and headed for the kitchen early to work their own magic.

Shay craftily skimmed over any mention of my otherworldly skills in hearing Ignatz's flute as she explained how the clues led to finding the instrument in the wind chimes.

Franz got curious. "Did the book that Jozef found contain anything about Ignatz and the flute? Or his death? Who wrote this second book? Did it tell you where the flute was hidden? How did you know otherwise?"

Jozef stayed honest yet managed to skirt the issue of clues since only he, Johnny and Shay knew Ignatz had been playing the flute for me. "That second journal was indeed written by Ignatz Jezek. That much is true. He explains that he poured his soul into crafting the flute and that he feared for his life while under the roof of Milos Duskova. Milos was a greedy man who believed with all his mind and heart that the flute was an alchemist's dream. It would turn metal to gold. Ignatz, in the last entry of the journal only says that he has hidden the flute because he will be murdered if Milos steals the flute."

Veronika choked back tears. "I am responsible. I bring Corbin Lerner here. He iss distant cousin of that branch of Duskova family. Milos, my ancestor. Another killer. I am so ashamed."

"Wait," I interrupted. "Are you saying you brought Corbin here to find the flute?"

She looked horrified. "No, no! I bring here to help with—how you say—identification—of dead in St. John Cemetery. I did not know he knew about flute or what evil man he iss. I did not know he would kill my sister and try to kill others and me and you."

Jozef patted her hand. "You are not at fault for Corbin's wickedness, Veronika. And remember, you also listened to me and brought Johnny to do the mural. That helped keep a balance."

"You'd met Johnny before?" I asked.

"Oh yes. He worked with me in the bookstore those few weeks he was filming his daytime drama. Sweet boy. I love his show. Yolanda is one of my favorite people and I knew she would persuade Veronika to bring Johnny to *Kouzlo Noc*." He smiled at Veronika. "I did not mean to interrupt you. Please, tell Abby what you think happened?"

Veronika continued, "We are of belief that centuries ago Milos was angry when flute is not with Ignatz and he throws him out of window in north wing." She paused. "I think that room needs redecorating?"

I couldn't look at Shay. If I did we'd both lose it and I, for one, was sure Veronika hadn't intended to be funny.

Veronika added, "We find other journal by my grandfather, Eduard, who says he hass theory that Ignatz is buried under boathouse. We look today and if we find him we will gif him Christian burial in the good cemetery."

I wondered whom "we" meant. I had a definite bond with Ignatz Jezek, whom I now felt certain was resting in peace since his flute had been discovered by people who wanted only to keep it as a family heirloom instead of test its powers. I had no desire to go on a grave-digging expedition. Since Corbin, the resident gravedigger, was in custody in the village of St. Agnes Crossing, I assumed Jozef would supervise the project, with Franz, Fritz, Mitchell and Johnny performing the actual labor.

Johnny. He hadn't joined us for breakfast. It was now eleven in the morning and I was getting worried. Had Corbin coshed him over the head harder than we'd thought? Was he now writhing in pain with a severe concussion—or worse?

Jozef caught me glancing at the door for the sixteenth time in two minutes. He rose, went into the ballroom, then returned moments later with a box. He handed it to me. "I am so sorry. I was supposed to give this to you an hour ago when you awoke."

Inside the box lay a cute little "stuffie"—a model of a *przewalski,* the miniature horses Johnny had told me he tended at the Prague Zoo in his guise as Gregory Noble. The horse was dressed in 18th Century garb, including a waistcoat, ruffled shirt and a wig that bore a striking resemblance to one that Mozart wore that's been depicted in hundreds of different images. And the horsey came with a prop—a small harpsichord nestled against its hooves. A tiny white handkerchief had been tucked into a pocket of the waistcoat. Embroidered in red was the word, *"Amadeus."* Now that indeed was sweet.

I held the horse up so all assembled could see. Jozef

gestured toward the tiny harpsichord. "Johnny said, 'Tell Abby to lift the lid.'"

I did. There was a rolled-up note resting on the strings. I unfolded it.

My darling St. Agnes. Had to rush off. Two phone calls in less than ten minutes early this morning and a major rush to the airport. The South Sarasota Retirees called to tell me they're moving up their production of Magic Flute *so I'm needed now before Yolanda blackmails me into heading to Alaska for a Gregory Noble stint as an ice road trucker catching igloo smugglers or polar bears.*

Gone? Well, hell. I continued reading.

You were sleeping the sleep of the righteous so I didn't want to wake you—don't be ticked. You've had a rough week. And good news! Second call was Yolanda. Says fans are clamoring for more Abby Fouchet. So "Vanessa Manilow" is back on Endless Time—*probably in the fall. The "why" of Vanessa's absence? She's been guiding tourists up Mt. Elbrus in Russia. Vanessa will return to run as a state representative from Staten Island (and no, darlin', I'm clueless as to what climbing mountains has to do with running for office.) Yolanda specifically requested a politician with chestnut and green hair.*
See you in a month. All my love.
Johnny

* * * * *

REQUEST YOUR FREE BOOKS!

2 FREE NOVELS
PLUS 2 FREE GIFTS!

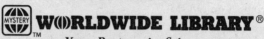

Your Partner in Crime

ReaderService.com

Manage your account online!

- Review your order history
- Manage your payments
- Update your address

---

*We've designed
the Harlequin® Reader Service
website just for you.*

Enjoy all the features!

- Reader excerpts from any series
- Respond to mailings and
  special monthly offers
- Discover new series available to you
- Browse the Bonus Bucks catalog
- Share your feedback

Visit us at:
ReaderService.com